Agatha Christie

Taken at
the Flood

HarperCollins*Publishers*

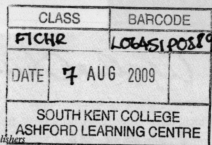
HarperCollins*Publishers*
77–85 Fulham Palace Road,
Hammersmith, London W6 8JB
www.**fire**and**water**.com

This *Agatha Christie Signature Edition* published 2002
8

First published in Great Britain by
Collins 1948

ISBN 0 00 712101 6

Typeset by Palimpsest Book Production Limited,
Polmont, Stirlingshire

Printed and bound in Great Britain by
Clays Ltd, St Ives plc

Taken at the Flood

Agatha Christie is known throughout the world as the Queen of Crime. Her books have sold over a billion copies in English with another billion in 100 foreign languages. She is the most widely published author of all time and in any language, outsold only by the Bible and Shakespeare. She is the author of 80 crime novels and short story collections, 19 plays, and six novels written under the name of Mary Westmacott.

Agatha Christie's first novel, *The Mysterious Affair at Styles*, was written towards the end of the First World War, in which she served as a VAD. In it she created Hercule Poirot, the little Belgian detective who was destined to become the most popular detective in crime fiction since Sherlock Holmes. It was eventually published by The Bodley Head in 1920.

In 1926, after averaging a book a year, Agatha Christie wrote her masterpiece. *The Murder of Roger Ackroyd* was the first of her books to be published by Collins and marked the beginning of an author-publisher relationship which lasted for 50 years and well over 70 books. *The Murder of Roger Ackroyd* was also the first of Agatha Christie's books to be dramatised – under the name *Alibi* – and to have a successful run in London's West End. *The Mousetrap*, her most famous play of all, opened in 1952 and is the longest-running play in history.

Agatha Christie was made a Dame in 1971. She died in 1976, since when a number of books have been published posthumously: the bestselling novel *Sleeping Murder* appeared later that year, followed by her autobiography and the short story collections *Miss Marple's Final Cases*, *Problem at Pollensa Bay* and *While the Light Lasts*. In 1998 *Black Coffee* was the first of her plays to be novelised by another author, Charles Osborne.

The Agatha Christie Collection

The Man In The Brown Suit
The Secret of Chimneys
The Seven Dials Mystery
The Mysterious Mr Quin
The Sittaford Mystery
The Hound of Death
The Listerdale Mystery
Why Didn't They Ask Evans?
Parker Pyne Investigates
Murder Is Easy
And Then There Were None
Towards Zero
Death Comes as the End
Sparkling Cyanide
Crooked House
They Came to Baghdad
Destination Unknown
Spider's Web *
The Unexpected Guest *
Ordeal by Innocence
The Pale Horse
Endless Night
Passenger To Frankfurt
Problem at Pollensa Bay
While the Light Lasts

Poirot

The Mysterious Affair at Styles
The Murder on the Links
Poirot Investigates
The Murder of Roger Ackroyd
The Big Four
The Mystery of the Blue Train
Black Coffee *
Peril at End House
Lord Edgware Dies
Murder on the Orient Express
Three-Act Tragedy
Death in the Clouds
The ABC Murders
Murder in Mesopotamia
Cards on the Table
Murder in the Mews
Dumb Witness
Death on the Nile
Appointment With Death
Hercule Poirot's Christmas
Sad Cypress
One, Two, Buckle My Shoe
Evil Under the Sun
Five Little Pigs

The Hollow
The Labours of Hercules
Taken at the Flood
Mrs McGinty's Dead
After the Funeral
Hickory Dickory Dock
Dead Man's Folly
Cat Among the Pigeons
The Adventure of the Christmas Pudding
The Clocks
Third Girl
Hallowe'en Party
Elephants Can Remember
Poirot's Early Cases
Curtain: Poirot's Last Case

Marple

The Murder at the Vicarage
The Thirteen Problems
The Body in the Library
The Moving Finger
A Murder is Announced
They Do It With Mirrors
A Pocket Full of Rye
The 4.50 from Paddington
The Mirror Crack'd from Side to Side
A Caribbean Mystery
At Bertram's Hotel
Nemesis
Sleeping Murder
Miss Marple's Final Cases

Tommy & Tuppence

The Secret Adversary
Partners in Crime
N or M?
By the Pricking of My Thumbs
Postern of Fate

Published as Mary Westmacott

Giant's Bread
Unfinished Portrait
Absent in the Spring
The Rose and the Yew Tree
A Daughter's a Daughter
The Burden

Memoirs

An Autobiography
Come, Tell Me How You Live

Play Collections

The Mousetrap and Selected Plays
Witness for the Prosecution and
   Selected Plays

* novelised by Charles Osborne

There is a tide in the affairs of men,
Which, taken at the flood, leads on to fortune;
Omitted, all the voyage of their life
Is bound in shallows and in miseries.
On such a full sea are we now afloat,
And we must take the current when it serves,
Or lose our ventures.

Prologue

I

In every club there is a club bore. The Coronation Club was no exception; and the fact that an air raid was in progress made no difference to normal procedure.

Major Porter, late Indian Army, rustled his newspaper and cleared his throat. Every one avoided his eye, but it was no use.

'I see they've got the announcement of Gordon Cloade's death in the *Times*,' he said. 'Discreetly put, of course. *On Oct. 5th, result of enemy action.* No address given. As a matter of fact it was just round the corner from my little place. One of those big houses on top of Campden Hill. I can tell you it shook me up a bit. I'm a Warden, you know. Cloade had only just got back from the States. He'd been over on that Government Purchase business. Got married while he was over there. A young widow – young enough to be his daughter. Mrs Underhay. As a matter of fact I knew her first husband out in Nigeria.'

Major Porter paused. Nobody displayed any interest or asked him to continue. Newspapers were held up sedulously in front of faces, but it took more than that to discourage Major Porter. He always had long histories to relate, mostly about people whom nobody knew.

'Interesting,' said Major Porter, firmly, his eyes fixed absently on a pair of extremely pointed patent-leather shoes – a type of footwear of which he profoundly disapproved. 'As I said, I'm a Warden. Funny business this blast. Never know what it's going to do. Blew the basement in and ripped off the roof. First floor practically wasn't touched. Six people in the house. Three servants: married couple and a housemaid, Gordon Cloade, his wife and the wife's brother. They were all down in the basement except the wife's brother – ex-Commando fellow – he preferred his own comfortable bedroom on the first floor – and by Jove, he escaped with a few bruises. The three servants were all killed by blast – Gordon Cloade must have been worth well over a million.'

Again Major Porter paused. His eyes had travelled up from the patent-leather shoes – striped trousers – black coat – egg-shaped head and colossal moustaches. Foreign, of course! That explained the shoes. 'Really,' thought Major Porter, 'what's the club coming to? Can't get away from foreigners even *here*.' This separate train of thought ran alongside his narrative.

The fact that the foreigner in question appeared to be giving him full attention did not abate Major Porter's prejudice in the slightest.

'She can't be more than about twenty-five,' he went on. 'And a widow for the second time. Or at any rate – that's what *she* thinks . . .'

He paused, hoping for curiosity – for comment. Not getting it, he nevertheless went doggedly on:

'Matter of fact I've got my own ideas about that. Queer business. As I told you, I knew her first husband, Underhay. Nice fellow – district commissioner in Nigeria at one time. Absolutely dead keen on his job – first-class chap. He married this girl in Cape Town. She was out there with some touring company. Very down on her luck, and pretty and helpless and all that. Listened to poor old Underhay raving about his district and the great wide-open spaces – and breathed out, "Wasn't it wonderful?" and how she wanted "to get away from everything." Well, she married him and got away from it. He was very much in love, poor fellow – but the thing didn't tick over from the first. She hated the bush and was terrified of the natives and was bored to death. Her idea of life was to go round to the local and meet the theatrical crowd and talk shop. Solitude à deux in the jungle wasn't at all her cup of tea. Mind you, I never met her myself – I heard all this from poor old Underhay. It hit him pretty hard. He did the decent thing, sent her home and agreed to give her a divorce. It was just after that I met him. He was all on edge and in the mood when a man's got to talk. He was a funny old-fashioned kind of chap in some ways – an R.C., and he didn't care for divorce. He said to me, "There are other ways of giving a woman her freedom." "Now, look here, old boy," I said, "don't go doing anything foolish. No woman in the world is worth putting a bullet through your head."

'He said that that wasn't his idea at all. "But I'm a lonely man," he said. "Got no relations to bother about me. If a report of my death gets back that will make Rosaleen a widow, which is what she wants." "And what about you?" I said. "Well," he said, "maybe a Mr Enoch Arden will turn up somewhere a thousand miles or so away and start life anew." "Might be awkward for her some day," I warned him. "Oh, no," he says, "I'd play the game. Robert Underhay would be dead all right."

'Well, I didn't think any more of it, but six months later I heard that Underhay had died of fever up in the bush somewhere. His natives were a trustworthy lot and they came back with a good circumstantial tale and a few last words scrawled in Underhay's writing saying they'd done all they could for him, and he was afraid he was pegging out, and praising up his headman. That man was devoted to him and so were all the others. Whatever he told them to swear to, they would swear to. So there it is . . . Maybe Underhay's buried up country in the midst of equatorial Africa but maybe he isn't – and if he isn't Mrs Gordon Cloade may get a shock one day. And serve her right, I say. I never met her, but I know the sound of a little gold-digger! She broke up poor old Underhay all right. It's an interesting story.'

Major Porter looked round rather wistfully for confirmation of this assertion. He met two bored and fishy stares, the half-averted gaze of young Mr Mellon and the polite attention of M. Hercule Poirot.

Then the newspaper rustled and a grey-haired man with a singularly impassive face rose quietly from his arm-chair by the fire and went out.

Major Porter's jaw dropped, and young Mr Mellon gave a faint whistle.

'Now you've done it!' he remarked. 'Know who that was?'

'God bless my soul,' said Major Porter in some agitation. 'Of course. I don't know him intimately but we are acquainted . . . Jeremy Cloade, isn't it, Gordon Cloade's brother? Upon my word, how extremely unfortunate! If I'd had any idea –'

'He's a solicitor,' said young Mr Mellon. 'Bet he sues you for slander or defamation of character or something.'

For young Mr Mellon enjoyed creating alarm and despondency in such places as it was not forbidden by the Defence of the Realm Act.

Major Porter continued to repeat in an agitated manner:

'Most unfortunate. *Most* unfortunate!'

'It will be all over Warmsley Heath by this evening,' said Mr Mellon. 'That's where all the Cloades hang out. They'll sit up late discussing what action to take.'

But at that moment the All Clear sounded, and young Mr Mellon stopped being malicious, and tenderly piloted his friend Hercule Poirot out into the street.

'Terrible atmosphere, these clubs,' he said. 'The most crashing collection of old bores. Porter's easily the worst, though. His description of the Indian rope trick takes three quarters of an hour, and he knows everybody whose mother ever passed through Poona!'

This was in the autumn of 1944. It was in late spring, 1946, that Hercule Poirot received a visit.

II

Hercule Poirot was sitting at his neat writing-desk on a pleasant May morning when his manservant George approached him and murmured deferentially:

'There is a lady, sir, asking to see you.'

'What kind of a lady?' Poirot asked cautiously.

He always enjoyed the meticulous accuracy of George's descriptions.

'She would be aged between forty and fifty, I should say, sir. Untidy and somewhat artistic in appearance. Good walking-shoes, brogues. A tweed coat and skirt – but a lace blouse. Some questionable Egyptian beads and a blue chiffon scarf.'

Poirot shuddered slightly.

'I do not think,' he said, 'that I wish to see her.'

'Shall I tell her, sir, that you are indisposed?'

Poirot looked at him thoughtfully.

'You have already, I gather, told her that I am engaged on important business and cannot be disturbed?'

George coughed again.

'She said, sir, that she had come up from the country specially, and did not mind how long she waited.'

Poirot sighed.

'One should never struggle against the inevitable,'

13

he said. 'If a middle-aged lady wearing sham Egyptian beads has made up her mind to see the famous Hercule Poirot, and has come up from the country to do so, nothing will deflect her. She will sit there in the hall till she gets her way. Show her in, George.'

George retreated, returning presently to announce formally:

'Mrs Cloade.'

The figure in the worn tweeds and the floating scarf came in with a beaming face. She advanced to Poirot with an outstretched hand, all her bead necklaces swinging and clinking.

'M. Poirot,' she said, 'I have come to you under spirit guidance.'

Poirot blinked slightly.

'Indeed, Madame. Perhaps you will take a seat and tell me –'

He got no further.

'Both ways, M. Poirot. With the automatic writing *and* with the ouija board. It was the night before last. Madame Elvary (a wonderful woman she is) and I were using the board. We got the same initials repeatedly. H.P. H.P. H.P. Of course I did not get the true significance at once. It takes, you know, a little *time*. One cannot, on this earthly plane, see clearly. I racked my brains thinking of someone with those initials. I knew it must connect up with the last séance – really a most poignant one, but it was some time before I got it. And then I bought a copy of *Picture Post* (Spirit guidance again, you see, because usually I buy the *New Statesman*) and there you were – a picture of you, and described, and on account of what you had done. It is wonderful, don't you think, M. Poirot, how everything has a *purpose*? Clearly, you are the person appointed by the Guides to elucidate this matter.'

Poirot surveyed her thoughtfully. Strangely enough the thing that really caught his attention was that she had remarkably shrewd light-blue eyes. They gave point, as it were, to her rambling method of approach.

'And what, Mrs – Cloade – is that right?' He frowned. 'I seem to have heard the name some time ago –'

She nodded vehemently.

'My poor brother-in-law – Gordon. Immensely rich and *often* mentioned in the press. He was killed in the Blitz over a year ago – a great blow to all of us. My husband is his younger brother. He is a doctor. Dr Lionel Cloade . . . Of course,' she added, lowering her voice, 'he has no idea that I am consulting you. He would not approve. Doctors, I find, have a very materialistic outlook. The spiritual seems to be strangely hidden from them. They pin their faith on Science – but what I say is . . . what *is* Science – what can it do?'

There seemed, to Hercule Poirot, to be no answer

Agatha Christie

to the question other than a meticulous and pains-taking description embracing Pasteur, Lister, Humphry Davy's safety lamp – the convenience of electricity in the home and several hundred other kindred items. But that, naturally, was not the answer Mrs Lionel Cloade wanted. In actual fact her question, like so many questions, was not really a question at all. It was a mere rhetorical gesture.

Hercule Poirot contented himself with inquiring in a practical manner:

'In what way do you believe I can help you, Mrs Cloade?'

'Do you believe in the reality of the spirit world, M. Poirot?'

'I am a good Catholic,' said Poirot cautiously.

Mrs Cloade waved aside the Catholic faith with a smile of pity.

'Blind! The Church is blind – prejudiced, foolish – not welcoming the reality and beauty of the world that lies behind this one.'

'At twelve o'clock,' said Hercule Poirot, 'I have an important appointment.'

It was a well-timed remark. Mrs Cloade leaned forward.

'I must come to the point at once. Would it be possible for you, M. Poirot, to find a missing person?'

Poirot's eyebrows rose.

'It might be possible – yes,' he replied cautiously. 'But the police, my dear Mrs Cloade, could do so a great deal more easily than I could. They have all the necessary machinery.'

Mrs Cloade waved away the police as she had waved away the Catholic Church.

'No, M. Poirot – it is to you I have been guided – by those beyond the veil. Now listen. My brother Gordon married some weeks before his death, a young widow – a Mrs Underhay. Her first husband (poor child, such a grief to her) was reported dead in Africa. A mysterious country – Africa.'

'A mysterious continent,' Poirot corrected her. 'Possibly. What part –'

She swept on.

'Central Africa. The home of voodoo, of the zombie –'

'The zombie is in the West Indies.'

Mrs Cloade swept on:

'– of black magic – of strange and secret practices – a country where a man could disappear and never be heard of again.'

'Possibly, possibly,' said Poirot. 'But the same is true of Piccadilly Circus.'

Mrs Cloade waved away Piccadilly Circus.

'Twice lately, M. Poirot, a communication has come through from a spirit who gives his name as Robert. The message was the same each time. *Not dead . . .*

17

We were puzzled, we knew no Robert. Asking for further guidance we got this. "*R.U. R.U. R.U.* – then *Tell R. Tell R.*" "Tell Robert?" we asked. "No, *from* Robert. R.U." "What does the U. stand for?" Then, M. Poirot, the most significant answer came. "*Little Boy Blue. Little Boy Blue. Ha ha ha!*" You see?'

'No,' said Poirot, 'I do not.'

She looked at him pityingly.

'The nursery rhyme *Little Boy Blue.* "*Under* the *Haycock* fast asleep" – *Underhay* – you see?'

Poirot nodded. He forbore to ask why, if the name Robert could be spelt out, the name Underhay could not have been treated the same way, and why it had been necessary to resort to a kind of cheap Secret Service spy jargon.

'And my sister-in-law's name is Rosaleen,' finished Mrs Cloade triumphantly. 'You see? Confusing all these Rs. But the *meaning* is quite plain. "*Tell Rosaleen that Robert Underhay is not dead.*"'

'Aha, and did you tell her?'

Mrs Cloade looked slightly taken aback.

'Er – well – no. You see, I mean – well, people are so *sceptical*. Rosaleen, I am sure, would be so. And then, poor child, it might upset her – wondering, you know, where he was – and what he was doing.'

'Besides projecting his voice through the ether? Quite so. A curious method, surely, of announcing his safety?'

'Ah, M. Poirot, you are not an initiate. And how do we know what the *circumstances* are? Poor Captain Underhay (or is it Major Underhay) may be a prisoner somewhere in the dark interior of Africa. But if he could be *found*, M. Poirot. If he could be restored to his dear young Rosaleen. Think of her happiness! Oh, M. Poirot, I have been *sent* to you – surely, *surely* you will not refuse the behest of the spiritual world.'

Poirot looked at her reflectively.

'My fees,' he said softly, 'are very expensive. I may say enormously expensive! And the task you suggest would not be easy.'

'Oh dear – but surely – it is most unfortunate. I and my husband are very badly off – very badly off indeed. Actually my own plight is worse than my dear husband knows. I bought some shares – under spirit guidance – and so far they have proved very disappointing – in fact, quite alarming. They have gone right down and are now, I gather, practically unsaleable.'

She looked at him with dismayed blue eyes.

'I have not dared to tell my husband. I simply tell *you* in order to explain how I am situated. But surely, dear M. Poirot, to reunite a young husband and wife – it is such a *noble* mission –'

'Nobility, *chère Madame*, will not pay steamer and railway and air travel fares. Nor will it cover the cost of long telegrams and cables, and the interrogations of witnesses.'

'But if he is found – if Captain Underhay is found alive and well – then – well, I think I may safely say that, once that was accomplished, there – there would be no difficulty about – er – reimbursing you.'

'Ah, he is rich, then, this Captain Underhay?'

'No. Well, no . . . But I can assure you – I can give you my *word* – that – that the money situation will not present difficulties.'

Slowly Poirot shook his head.

'I am sorry, Madame. The answer is No.'

He had a little difficulty in getting her to accept that answer.

When she had finally gone away, he stood lost in thought, frowning to himself. He remembered now why the name of Cloade was familiar to him. The conversation at the club the day of the air raid came back to him. The booming boring voice of Major Porter, going on and on, telling a story to which nobody wanted to listen.

He remembered the rustle of a newspaper and Major Porter's suddenly dropped jaw and expression of con-sternation.

But what worried him was trying to make up his mind about the eager middle-aged lady who had just left him. The glib spiritualistic patter, the vagueness, the floating scarves, the chains and amulets jingling round her neck – and finally, slightly at variance with all this, that sudden shrewd glint in a pair of pale-blue eyes.

'Just why exactly did she come to me?' he said to himself. 'And what, I wonder, has been going on in' – he looked down at the card on his desk – 'Warmsley Vale?'

III

It was exactly five days later that he saw a small paragraph in an evening paper – it referred to the death of a man called Enoch Arden – at Warmsley Vale, a small old-world village about three miles from the popular Warmsley Heath Golf Course.

Hercule Poirot said to himself again:

'I wonder what has been going on in Warmsley Vale . . .'

Book I

Chapter 1

I

Warmsley Heath consists of a golf course, two hotels, some very expensive modern villas giving on to the golf course, a row of what were, before the war, luxury shops, and a railway station.

Emerging from the railway station, a main road roars its way to London on your left – to your right a small path across a field is signposted

Footpath to Warmsley Vale.

Warmsley Vale, tucked away amongst wooded hills, is as unlike Warmsley Heath as well can be. It is in essence a microscopic old-fashioned market town now degenerated into a village. It has a main street of Georgian houses, several pubs, a few unfashionable shops and a general air of being a hundred and fifty instead of twenty-eight miles from London.

Its occupants one and all unite in despising the mushroom growth of Warmsley Heath.

On the outskirts are some charming houses with pleasant old-world gardens. It was to one of these houses, the White House, that Lynn Marchmont returned in the early spring of 1946 when she was demobbed from the Wrens.

On her third morning she looked out of her bedroom window, across the untidy lawn to the elms in the meadow beyond, and sniffed the air happily. It was a gentle grey morning with a smell of soft wet earth. The kind of smell that she had been missing for the past two years and a half.

Wonderful to be home again, wonderful to be here in her own little bedroom which she had thought of so often and so nostalgically whilst she had been overseas. Wonderful to be out of uniform, to be able to get into a tweed skirt and a jumper – even if the moths *had* been rather too industrious during the war years!

It was good to be out of the Wrens and a free woman again, although she had really enjoyed her overseas service very much. The work had been reasonably interesting, there had been parties, plenty of fun, but there had also been the irksomeness of routine and the feeling of being herded together with her companions which had sometimes made her feel desperately anxious to escape.

It was then, during the long scorching summer out East, that she had thought so longingly of Warmsley Vale and the shabby cool pleasant house, and of dear Mums.

Lynn both loved her mother and was irritated by her. Far away from home, she had loved her still and had forgotten the irritation, or remembered it only with an additional homesick pang. Darling Mums, so completely maddening! What she would not have given to have heard Mums enunciate one cliché in her sweet complaining voice. Oh, to be at home again and never, *never* to have to leave home again!

And now here she was, out of the Service, free, and back at the White House. She had been back three days. And already a curious dissatisfied restlessness was creeping over her. It was all the same – almost too much all the same – the house and Mums and Rowley and the farm and the family. The thing that was different and that ought not to be different was herself . . .

'Darling . . .' Mrs Marchmont's thin cry came up the stairs. 'Shall I bring my girl a nice tray in bed?'

Lynn called out sharply:

'Of course not. I'm coming down.'

'And why,' she thought, 'has Mums got to say "my girl". It's so *silly*!'

She ran downstairs and entered the dining-room.

It was not a very good breakfast. Already Lynn was realizing the undue proportion of time and interest taken by the search for food. Except for a rather unreliable woman who came four mornings a week, Mrs Marchmont was alone in the house, struggling with cooking and cleaning. She had been nearly forty when Lynn was born and her health was not good. Also Lynn realized with some dismay how their financial position had changed. The small but adequate fixed income which had kept them going comfortably before the war was now almost halved by taxation. Rates, expenses, wages had all gone up.

'Oh! brave new world,' thought Lynn grimly. Her eyes rested lightly on the columns of the daily paper.

'Ex-W.A.A.F. seeks post where initiative and drive will be appreciated.' 'Former W.R.E.N. seeks post where organizing ability and authority are needed.'

Enterprise, initiative, command, those were the commodities offered. But what was wanted? People who could cook and clean, or write decent shorthand. Plodding people who knew a routine and could give good service.

Well, it didn't affect her. Her way ahead lay clear. Marriage to her cousin Rowley Cloade. They had got engaged seven years ago, just before the outbreak of war. Almost as long as she could remember, she had meant to marry Rowley. His choice of a farming life had been acquiesced in readily by her. A good life – not exciting perhaps, and with plenty of hard work, but they both loved the open air and the care of animals.

Not that their prospects were quite what they had been – Uncle Gordon had always promised . . .

Mrs Marchmont's voice broke in plaintively apposite:

'It's been the most dreadful blow to us all, Lynn darling, as I wrote you. Gordon had only been in England two days. We hadn't even *seen* him. If *only* he hadn't stayed in London. If he'd come straight down here.'

II

'Yes, if only . . .'

Far away, Lynn had been shocked and grieved by the news of her uncle's death, but the true significance of it was only now beginning to come home to her.

For as long as she could remember, her life, all their lives, had been dominated by Gordon Cloade. The rich, childless man had taken all his relatives completely under his wing.

Agatha Christie

Even Rowley . . . Rowley and his friend Johnnie Vavasour had started in partnership on the farm. Their capital was small, but they had been full of hope and energy. And Gordon Cloade had approved.

To her he had said more.

'You can't get anywhere in farming without capital. But the first thing to find out is whether these boys have really got the will and the energy to make a go of it. If I set them up now, I wouldn't know that – maybe for years. If they've got the right stuff in them, if I'm satisfied that their side of it is all right, well then, Lynn, you needn't worry. I'll finance them on the proper scale. So don't think badly of your prospects, my girl. You're just the wife Rowley needs. But keep what I've told you under your hat.'

Well, she had done that, but Rowley himself had sensed his uncle's benevolent interest. It was up to him to prove to the old boy that Rowley and Johnnie were a good investment for money.

Yes, they had all depended on Gordon Cloade. Not that any of the family had been spongers or idlers. Jeremy Cloade was senior partner in a firm of solicitors, Lionel Cloade was in practice as a doctor.

But behind the workaday life was the comforting assurance of money in the background. There was never any need to stint or to save. The future was assured. Gordon Cloade, a childless widower, would see to that. He had told them all, more than once, that that was so.

His widowed sister, Adela Marchmont, had stayed on at the White House when she might, perhaps, have moved into a smaller, more labour-saving house. Lynn went to first-class schools. If the war had not come, she would have been able to take any kind of expensive training she had pleased. Cheques from Uncle Gordon flowed in with comfortable regularity to provide little luxuries.

Everything had been so *settled*, so *secure*. And then had come Gordon Cloade's wholly unexpected marriage.

'Of course, darling,' Adela went on, 'we were all flabbergasted. If there was one thing that seemed quite certain, it was that Gordon would never marry again. It wasn't, you see, as though he hadn't got plenty of family ties.'

Yes, thought Lynn, plenty of family. Sometimes, possibly, rather too much family?

'He was so kind always,' went on Mrs Marchmont. 'Though perhaps just a weeny bit tyrannical on occasions. He never liked the habit of dining off a polished table. Always insisted on my sticking to the old-fashioned tablecloths. In fact, he sent me the most beautiful Venetian lace ones when he was in Italy.'

'It certainly paid to fall in with his wishes,' said Lynn

dryly. She added with some curiosity, 'How did he meet this – second wife? You never told me in your letters.'

'Oh, my dear, on some boat or plane or other. Coming from South America to New York, I believe. After all those years! And after all those secretaries and typists and housekeepers and everything.'

Lynn smiled. Ever since she could remember, Gordon Cloade's secretaries, housekeepers and office staff had been subjected to the closest scrutiny and suspicion.

She asked curiously, 'She's good-looking, I suppose?'

'Well, dear,' said Adela, '*I* think myself she has rather a *silly* face.'

'You're not a man, Mums!'

'Of course,' Mrs Marchmont went on, 'the poor girl was blitzed and had shock from blast and was really frightfully ill and all that, and it's my opinion she's never really quite recovered. She's a mass of nerves, if you know what I mean. And really, sometimes, she looks quite half-witted. I don't feel she could ever have made much of a companion for poor Gordon.

Lynn smiled. She doubted whether Gordon Cloade had chosen to marry a woman years younger than himself for her intellectual companionship.

'And then, dear,' Mrs Marchmont lowered her voice, 'I hate to say it, but of course she's *not* a lady!'

'What an expression, Mums! What does that matter nowadays?'

'It still matters in the country, dear,' said Adela placidly. 'I simply mean that she isn't exactly one of *us*!'

'Poor little devil!'

'Really, Lynn, I don't know what you mean. We have all been *most* careful to be kind and polite and to welcome her amongst us for Gordon's sake.'

'She's at Furrowbank, then?' Lynn asked curiously.

'Yes, naturally. Where else was there for her to go when she came out of the nursing home? The doctors said she must be out of London. She's at Furrowbank with her brother.'

'What's *he* like?' Lynn asked.

'A *dreadful* young man!' Mrs Marchmont paused, and then added with a good deal of intensity: '*Rude.*'

A momentary flicker of sympathy crossed Lynn's mind. She thought: 'I bet *I'd* be rude in his place!'

She asked: 'What's his name?'

'Hunter. David Hunter. Irish, I believe. Of course they are not people one has ever heard of. She was a widow – a Mrs Underhay. One doesn't wish to be *uncharitable*, but one can't help asking oneself – what *kind* of a widow would be likely to be travelling about from South America in wartime? One can't help feeling, you know, that she was just *looking* for a rich husband.'

'In which case, she didn't look in vain,' remarked Lynn.

Mrs Marchmont sighed.

'It seems so extraordinary. Gordon was such a shrewd man always. And it wasn't, I mean, that women hadn't *tried*. That last secretary but one, for instance. Really quite *blatant*. She was very efficient, I believe, but he had to get rid of her.'

Lynn said vaguely: 'I suppose there's always a Waterloo.'

'Sixty-two,' said Mrs Marchmont. 'A very dangerous age. And a war, I imagine, is unsettling. But I can't tell you what a *shock* it was when we got his letter from New York.'

'What did it say exactly?'

'He wrote to Frances – I really can't *think* why. Perhaps he imagined that owing to her upbringing she might be more sympathetic. He said that we'd probably be surprised to hear that he was married. It had all been rather sudden, but he was sure we should all soon grow very fond of Rosaleen (such a very *theatrical* name, don't you think, dear? I mean definitely rather bogus). She had had a very sad life, he said, and had gone through a lot although she was so young. Really it was wonderful the plucky way she had stood up to life.'

'Quite a well-known gambit,' murmured Lynn.

'Oh, I know. I do agree. One has heard it so *many* times. But one would really think that *Gordon* with all his experience – still, there it is. She has the most enormous eyes – dark blue and what they call put in with a smutty finger.'

'Attractive?'

'Oh, yes, she is certainly very *pretty*. It's not the kind of prettiness *I* admire.'

'It never is,' said Lynn with a wry smile.

'No, dear. Really, *men* – but well, there's no accounting for men! Even the most well-balanced of them do the most incredibly foolish things! Gordon's letter went on to say that we mustn't think for a moment that this would mean any loosening of old ties. He still considered us all his special responsibility.'

'But he didn't,' said Lynn, 'make a will after his marriage?'

Mrs Marchmont shook her head.

'The last will he made was in 1940. I don't know any details, but he gave us to understand at the time that we were all taken care of by it if anything should happen to him. That will, of course, was revoked by his marriage. I suppose he would have made a new will when he got home – but there just wasn't time. He was killed practically the day after he landed in this country.'

'And so she – Rosaleen – gets everything?'

'Yes. The old will was invalidated by his marriage.'

Lynn was silent. She was not more mercenary than most, but she would not have been human if she had not resented the new state of affairs. It was not, she felt, at all what Gordon Cloade himself would have envisaged. The bulk of his fortune he might have left to his young wife, but certain provisions he would certainly have made for the family he had encouraged to depend upon him. Again and again he had urged them not to save, not to make provision for the future. She had heard him say to Jeremy, 'You'll be a rich man when I die.' To her mother he had often said, 'Don't worry, Adela. I'll always look after Lynn – you know that, and I'd hate you to leave this house – it's your *home*. Send all the bills for repairs to me.' Rowley he had encouraged to take up farming. Antony, Jeremy's son, he had insisted should go into the Guards and he had always made him a handsome allowance. Lionel Cloade had been encouraged to follow up certain lines of medical research that were not immediately profitable and to let his practice run down.

Lynn's thoughts were broken into. Dramatically, and with a trembling lip, Mrs Marchmont produced a sheaf of bills.

'And look at all these,' she wailed. 'What am I to *do*? What on earth am I to do, Lynn? The bank manager wrote me only this morning that I'm overdrawn. I don't see how I *can* be. I've been so careful. But it seems my investments just aren't producing what they used to. Increased taxation he says. And all these yellow things, War Damage Insurance or something – one has to pay them whether one wants to or not.'

Lynn took the bills and glanced through them. There were no records of extravagance amongst them. They were for slates replaced on the roof; the mending of fences, replacement of a worn-out kitchen boiler – a new main water pipe. They amounted to a considerable sum.

Mrs Marchmont said piteously:

'I suppose I ought to move from here. But where could I go? There isn't a small house anywhere – there just *isn't* such a thing. Oh, I don't want to worry you with all this, Lynn. Not just as soon as you've come home. But I don't know what to do. I really don't.'

Lynn looked at her mother. She was over sixty. She had never been a very strong woman. During the war she had taken in evacuees from London, had cooked and cleaned for them, had worked with the W.V.S., made jam, helped with school meals. She had worked fourteen hours a day in contrast to a pleasant easy life before the war. She was now, as Lynn saw, very near a breakdown. Tired out and frightened of the future.

A slow quiet anger rose in Lynn. She said slowly:

'Couldn't this Rosaleen – help?'

Mrs Marchmont flushed.

'We've no right to anything – anything at all.'

Lynn demurred.

'I think you've a moral right. Uncle Gordon always helped.'

Mrs Marchmont shook her head. She said:

'It wouldn't be very nice, dear, to ask favours – not of someone one doesn't like very much. And anyway that brother of hers would never let her give away a penny!'

And she added, heroism giving place to pure female cattiness: 'If he really *is* her brother, that is to say!'

Chapter 2

Frances Cloade looked thoughtfully across the dinner table at her husband.

Frances was forty-eight. She was one of those lean greyhound women who look well in tweeds. There was a rather arrogant ravaged beauty about her face which had no make-up except a little carelessly applied lipstick. Jeremy Cloade was a spare grey-haired man of sixty-three, with a dry expressionless face.

It was, this evening, even more expressionless than usual.

His wife registered the fact with a swift flashing glance.

A fifteen-year-old girl shuffled round the table, handing the dishes. Her agonized gaze was fixed on Frances. If Frances frowned, she nearly dropped something, a look of approval set her beaming.

It was noted enviously in Warmsley Vale that if any

one had servants it would be Frances Cloade. She did not bribe them with extravagant wages, and she was exacting as to performance – but her warm approval of endeavour and her infectious energy and drive made of domestic service something creative and personal. She had been so used to being waited on all her life that she took it for granted without self-consciousness, and she had the same appreciation of a good cook or a good parlourmaid as she would have had for a good pianist.

Frances Cloade had been the only daughter of Lord Edward Trenton, who had trained his horses in the neighbourhood of Warmsley Heath. Lord Edward's final bankruptcy was realized by those in the know to be a merciful escape from worse things. There had been rumours of horses that had signally failed to stay at unexpected moments, other rumours of inquiries by the Stewards of the Jockey Club. But Lord Edward had escaped with his reputation only lightly tarnished and had reached an arrangement with his creditors which permitted him to live exceedingly comfortably in the South of France. And for these unexpected blessings he had to thank the shrewdness and special exertions of his solicitor, Jeremy Cloade. Cloade had done a good deal more than a solicitor usually does for a client, and had even advanced guarantees of his own. He had made it clear that he had a deep admiration for Frances Trenton, and in due course, when her father's affairs had been satisfactorily wound up, Frances became Mrs Jeremy Cloade.

What she had felt about it no one had ever known. All that could be said was that she had kept her side of the bargain admirably. She had been an efficient and loyal wife to Jeremy, a careful mother to his son, had forwarded Jeremy's interests in every way and had never once suggested by word or deed that the match was anything but a freewill impulse on her part.

In response the Cloade family had an enormous respect and admiration for Frances. They were proud of her, they deferred to her judgment – but they never felt really quite intimate with her.

What Jeremy Cloade thought of his marriage nobody knew, because nobody ever did know what Jeremy Cloade thought or felt. 'A dry stick' was what people said about Jeremy. His reputation both as a man and a lawyer was very high. Cloade, Brunskill and Cloade never touched any questionable legal business. They were not supposed to be brilliant but were considered very sound. The firm prospered and the Jeremy Cloades lived in a handsome Georgian house just off the Market Place with a big old-fashioned walled garden behind it where the pear trees in spring showed a sea of white blossom.

It was to a room overlooking the garden at the back of the house that the husband and wife went when they rose from the dinner table. Edna, the fifteen-year-old, brought in coffee, breathing excitedly and adenoidally.

Frances poured a little coffee into the cup. It was strong and hot. She said to Edna, crisply and approvingly:

'Excellent, Edna.'

Edna went crimson with pleasure and went out marvelling nevertheless at what some people liked. Coffee, in Edna's opinion, ought to be a pale cream colour, ever so sweet, with lots of milk!

In the room overlooking the garden, the Cloades drank their coffee, black and without sugar. They had talked in a desultory way during dinner, of acquaintances met, of Lynn's return, of the prospects of farming in the near future, but now, alone together, they were silent.

Frances leaned back in her chair, watching her husband. He was quite oblivious of her regard. His right hand stroked his upper lip. Although Jeremy Cloade did not know it himself the gesture was a characteristic one and coincided with inner perturbation. Frances had not observed it very often. Once when Antony, their son, had been seriously ill as a child; once when waiting for a jury to consider their verdict; at the outbreak of war, waiting to hear the irrevocable words over the wireless; on the eve of Antony's departure after embarkation leave.

Frances thought a little while before she spoke. Their

married life had been happy, but never intimate in so far as the spoken word went. She had respected Jeremy's reserves and he hers. Even when the telegram had come announcing Antony's death on active service, they had neither of them broken down.

He had opened it, then he had looked up at her. She had said, 'Is it –?'

He had bowed his head, then crossed and put the telegram into her outstretched hand.

They had stood there quite silently for a while. Then Jeremy had said: 'I wish I could help you, my dear.' And she had answered, her voice steady, her tears unshed, conscious only of the terrible emptiness and aching: 'It's just as bad for you.' He had patted her shoulder: 'Yes,' he said. 'Yes . . .' Then he had moved towards the door, walking a little awry, yet stiffly, suddenly an old man . . . saying as he did so, 'There's nothing to be said – nothing to be said . . .'

She had been grateful to him, passionately grateful, for understanding so well, and had been torn with pity for him, seeing him suddenly turn into an old man. With the loss of her boy, something had hardened in her – some ordinary common kindness had dried up. She was more efficient, more energetic than ever – people became sometimes a little afraid of her ruthless common sense . . .

Jeremy Cloade's finger moved along his upper lip

again – irresolutely, searching. And crisply, across the room, Frances spoke.

'Is anything the matter, Jeremy?'

He started. His coffee cup almost slipped from his hand. He recovered himself, put it firmly down on the tray. Then he looked across at her.

'What do you mean, Frances?'

'I'm asking you if anything is the matter?'

'What should be the matter?'

'It would be foolish to guess. I would rather you told me.'

She spoke without emotion in a businesslike way.

He said unconvincingly:

'There is nothing the matter –'

She did not answer. She merely waited inquiringly. His denial, it seemed, she put aside as negligible. He looked at her uncertainly.

And just for a moment the imperturbable mask of his grey face slipped, and she caught a glimpse of such turbulent agony that she almost exclaimed aloud. It was only for a moment but she didn't doubt what she had seen.

She said quietly and unemotionally:

'I think you had better tell me –'

He sighed – a deep unhappy sigh.

'You will have to know, of course,' he said, 'sooner or later.'

And he added what was to her a very astonishing phrase.

'I'm afraid you've made a bad bargain, Frances.'

She went right past an implication she did not understand to attack hard facts.

'What is it,' she said; 'money?'

She did not know why she put money first. There had been no special signs of financial stringency other than were natural to the times. They were short-staffed at the office with more business than they could cope with, but that was the same everywhere and in the last month they had got back some of their people released from the Army. It might just as easily have been illness that he was concealing – his colour had been bad lately, and he had been overworked and overtired. But nevertheless Frances' instinct went towards money, and it seemed she was right.

Her husband nodded.

'I see.' She was silent a moment, thinking. She herself did not really care about money at all – but she knew that Jeremy was quite incapable of realizing that. Money meant to him a four-square world – stability – obligations – a definite place and status in life.

Money to her was a toy tossed into one's lap to play with. She had been born and bred in an atmosphere of financial instability. There had been wonderful times when the horses had done what was expected of them.

Agatha Christie

There had been difficult times when the tradesmen wouldn't give credit and Lord Edward had been forced to ignominious straits to avoid the bailiffs on the front-door step. Once they had lived on dry bread for a week and sent all the servants away. They had had the bailiffs in the house for three weeks once when Frances was a child. She had found the bum in question very agreeable to play with and full of stories of his own little girl.

If one had no money one simply scrounged, or went abroad, or lived on one's friends and relations for a bit. Or somebody tided you over with a loan . . .

But looking across at her husband Frances realized that in the Cloade world you didn't do that kind of thing. You didn't beg or borrow or live on other people. (And conversely you didn't expect them to beg or borrow or live off you!)

Frances felt terribly sorry for Jeremy and a little guilty about being so unperturbed herself. She took refuge in practicality.

'Shall we have to sell up everything? Is the firm going smash?'

Jeremy Cloade winced, and she realized she had been too matter-of-fact.

'My dear,' she said gently, 'do tell me. I can't go on guessing.'

Cloade said stiffly, 'We went through rather a bad crisis two years ago. Young Williams, you remember,

46

absconded. We had some difficulty getting straight again. Then there were certain complications arising out of the position in the Far East after Singapore –'

She interrupted him.

'Never mind the whys – they are so unimportant. You were in a jam. And you haven't been able to snap out of it?'

He said, 'I relied on Gordon. Gordon would have put things straight.'

She gave a quick impatient sigh.

'Of course. I don't want to blame the poor man – after all, it's only human nature to lose your head about a pretty woman. And why on earth shouldn't he marry again if he wanted to? But it was unfortunate his being killed in that air raid before he'd settled anything or made a proper will or adjusted his affairs. The truth is that one never believes for a minute, no matter what danger you're in, that you yourself are going to be killed. The bomb is always going to hit the other person!'

'Apart from his loss, and I was very fond of Gordon – and proud of him too,' said Gordon Cloade's elder brother, 'his death was a catastrophe for me. It came at a moment –'

He stopped.

'Shall we be bankrupt?' Frances asked with intelligent interest.

Jeremy Cloade looked at her almost despairingly. Though she did not realize it, he could have coped much better with tears and alarm. This cool detached practical interest defeated him utterly.

He said harshly, 'It's a good deal worse than that . . .'

He watched her as she sat quite still, thinking over that. He said to himself, 'In another minute I shall have to tell her. She'll know what I am . . . She'll have to know. Perhaps she won't believe it at first.'

Frances Cloade sighed and sat up straight in her big arm-chair.

'I see,' she said. 'Embezzlement. Or if that isn't the right word, that kind of thing . . . like young Williams.'

'Yes, but this time – you don't understand – *I'm* responsible. I've used trust funds that were committed to my charge. So far, I've covered my tracks –'

'But now it's all going to come out?'

'Unless I can get the necessary money – quickly.'

The shame he felt was the worst he had known in his life. How would she take it?

At the moment she was taking it very calmly. But then, he thought, Frances would never make a scene. Never reproach or upbraid.

Her hand to her cheek, she was frowning.

'It's so stupid,' she said, 'that I haven't got any money of my own at all . . .'

He said stiffly, 'There is your marriage settlement, but –'

She said absently, 'But I suppose that's gone too.'

He was silent. Then he said with difficulty, in his dry voice: 'I'm sorry, Frances. More sorry than I can say. You made a bad bargain.'

She looked up sharply.

'You said that before. What do you mean by that?'

Jeremy said stiffly:

'When you were good enough to marry me, you had the right to expect – well, integrity – and a life free from sordid anxieties.'

She was looking at him with complete astonishment.

'Really, Jeremy! What on earth do you think I married you for?'

He smiled slightly.

'You have always been a most loyal and devoted wife, my dear. But I can hardly flatter myself that you would have accepted me in – er – different circumstances.'

She stared at him and suddenly burst out laughing.

'You funny old stick! What a wonderful novelettish mind you must have behind that legal façade! Do you really think that I married you as the price of saving Father from the wolves – or the Stewards of the Jockey Club, et cetera?'

'You were very fond of your father, Frances.'

'I was devoted to Daddy! He was terribly attractive and the greatest fun to live with! But I always knew he was a bad hat. And if you think that I'd sell myself to the family solicitor in order to save him from getting what was always coming to him, then you've never understood the first thing about me. Never!'

She stared at him. Extraordinary, she thought, to have been married to someone for over twenty years and not have known what was going on in their minds. But how could one know when it was a mind so different from one's own? A romantic mind, of course, well camouflaged, but essentially romantic. She thought: 'All those old Stanley Weymans in his bedroom. I might have known from *them*! The poor idiotic darling!'

Aloud she said:

'I married you because I was in love with you, of course.'

'In love with me? But what could you see in me?'

'If you ask me that, Jeremy, I really don't know. You were such a *change*, so different from all Father's crowd. You never talked about horses for one thing. You've no idea how *sick* I was of horses – and what the odds were likely to be for the Newmarket Cup! You came to dinner one night – do you remember? – and I sat next to you and asked you what bimetallism was, and you told me – really *told* me! It took the whole of dinner – six courses – we were in funds at the moment and had a French chef!'

'It must have been extremely boring,' said Jeremy.

'It was fascinating! Nobody had ever treated me seriously before. And you were so polite and yet never seemed to look at me or think I was nice or good-looking or anything. It put me on my mettle. I *swore* I'd make you notice me.'

Jeremy Cloade said grimly . . . 'I noticed you all right. I went home that evening and didn't sleep a wink. You had a blue dress with cornflowers . . .'

There was silence for a moment or two, then Jeremy cleared his throat.

'Er – all that is a long time ago . . .'

She came quickly to the rescue of his embarrassment.

'And we're now a middle-aged married couple in difficulties, looking for the best way out.'

'After what you've just told me, Frances, it makes it a thousand times worse that this – this disgrace –'

She interrupted him.

'Let us please get things clear. You are being apologetic because you've fallen foul of the law. You may be prosecuted – go to prison.' (He winced.) 'I don't want that to happen. I'll fight like anything to stop it, but don't credit me with moral indignation. We're

51

not a moral family, remember. Father, in spite of his attractiveness, was a bit of a crook. And there was Charles – my cousin. They hushed it up and he wasn't prosecuted, and they hustled him off to the Colonies. And there was my cousin Gerald – *he* forged a cheque at Oxford. But he went to fight and got a posthumous V.C. for complete bravery and devotion to his men and superhuman endurance. What I'm trying to say is people are *like* that – not quite bad or quite good. I don't suppose I'm particularly straight myself – I have been because there hasn't been any temptation to be otherwise. But what I have got is plenty of courage and' (she smiled at him) 'I'm *loyal*!'

'My dear!' He got up and came over to her. He stopped and put his lips to her hair.

'And now,' said Lord Edward Trenton's daughter, smiling up at him, 'what are we going to do? Raise money somehow?'

Jeremy's face stiffened.

'I don't see how.'

'A mortgage on this house. Oh, I see,' she was quick, 'that's been done. I'm stupid. Of course you've done all the obvious things. It's a question then of a *touch*? Who *can* we touch? I suppose there's only one possibility. Gordon's widow – the dark Rosaleen!'

Jeremy shook his head dubiously.

'It would have to be a large sum . . . And it can't

come out of capital. The money's only in trust for her for her life.'

'I hadn't realized that. I thought she had it absolutely. What happens when she dies?'

'It comes to Gordon's next of kin. That is to say it is divided between myself, Lionel, Adela, and Maurice's son, Rowley.'

'It comes to *us* . . .' said Frances slowly.

Something seemed to pass through the room – a cold air – the shadow of a thought . . .

Frances said: 'You didn't tell me that . . . I thought she got it for keeps – that she could leave it to any one she liked?'

'No. By the statute relating to intestacy of 1925 . . .'

It is doubtful whether Frances listened to his explanation. She said when his voice stopped:

'It hardly matters to us personally. We'll be dead and buried, long before she's middle-aged. How old is she? Twenty-five – twenty-six? She'll probably live to be seventy.'

Jeremy Cloade said doubtfully:

'We might ask her for a loan – putting it on family grounds? She may be a generous-minded girl – really we know so little of her –'

Frances said: 'At any rate we have been reasonably nice to her – not catty like Adela. She might respond.'

Agatha Christie

Her husband said warningly:

'There must be no hint of – er – real urgency.'

Frances said impatiently: 'Of course not! The trouble is that it's not the girl herself we shall have to deal with. She's completely under the thumb of that brother of hers.'

'A very unattractive young man,' said Jeremy Cloade.

Frances' sudden smile flashed out.

'Oh, no,' she said. 'He's attractive. *Most* attractive. Rather unscrupulous, too, I should imagine. But then as far as that goes, *I'm* unscrupulous too!'

Her smile hardened. She looked up at her husband.

'We're not going to be beaten, Jeremy,' she said. 'There's bound to be *some* way . . . if I have to rob a bank!'

Chapter 3

'Money!' said Lynn.

Rowley Cloade nodded. He was a big square young man with a brick-red skin, thoughtful blue eyes and very fair hair. He had a slowness that seemed more purposeful than ingrained. He used deliberation as others use quickness of repartee.

'Yes,' he said, 'everything seems to boil down to money these days.'

'But I thought farmers had done so well during the war?'

'Oh, yes – but that doesn't do you any permanent good. In a year we'll be back where we were – with wages up, workers unwilling, everybody dissatisfied and nobody knowing where they are. Unless, of course, you can farm in a really big way. Old Gordon knew. That was where he was preparing to come in.'

'And now –' Lynn asked.

Rowley grinned.

'And now Mrs Gordon goes to London and spends a couple of thousand on a nice mink coat.'

'It's – it's wicked!'

'Oh, no –' He paused and said: 'I'd rather like to give *you* a mink coat, Lynn –'

'What's she like, Rowley?' She wanted to get a contemporary judgment.

'You'll see her tonight. At Uncle Lionel's and Aunt Kathie's party.'

'Yes, I know. But I want *you* to tell me. Mums says she's half-witted?'

Rowley considered.

'Well – I shouldn't say intellect was her strong point. But I think really she only seems half-witted because she's being so frightfully careful.'

'Careful? Careful about what?'

'Oh, just careful. Mainly, I imagine, about her accent – she's got quite a brogue, you know, or else about the right fork, and any literary allusions that might be flying around.'

'Then she really is – quite – well, uneducated?'

Rowley grinned.

'Oh, she's not a lady, if that's what you mean. She's got lovely eyes, and a very good complexion – and I suppose old Gordon fell for that, with her extraordinary air of being quite unsophisticated. I don't

think it's put on – though of course you never know.
She just stands around looking dumb and letting David
run her.'

'David?'

'That's the brother. I should say there's nothing
much about sharp practice *he* doesn't know!' Rowley
added: 'He doesn't like any of us much.'

'Why should he?' said Lynn sharply, and added as
he looked at her, slightly surprised, 'I mean *you* don't
like *him*.'

'I certainly don't. You won't either. He's not our
sort.'

'You don't know who I like, Rowley, or who I don't!
I've seen a lot of the world in the last three years. I –
I think my outlook has broadened.'

'You've seen more of the world than I have, that's
true.'

He said it quietly – but Lynn looked up sharply.

There had been something – behind those even
tones.

He returned her glance squarely, his face unemotional. It had never, Lynn remembered, been easy to
know exactly what Rowley was thinking.

What a queer topsy-turvy world it was, thought
Lynn. It used to be the man who went to the wars,
the woman who stayed at home. But here the positions
were reversed.

Of the two young men, Rowley and Johnnie, one had had perforce to stay on the farm. They had tossed for it and Johnnie Vavasour had been the one to go. He had been killed almost at once – in Norway. All through the years of war Rowley had never been more than a mile or two from home.

And she, Lynn, had been to Egypt, to North Africa, to Sicily. She had been under fire more than once.

Here was Lynn Home-from-the-wars, and here was Rowley Stay-at-home.

She wondered, suddenly, if he minded . . .

She gave a nervous little half laugh. 'Things seem sometimes a bit upside down, don't they?'

'Oh, I don't know.' Rowley stared vacantly out over the countryside. 'Depends.'

'Rowley,' she hesitated, 'did you *mind* – I mean – Johnnie –'

His cold level gaze threw her back on herself.

'Let's leave Johnnie out of it! The war's over – and I've been lucky.'

'Lucky, you mean' – she paused doubtfully – 'not to have had to – to go?'

'Wonderful luck, don't you think so?' She didn't know quite how to take that. His voice was smooth with hard edges. He added with a smile, 'But, of course, you service girls will find it hard to settle down at home.'

She said irritably, 'Oh, don't be stupid, Rowley.'

(But why be irritable? Why – unless, because his words touched a raw nerve of truth somewhere.)

'Oh well,' said Rowley. 'I suppose we might as well consider getting married. Unless you've changed your mind?'

'Of course I haven't changed my mind. Why should I?'

He said vaguely:

'One never knows.'

'You mean you think I'm' – Lynn paused – 'different?'

'Not particularly.'

'Perhaps *you've* changed your mind?'

'Oh, no, *I've* not changed. Very little change down on the farm, you know.'

'All right, then,' said Lynn – conscious, somehow, of anticlimax, 'let's get married. Whenever you like.'

'June or thereabouts?'

'Yes.'

They were silent. It was settled. In spite of herself, Lynn felt terribly depressed. Yet Rowley was Rowley – just as he always had been. Affectionate, unemotional, painstakingly given to understatement.

They loved each other. They had always loved each other. They had never talked about their love very much – so why should they begin now?

They would get married in June and live at Long

Agatha Christie

Willows (a nice name, she had always thought) and she would never go away again. Go away, that is to say, in the sense that the words now held for her. The excitement of gangplanks being pulled up, the racing of a ship's screw, the thrill as an aeroplane became airborne and soared up and over the earth beneath. Watching a strange coastline take form and shape. The smell of hot dust, and paraffin, and garlic – the clatter and gabble of foreign tongues. Strange flowers, red poinsettias rising proudly from a dusty garden . . . Packing, unpacking – where next?

All that was over. The war was over. Lynn Marchmont had come home. Home is the sailor, home from the sea . . . But I'm not the same Lynn who went away, she thought.

She looked up and saw Rowley watching her . . .

Chapter 4

Aunt Kathie's parties were always much the same. They had a rather breathless amateurish quality about them characteristic of the hostess. Dr Cloade had an air of holding irritability in check with difficulty. He was invariably courteous to his guests – but they were conscious of his courtesy being an effort.

In appearance Lionel Cloade was not unlike his brother Jeremy. He was spare and grey-haired – but he had not the lawyer's imperturbability. His manner was brusque and impatient – and his nervous irritability had affronted many of his patients and blinded them to his actual skill and kindliness. His real interests lay in research and his hobby was the use of medicinal herbs throughout history. He had a precise intellect and found it hard to be patient with his wife's vagaries.

Though Lynn and Rowley always called Mrs Jeremy Cloade 'Frances,' Mrs Lionel Cloade was invariably

'Aunt Kathie.' They were fond of her but found her rather ridiculous.

This 'party', arranged ostensibly to celebrate Lynn's home-coming, was merely a family affair.

Aunt Kathie greeted her niece affectionately:

'So nice and *brown* you look, my dear. Egypt, I suppose. Did you read the book on the Pyramid prophecies I sent you? *So* interesting. Really explains everything, don't you think?'

Lynn was saved from replying by the entrance of Mrs Gordon Cloade and her brother David.

'This is my niece, Lynn Marchmont, Rosaleen.'

Lynn looked at Gordon Cloade's widow with decorously veiled curiosity.

Yes, she *was* lovely, this girl who had married old Gordon Cloade for his money. And it was true what Rowley had said, that she had an air of innocence. Black hair, set in loose waves, Irish blue eyes put in with the smutty finger – half-parted lips.

The rest of her was predominantly expensive. Dress, jewels, manicured hands, fur cape. Quite a good figure, but she didn't, really, know how to wear expensive clothes. Didn't wear them as Lynn Marchmont could have worn them, given half a chance! (But you never *will* have a chance, said a voice in her brain.)

'How do you do,' said Rosaleen Cloade.

She turned hesitatingly to the man behind her.

She said: 'This – this is my brother.'

'How do you do,' said David Hunter.

He was a thin young man with dark hair and dark eyes. His face was unhappy and defiant and slightly insolent.

Lynn saw at once why all the Cloades disliked him so much. She had met men of that stamp abroad. Men who were reckless and slightly dangerous. Men whom you couldn't depend upon. Men who made their own laws and flouted the universe. Men who were worth their weight in gold in a push – and who drove their C.O.s to distraction out of the firing line!

Lynn said conversationally to Rosaleen:

'And how do you like living at Furrowbank?'

'I think it's a wonderful house,' said Rosaleen.

David Hunter gave a faint sneering laugh.

'Poor old Gordon did himself well,' he said. 'No expense spared.'

It was literally the truth. When Gordon had decided to settle down in Warmsley Vale – or rather had decided to spend a small portion of his busy life there, he had chosen to build. He was too much of an individualist to care for a house that was impregnated with other people's history.

He had employed a young modern architect and given him a free hand. Half Warmsley Vale thought

Furrowbank a dreadful house, disliking its white square-
ness, its built-in furnishing, its sliding doors, and glass
tables and chairs. The only part of it they really admired
wholeheartedly were the bathrooms.

There had been awe in Rosaleen's, 'It's a wonderful
house.' David's laugh made her flush.

'You're the returned Wren, aren't you?' said David
to Lynn.

'Yes.'

His eyes swept over her appraisingly – and for some
reason she flushed.

Aunt Katherine appeared again suddenly. She had
a trick of seeming to materialize out of space. Perhaps she had caught the trick of it from many of the
spiritualistic séances she attended.

'Supper,' she said, rather breathlessly, and added,
parentheticaly, 'I think it's better than calling it dinner.
People don't *expect* so much. Everything's very difficult, isn't it? Mary Lewis tells me she slips the fishman
ten shillings every other week. *I* think that's immoral.'

Dr Lionel Cloade was giving his irritable nervous
laugh as he talked to Frances Cloade. 'Oh, come,
Frances,' he said. 'You can't expect me to believe you
really think *that* – let's go in.'

They went into the shabby and rather ugly dining-
room. Jeremy and Frances, Lionel and Katherine,
Adela, Lynn and Rowley. A family party of Cloades

– with two outsiders. For Rosaleen Cloade, though she bore the name, had not become a Cloade as Frances and Katherine had done.

She was the stranger, ill at ease, nervous. And David – David was the outlaw. By necessity, but also by choice. Lynn was thinking these things as she took her place at the table.

There were waves in the air of feeling – a strong electrical current of – what was it? Hate? Could it really be *hate*?

Something at any rate – *destructive*.

Lynn thought suddenly, 'But that's what's the matter everywhere. I've noticed it ever since I got home. It's the aftermath war has left. Ill will. Ill feeling. It's everywhere. On railways and buses and in shops and amongst workers and clerks and even agricultural labourers. And I suppose worse in mines and factories. Ill will. But here it's more than that. Here it's particular. It's *meant*!'

And she thought, shocked: '*Do* we hate them so much? These strangers who have taken what we think is ours?'

And then – 'No, not yet. We might – but not yet. No, it's *they* who hate *us*.'

It seemed to her so overwhelming a discovery that she sat silent thinking about it and forgetting to talk to David Hunter who was sitting beside her.

Presently he said: 'Thinking out something?'

His voice was quite pleasant, slightly amused, but she felt conscience-stricken. He might think that she was going out of her way to be ill-mannered.

She said, 'I'm sorry. I was having thoughts about the state of the world.'

David said coolly, 'How extremely unoriginal!'

'Yes, is is rather. We are all so earnest nowadays. And it doesn't seem to do much good either.'

'It is usually more practical to wish to do harm. We've thought up one or two rather practical gadgets in that line during the last few years – including that *pièce de résistance*, the Atom Bomb.'

'That was what I was thinking about – oh, I don't mean the Atom Bomb. I meant ill will. Definite practical ill will.'

David said calmly:

'Ill will certainly – but I rather take issue to the word practical. They were more practical about it in the Middle Ages.'

'How do you mean?'

'Black magic generally. Ill wishing. Wax figures. Spells at the turn of the moon. Killing off your neighbour's cattle. Killing off your neighbour himself.'

'You don't really believe there *was* such a thing as black magic?' asked Lynn incredulously.

'Perhaps not. But at any rate people did *try* hard.

Nowadays, well –' He shrugged his shoulders. 'With all the ill will in the world you and your family can't do much about Rosaleen and myself, can you?'

Lynn's head went back with a jerk. Suddenly she was enjoying herself.

'It's a little late in the day for that,' she said politely.

David Hunter laughed. He, too, sounded as though he were enjoying himself.

'Meaning we've got away with the booty? Yes, we're sitting pretty all right.'

'*And* you get a kick out of it!'

'Out of having a lot of money? I'll say we do.'

'I didn't mean only the money. I meant out of *us*.'

'Out of having scored off you? Well, perhaps. You'd all have been pretty smug and complacent about the old boy's cash. Looked upon it as practically in your pockets already.'

Lynn said:

'You must remember that we'd been taught to think so for years. Taught not to save, not to think of the future – encouraged to go ahead with all sorts of schemes and projects.'

(Rowley, she thought, Rowley and the farm.)

'Only one thing, in fact, that you hadn't learnt,' said David pleasantly.

'What's that?'

'That nothing's safe.'

67

'Lynn,' cried Aunt Katherine, leaning forward from the head of the table, 'one of Mrs Lester's controls is a fourth-dynasty priest. He's told us such wonderful things. You and I, Lynn, must have a long talk. Egypt, I feel, must have affected you physically.'

Dr Cloade said sharply:

'Lynn's had better things to do than play about with all this superstitious tomfoolery.'

'You are so biased, Lionel,' said his wife.

Lynn smiled at her aunt – then sat silent with the refrain of the words David had spoken swimming in her brain.

'*Nothing's safe . . .*'

There were people who lived in such a world – people to whom everything was dangerous. David Hunter was such a person . . . It was not the world that Lynn had been brought up in – but it was a world that held attractions for her nevertheless.

David said presently in the same low amused voice:

'Are we still on speaking terms?'

'Oh, yes.'

'Good. And do you still grudge Rosaleen and myself our ill-gotten access to wealth?'

'Yes,' said Lynn with spirit.

'Splendid. What are you going to do about it?'

'Buy some wax and practise black magic!'

He laughed.

'Oh, no, you won't do that. You aren't one of those who rely on old outmoded methods. Your methods will be modern and probably very efficient. But you won't win.'

'What makes you think there is going to be a fight? Haven't we all accepted the inevitable?'

'You all behave beautifully. It is very amusing.'

'Why,' said Lynn, in a low tone, 'do you hate us?'

Something flickered in those dark unfathomable eyes.

'I couldn't possibly make you understand.'

'I think you could,' said Lynn.

David was silent for a moment or two, then he asked in a light conversational tone:

'Why are you going to marry Rowley Cloade? He's an oaf.'

She said sharply:

'You know nothing about it – or about him. You couldn't begin to know!'

Without any air of changing the conversation David asked:

'What do you think of Rosaleen?'

'She's very lovely.'

'What else?'

'She doesn't seem to be enjoying herself.'

'Quite right,' said David, 'Rosaleen's rather stupid. She's scared. She always has been rather scared. She

69

drifts into things and then doesn't know what it's all about. Shall I tell you about Rosaleen?'

'If you like,' said Lynn politely.

'I do like. She started by being stage-struck and drifted on to the stage. She wasn't any good, of course. She got into a third-rate touring company that was going out to South Africa. She liked the sound of South Africa. The company got stranded in Cape Town. Then she drifted into marriage with a Government official from Nigeria. She didn't like Nigeria – and I don't think she liked her husband much. If he'd been a hearty sort of fellow who drank and beat her, it would have been all right. But he was rather an intellectual man who kept a large library in the wilds and who liked to talk metaphysics. So she drifted back to Cape Town again. The fellow behaved very well and gave her an adequate allowance. He might have given her a divorce, but again he might not for he was a Catholic; but anyway he rather fortunately died of fever, and Rosaleen got a small pension. Then the war started and she drifted on to a boat for South America. She didn't like South America very much, so she drifted on to another boat and there she met Gordon Cloade and told him all about her sad life. So they got married in New York and lived happily for a fortnight, and a little later he was killed by a bomb and she was left a large house, a lot of expensive jewellery, and an immense income.'

'It's nice that the story has such a happy ending,' said Lynn.

'Yes,' said David Hunter. 'Possessing no intellect at all, Rosaleen has always been a lucky girl – which is just as well. Gordon Cloade was a strong old man. He was sixty-two. He might easily have lived for twenty years. He might have lived even longer. That wouldn't have been much fun for Rosaleen, would it? She was twenty-four when she married him. She's only twenty-six now.'

'She looks even younger,' said Lynn.

David looked across the table. Rosaleen Cloade was crumbling her bread. She looked like a nervous child.

'Yes,' he said thoughtfully. 'She does. Complete absence of thought, I suppose.'

'Poor thing,' said Lynn suddenly.

David frowned.

'Why the pity?' he said sharply. '*I'll* look after Rosaleen.'

'I expect you will.'

He scowled.

'Any one who tries to do down Rosaleen has got me to deal with! And I know a good many ways of making war – some of them not strictly orthodox.'

'Am I going to hear *your* life history now?' asked Lynn coldly.

'A very abridged edition.' He smiled. 'When the war

71

broke out I saw no reason why I should fight for England. I'm Irish. But like all the Irish, I like fighting. The Commandos had an irresistible fascination for me. I had some fun but unfortunately I got knocked out with a bad leg wound. Then I went to Canada and did a job of training fellows there. I was at a loose end when I got Rosaleen's wire from New York saying she was getting married! She didn't actually announce that there would be pickings, but I'm quite sharp at reading between the lines. I flew there, tacked myself on to the happy pair and came back with them to London. And now' – he smiled insolently at her – '*Home is the sailor, home from the sea.* That's you! *And the Hunter home from the Hill.* What's the matter?'

'Nothing,' said Lynn.

She got up with the others. As they went into the drawing-room, Rowley said to her: 'You seemed to be getting on quite well with David Hunter. What were you talking about?'

'Nothing particular,' said Lynn.

Chapter 5

'David, when are we going back to London? When are we going to America?'

Across the breakfast table, David Hunter gave Rosaleen a quick surprised glance.

'There's no hurry, is there? What's wrong with this place?'

He gave a swift appreciative glance round the room where they were breakfasting. Furrowbank was built on the side of a hill and from the windows one had an unbroken panorama of sleepy English countryside. On the slope of the lawn thousands of daffodils had been planted. They were nearly over now, but a sheet of golden bloom still remained.

Crumbling the toast on her plate, Rosaleen murmured:

'You said we'd go to America – soon. As soon as it could be managed.'

'Yes – but actually it isn't managed so easily. There's priority. Neither you nor I have any business reasons to put forward. Things are always difficult after a war.'

He felt faintly irritated with himself as he spoke. The reasons he advanced, though genuine enough, had the sound of excuses. He wondered if they sounded that way to the girl who sat opposite him. And why was she suddenly so keen to go to America?

Rosaleen murmured: 'You said we'd only be here for a short time. You didn't say we were going to live here.'

'What's wrong with Warmsley Vale – and Furrow-bank? Come now?'

'Nothing. It's *them* – all of them!'

'The Cloades?'

'Yes.'

'That's just what I get a kick out of,' said David. 'I like seeing their smug faces eaten up with envy and malice. Don't grudge me my fun, Rosaleen.'

She said in a low troubled voice:

'I wish you didn't feel like that. I don't like it.'

'Have some spirit, girl. We've been pushed around enough, you and I. The Cloades have lived soft – soft. Lived on big brother Gordon. Little fleas on a big flea. I hate their kind – I always have.'

She said, shocked:

'I don't like hating people. It's wicked.'

'Don't you think they hate you? Have they been kind to you – friendly?'

She said doubtfully:

'They haven't been unkind. They haven't done me any harm.'

'But they'd like to, babyface. They'd like to.' He laughed recklessly. 'If they weren't so careful of their own skins, you'd be found with a knife in your back one fine morning.'

She shivered.

'Don't say such dreadful things.'

'Well – perhaps not a knife. Strychnine in the soup.'

She stared at him, her mouth tremulous.

'You're joking . . .'

He became serious again.

'Don't worry, Rosaleen. I'll look after you. They've got me to deal with.'

She said, stumbling over the words, 'If it's true what you say – about their hating us – hating *me* – why don't we go to London? We'd be safe there – away from them all.'

'The country's good for you, my girl. You know it makes you ill being in London.'

'That was when the bombs were there – the bombs.' She shivered, closed her eyes. 'I'll never forget – *never* . . .'

'Yes, you will.' He took her gently by the shoulders,

shook her slightly. 'Snap out of it, Rosaleen. You were badly shocked, but it's over now. There are no more bombs. Don't think about it. Don't remember. The doctor said country air and a country life for a long time to come. That's why I want to keep you away from London.'

'Is that really why? Is it, David? I thought – perhaps –'

'What did you think?'

Rosaleen said slowly:

'I thought perhaps it was because of *her* you wanted to be here . . .'

'Her?'

'You know the one I mean. The girl the other night. The one who was in the Wrens.'

His face was suddenly black and stern.

'Lynn? Lynn Marchmont.'

'She means something to you, David.'

'Lynn Marchmont? She's Rowley's girl. Good old stay-at-home Rowley. That bovine slow-witted good-looking ox.'

'I watched you talking to her the other night.'

'Oh, for Heaven's sake, Rosaleen.'

'And you've seen her since, haven't you?'

'I met her near the farm the other morning when I was out riding.'

'And you'll meet her again.'

'Of course I'll always be meeting her! This is a

tiny place. You can't go two steps without falling over a Cloade. But if you think I've fallen for Lynn Marchmont, you're wrong. She's a proud stuck-up unpleasant girl without a civil tongue in her head. I wish old Rowley joy of her. No, Rosaleen, my girl, she's not my type.'

She said doubtfully, 'Are you sure, David?'

'Of course I'm sure.'

She said half-timidly:

'I know you don't like my laying out the cards . . . But they come true, they do indeed. There was a girl bringing trouble and sorrow – a girl would come from over the sea. There was a dark stranger, too, coming into our lives, and bringing danger with him. There was the death card, and –'

'You and your dark strangers!' David laughed. 'What a mass of superstition you are. Don't have any dealings with a dark stranger, that's my advice to you.'

He strolled out of the house laughing, but when he was away from the house, his face clouded over and he frowned to himself, murmuring:

'Bad luck to you, Lynn. Coming home from abroad and upsetting the apple cart.'

For he realized that at this very moment he was deliberately making a course on which he might hope to meet the girl he had just apostrophized so savagely.

Rosaleen watched him stroll away across the garden and out through the small gate that gave on to a public footpath across the fields. Then she went up to her bedroom and looked through the clothes in her wardrobe. She always enjoyed touching and feeling her new mink coat. To think she should own a coat like that – she could never quite get over the wonder of it. She was in her bedroom when the parlourmaid came up to tell her that Mrs Marchmont had called.

Adela was sitting in the drawing-room with her lips set tightly together and her heart beating at twice its usual speed. She had been steeling herself for several days to make an appeal to Rosaleen but true to her nature had procrastinated. She had also been bewildered by finding that Lynn's attitude had unaccountably changed and that she was now rigidly opposed to her mother seeking relief from her anxieties by asking Gordon's widow for a loan.

However another letter from the bank manager that morning had driven Mrs Marchmont into positive action. She could delay no longer. Lynn had gone out early, and Mrs Marchmont had caught sight of David Hunter walking along the footpath – so the coast was clear. She particularly wanted to get Rosaleen alone, without David, rightly judging that Rosaleen alone would be a far easier proposition.

Nevertheless she felt dreadfully nervous as she waited

in the sunny drawing-room, though she felt slightly better when Rosaleen came in with what Mrs Marchmont always thought of as her 'half-witted look' more than usually marked.

'I wonder,' thought Adela to herself, 'if the blast did it or if she was always like that?'

'Rosaleen stammered.

'Oh, g-g-ood morning. Is there anything? Do sit down.'

'Such a lovely morning,' said Mrs Marchmont brightly. 'All my early tulips are out. Are yours?'

The girl stared at her vacantly.

'I don't know.'

What was one to do, thought Adela, with someone who didn't talk gardening or dogs – those standbys of rural conversation?

Aloud she said, unable to help the tinge of acidity that crept into her tone:

'Of course you have so many gardeners – they attend to all that.'

'I believe we're shorthanded. Old Mullard wants two more men, he says. But there seems a terrible shortage still of labour.'

The words came out with a kind of glib parrot-like delivery – rather like a child who repeats what it has heard a grown-up person say.

Yes, she *was* like a child. Was that, Adela wondered,

her charm? Was that what had attracted that hard-headed shrewd business man, Gordon Cloade, and blinded him to her stupidity and her lack of breeding? After all, it couldn't only be looks. Plenty of good-looking women had angled unsuccessfully to attract him.

But childishness, to a man of sixty-two, *might* be an attraction. Was it, could it be, real – or was it a pose – a pose that had paid and so had become second nature?

Rosaleen was saying, 'David's out, I'm afraid . . .' and the words recalled Mrs Marchmont to herself. David might return. Now was her chance and she must not neglect it. The words stuck in her throat but she got them out.

'I wonder – if you would help me?'

'Help you?'

Rosaleen looked surprised, uncomprehending.

'I – things are very difficult – you see, Gordon's death has made a great difference to us all.'

'You silly idiot,' she thought. 'Must you go on gaping at me like that? You know what I mean! You *must* know what I mean. After all, you've been poor yourself . . .'

She hated Rosaleen at that moment. Hated her because she, Adela Marchmont, was sitting here whining for money. She thought, 'I can't do it – I can't do it after all.'

In one brief instant all the long hours of thought and worry and vague planning flashed again across her brain.

Sell the house – (But move where? There weren't any small houses on the market – certainly not any cheap houses). Take paying guests – (But you couldn't get staff – and she simply couldn't – she just *couldn't* deal with all the cooking and housework involved. If Lynn helped – but Lynn was going to marry Rowley). Live with Rowley and Lynn herself? (No, she'd never do that!) Get a job. What job? Who wanted an untrained elderly tired-out woman?

She heard her voice, belligerent because she despised herself.

'I mean money,' she said.

'Money?' said Rosaleen.

She sounded ingenuously surprised, as though money was the last thing she expected to be mentioned.

Adela went on doggedly, tumbling the words out:

'I'm overdrawn at the bank, and I owe bills – repairs to the house – and the rates haven't been paid yet. You see, everything's halved – my income, I mean. I suppose it's taxation. Gordon, you see, used to help. With the house, I mean. He did all the repairs and the roof and painting and things like that. And an allowance as well. He paid it into the bank every quarter. He always said not to worry and of course

81

I never did. I mean, it was all right when he was alive, but now –'

She stopped. She was ashamed – but at the same time relieved. After all, the worst was over. If the girl refused, she refused, and that was that.

Rosaleen was looking very uncomfortable.

'Oh, dear,' she said. 'I didn't know. I never thought . . . I – well, of course, I'll ask David . . .'

Grimly gripping the sides of her chair, Adela said, desperately:

'Couldn't you give me a cheque – now . . .'

'Yes – yes, I suppose I could.' Rosaleen, looking startled, got up, went to the desk. She hunted in various pigeon-holes and finally produced a cheque-book. 'Shall I – how much?'

'Would – would five hundred pounds –' Adela broke off.

'Five hundred pounds,' Rosaleen wrote obediently.

A load slipped off Adela's back. After all, it had been easy! She was dismayed as it occurred to her that it was less gratitude that she felt than a faint scorn for the easiness of her victory! Rosaleen was surely strangely simple.

The girl rose from the writing-desk and came across to her. She held out the cheque awkwardly. The embarrassment seemed now entirely on her side.

'I hope this is all right. I'm really so sorry –'

Adela took the cheque. The unformed childish hand straggled across the pink paper. Mrs Marchmont. Five hundred pounds £500. Rosaleen Cloade.

'It's very good of you, Rosaleen. Thank you.'

'Oh please – I mean – I ought to have *thought* –'

'*Very* good of you, my dear.'

With the cheque in her handbag Adela Marchmont felt a different woman. The girl had really been very sweet about it. It would be embarrassing to prolong the interview. She said goodbye and departed. She passed David in the drive, said 'Good morning' pleasantly, and hurried on.

Chapter 6

'What was the Marchmont woman doing here?' demanded David as soon as he got in.

'Oh, David. She wanted money dreadfully badly. I'd never thought –'

'And you gave it her, I suppose.'

He looked at her in half-humorous despair.

'You're not to be trusted alone, Rosaleen.'

'Oh, David, I couldn't refuse. After all –'

'After all – what? How much?'

In a small voice Rosaleen murmured, 'Five hundred pounds.'

To her relief David laughed.

'A mere fleabite!'

'Oh, David, it's a lot of money.'

'Not to us nowadays, Rosaleen. You never really seem to grasp that you're a very rich woman. All the same if she asked five hundred she'd have gone away perfectly satisfied with two-fifty. You must learn the language of borrowing!'

She murmured, 'I'm sorry, David.'

'My dear girl! After all, it's *your* money.'

'It isn't. Not really.'

'Now don't begin that all over again. Gordon Cloade died before he had time to make a will. That's what's called the luck of the game. We win, you and I. The others – lose.'

'It doesn't seem – right.'

'Come now, my lovely sister Rosaleen, aren't you enjoying all this? A big house, servants – jewellery? Isn't it a dream come true? Isn't it? Glory be to God, sometimes I think I'll wake up and find it *is* a dream.'

She laughed with him, and watching her narrowly, he was satisfied. He knew how to deal with his Rosaleen. It was inconvenient, he thought, that she should have a conscience, but there it was.

'It's quite true, David, it is like a dream – or like something on the pictures. I do enjoy it all. I do really.'

'But what we have we hold,' he warned her. 'No more gifts to the Cloades, Rosaleen. Every one of them has got far more money than either you or I ever had.'

'Yes, I suppose that's true.'

'Where was Lynn this morning?' he asked.

'I think she'd gone to Long Willows.'

To Long Willows – to see Rowley – the oaf – the clodhopper! His good humour vanished. Set on marrying the fellow, was she?

Moodily he strolled out of the house, up through massed azaleas and out through the small gate on the top of the hill. From there the footpath dipped down the hill and past Rowley's farm.

As David stood there, he saw Lynn Marchmont coming up from the farm. He hesitated for a minute, then set his jaw pugnaciously and strolled down the hill to meet her. They met by a stile just half-way up the hill.

'Good morning,' said David. 'When's the wedding?'

'You've asked that before,' she retorted. 'You know well enough. It's in June.'

'You're going through with it?'

'I don't know what you mean, David.'

'Oh, yes, you do.' He gave a contemptuous laugh. 'Rowley. What's Rowley?'

'A better man than you – touch him if you dare,' she said lightly.

'I've no doubt he's a better man than me – but I do dare. I'd dare anything for you, Lynn.'

She was silent for a moment or two. She said at last:

'What you don't understand is that I love Rowley.'

'I wonder.'

She said vehemently:

'I do, I tell you. I do.'

David looked at her searchingly.

'We all see pictures of ourselves – of ourselves as we want to be. You see yourself in love with Rowley, settling down with Rowley, living here contented with Rowley, never wanting to get away. But that's not the real you, is it, Lynn?'

'Oh, what is the real me? What's the real *you*, if it comes to that? What do *you* want?'

'I'd have said I wanted safety, peace after storm, ease after troubled seas. But I don't know. Sometimes I suspect, Lynn, that both you and I want – trouble.' He added moodily, 'I wish you'd never turned up here. I was remarkably happy until you came.'

'Aren't you happy now?'

He looked at her. She felt excitement rising in her. Her breath became faster. Never had she felt so strongly David's queer moody attraction. He shot out a hand, grasped her shoulder, swung her round . . .

Then as suddenly she felt his grasp slacken. He was staring over her shoulder up the hill. She twisted her head to see what it was that had caught his attention.

A woman was just going through the small gate above Furrowbank. David said sharply: 'Who's that?'

Lynn said:

'It looks like Frances.'

'Frances?' He frowned. 'What does Frances want? My dear Lynn! Only those who want something drop in to see Rosaleen. Your mother has already dropped in this morning.'

'*Mother?*' Lynn drew back. She frowned. 'What did she want?'

'Don't you know? Money!'

'Money?' Lynn stiffened.

'She got it all right,' said David. He was smiling now the cool cruel smile that fitted his face so well.

They had been near a moment or two ago, now they were miles apart, divided by a sharp antagonism.

Lynn cried out, 'Oh, no, no, *no!*'

He mimicked her.

'Yes, yes, yes!'

'I don't believe it! How much?'

'Five hundred pounds.'

She drew her breath in sharply.

David said musingly:

'I wonder how much Frances is going to ask for? Really it's hardly safe to leave Rosaleen alone for five minutes! The poor girl doesn't know how to say No.'

'Have there been – who else?'

David smiled mockingly.

'Aunt Kathie had incurred certain debts – oh, nothing much, a mere two hundred and fifty covered them – but she was afraid it might get to the doctor's ears! Since they had been occasioned by payments to mediums, he might not have been sympathetic. She didn't know, of course,' added David, 'that the doctor himself had applied for a loan.'

Lynn said in a low voice, 'What you must think of us – what you must think of us!' Then, taking him by surprise, she turned and ran helter-skelter down the hill to the farm.

He frowned as he watched her go. She had gone to Rowley, flown there as a homing pigeon flies, and the fact disturbed him more than he cared to acknowledge.

He looked up the hill again and frowned.

'No, Frances,' he said under his breath. 'I think not. You've chosen a bad day,' and he strode purposefully up the hill.

He went through the gate and down through the azaleas – crossed the lawn, and came quietly in through the window of the drawing-room just as Frances Cloade was saying:

'– I wish I could make it all clearer. But you see, Rosaleen, it really is frightfully difficult to explain –'

A voice from behind her said:

'*Is it?*'

Frances Cloade turned sharply. Unlike Adela Marchmont she had not deliberately tried to find Rosaleen alone. The sum needed was sufficiently large to make it unlikely that Rosaleen would hand it over without consulting her brother. Actually, Frances would far rather have discussed the matter with David and Rosaleen together, than have David feel that she had tried to get money out of Rosaleen during his absence from the house.

She had not heard him come through the window, absorbed as she was in the presentation of a plausible case. The interruption startled her, and she realized also that David Hunter was, for some reason, in a particularly ugly mood.

'Oh, David,' she said easily, 'I'm glad you've come. I've just been telling Rosaleen. Gordon's death has left Jeremy in no end of a hole, and I'm wondering if she could possibly come to the rescue. It's like this –'

Her tongue flowed on swiftly – the large sum involved – Gordon's backing – promised verbally – Government restrictions – mortgages –

A certain admiration stirred in the darkness of David's mind. What a damned good liar the woman was! Plausible, the whole story. But not the truth. No, he'd take his oath on that. Not the truth! What, he wondered, *was* the truth? Jeremy been getting himself into Queer Street? It must be something pretty desperate, if he was allowing Frances to come and try this stunt. She was a proud woman, too –

He said, '*Ten thousand*?'

Rosaleen murmured in an awed voice:

'That's a lot of money.'

Frances said swiftly:

'Oh, I know it is. I wouldn't come to you if it wasn't such a difficult sum to raise. But Jeremy would never have gone into the deal if it hadn't been for Gordon's backing. It's so dreadfully unfortunate that Gordon should have died so suddenly –'

'Leaving you all out in the cold?' David's voice was unpleasant. 'After a sheltered life under his wing.'

There was a faint flash in Frances' eyes as she said:

'You put things so picturesquely!'

'Rosaleen can't touch the capital, you know. Only the income. And she pays about nineteen and six in the pound income tax.'

'Oh, I know. Taxation's dreadful these days. But it *could* be managed, couldn't it? We'd repay –'

He interrupted:

'It *could* be managed. *But it won't be!*'

Frances turned swiftly to Rosaleen.

'Rosaleen, you're such a generous –'

David's voice cut across her speech.

'What do you Cloades think Rosaleen is – a milch cow? All of you at her – hinting, asking, begging. And behind her back? Sneering at her, patronizing her, hating her, *wishing her dead* –'

'That's not true,' Frances cried.

'Isn't it? I tell you I'm sick of you all! *She's* sick of you all. You'll get no money out of us, so you can stop coming and whining for it? Understand?'

His face was black with fury.

Frances stood up. Her face was wooden and expressionless. She drew on a wash-leather glove absently, yet with attention, as though it was a significant action.

'You make your meaning quite plain, David,' she said.

Rosaleen murmured:

'I'm sorry. I'm really sorry . . .'

Frances paid no attention to her. Rosaleen might not have been in the room. She took a step towards the window and paused, facing David.

'You have said that I resent Rosaleen. That is not true. I have not resented Rosaleen – but I do resent – *you*!'

'What do you mean?'

He scowled at her.

'Women must live. Rosaleen married a very rich man, years older than herself. Why not? But *you*! You must live on your sister, live on the fat of the land, live softly – on *her*.'

'I stand between her and harpies.'

They stood looking at each other. He was aware of her anger and the thought flashed across him that

Agatha Christie

Frances Cloade was a dangerous enemy, one who could be both unscrupulous and reckless.

When she opened her mouth to speak, he even felt a moment's apprehension. But what she said was singularly noncommittal.

'I shall remember what you have said, David.'

Passing him, she went out of the window.

He wondered why he felt so strongly that the words had been a threat.

Rosaleen was crying.

'Oh, David, David – you oughtn't to have been saying those things to her. She's the one of them that's been the nicest to me.'

He said furiously: 'Shut up, you little fool. Do you want them to trample all over you and bleed you of every penny?'

'But the money – if – if it isn't rightfully mine –'

She quailed before his glance.

'I – I didn't mean that, David.'

'I should hope not.'

Conscience, he thought, was the devil!

He hadn't reckoned with the item of Rosaleen's conscience. It was going to make things awkward in the future.

The future? He frowned as he looked at her and let his thoughts race ahead. Rosaleen's future . . . His own . . . He'd always known what he wanted . . . he knew now . . . But Rosaleen? What future was there for Rosaleen?

As his face darkened – she cried out – suddenly shivering:

'Oh! Someone's walking over my grave.'

He said, looking at her curiously:

'So you realize it may come to that?'

'What do you mean, David?'

'I mean that five – six – seven people have every intention to hurry you into your grave before you're due there!'

'You don't mean – murder –' Her voice was horrified. 'You think these people would do murder – not nice people like the Cloades.'

'I'm not sure that it isn't just nice people like the Cloades who do do murder. But they won't succeed in murdering you while I'm here to look after you. They'd have to get me out of the way first. But if they did get me out of the way – well – look out for yourself!'

'David – don't say such awful things.'

'Listen,' he gripped her arm. 'If ever I'm not here, look after yourself, Rosaleen. Life isn't safe, remember – it's dangerous, damned dangerous. And I've an idea it's specially dangerous for you.'

Chapter 7

I

'Rowley, can you let me have five hundred pounds?'

Rowley stared at Lynn. She stood there, out of breath from running, her face pale, her mouth set.

He sat soothingly and rather as he would speak to a horse:

'There, there, ease up, old girl. What's all this about?'

'I want five hundred pounds.'

'I could do with it myself, for that matter.'

'But Rowley, this is *serious*. Can't you lend me five hundred pounds?'

'I'm overdrawn as it is. That new tractor –'

'Yes, yes –' She pushed aside the farming details. 'But you could raise money somehow – if you had to, couldn't you?'

'What do you want it for, Lynn? Are you in some kind of a hole?'

Agatha Christie

'I want it for him –' She jerked her head backwards towards the big square house on the hill.

'Hunter? Why on earth –'

'It's Mums. She's been borrowing from him. She's – she's in a bit of a jam about money.'

'Yes, I expect she is.' Rowley sounded sympathetic. 'Damned hard lines on her. I wish I could help a bit – but I can't.'

'I can't stand her borrowing money from David!'

'Hold hard, old girl. It's Rosaleen who actually has to fork out the cash. And after all, why not?'

'Why not? You say, "*Why not*," Rowley?'

'I don't see why Rosaleen shouldn't come to the rescue once in a while. Old Gordon put us all in a spot by pegging out without a will. If the position is put clearly to Rosaleen she must see herself that a spot of help all round is indicated.'

'*You* haven't borrowed from her?'

'No – well – that's different. I can't very well go and ask a woman for money. Sort of thing you don't like doing.'

'Can't you see that I don't like being – being beholden to David Hunter?'

'But you're not. It isn't his money.'

'That's just what it is, actually. Rosaleen's completely under his thumb.'

'Oh, I dare say. But it isn't his legally.'

'And you won't, you can't – lend me some money?'

'Now look here, Lynn – if you were in some real jam – blackmail or debts – I might be able to sell land or stock – but it would be a pretty desperate proceeding. I'm only just keeping my head above water as it is. And what with not knowing what this damned Government is going to do next – hampered at every turn – snowed under with forms, up to midnight trying to fill them in sometimes – it's too much for one man.'

Lynn said bitterly:

'Oh, I know! If only Johnnie hadn't been killed –'

He shouted out:

'Leave Johnnie out of it! Don't talk about that!'

She stared at him, astonished. His face was red and congested. He seemed beside himself with rage.

Lynn turned away and went slowly back to the White House.

II

'Can't you give it back, Mums?'

'Really, Lynn darling! I went straight to the bank with it. And then I paid Arthurs and Bodgham and Knebworth. Knebworth was getting quite abusive. Oh, my dear, the *relief*! I haven't been able to sleep for nights and nights. Really, Rosaleen was most understanding and nice about it.'

Lynn said bitterly:

'And I suppose you'll go to her again and again now.'

'I hope it won't be necessary, dear. I shall try to be very economical, you know that. But of course everything is so expensive nowadays. And it gets worse and worse.'

'Yes, and *we* shall get worse and worse. Going on cadging.'

Adela flushed.

'I don't think that's a nice way of putting it, Lynn. As I explained to Rosaleen, we had always depended on Gordon.'

'We shouldn't have. That's what's wrong, we shouldn't have,' Lynn added, 'He's right to despise us.'

'Who despises us?'

'That odious David Hunter.'

'Really,' said Mrs Marchmont with dignity, 'I don't see that it can matter in the least *what* David Hunter thinks. Fortunately he wasn't at Furrowbank this morning – otherwise I dare say he would have influenced that girl. She's completely under his thumb, of course.'

Lynn shifted from one foot to the other.

'What did you mean, Mums, when you said – that first morning I was home – "If he *is* her brother"?'

'Oh, *that*.' Mrs Marchmont looked slightly embarrassed. 'Well, there's been a certain amount of gossip, you know.'

Lynn merely waited inquiringly. Mrs Marchmont coughed.

'That type of young woman – the adventuress type (of course poor Gordon was completely taken in) – they've usually got a – well, a young man of their own in the background. Suppose she says to Gordon she's got a brother – wires to him in Canada or wherever he was. This man turns up. How is *Gordon* to know whether he's her brother or not? Poor Gordon, absolutely infatuated no doubt, and believing everything she said. And so her "brother" comes with them to England – poor Gordon quite unsuspecting.'

Lynn said fiercely:

'I don't believe it. I don't *believe* it!'

Mrs Marchmont raised her eyebrows.

'Really, my dear –'

'He's not like that. And she – she isn't either. She's a fool perhaps, but she's sweet – yes, she's really sweet. It's just people's foul minds. I don't believe it, I tell you.'

Mrs Marchmont said with dignity:

'There's really no need to *shout*.'

Chapter 8

I

It was a week later that the 5.20 train drew into Warmsley Heath Station and a tall bronzed man with a knapsack got out.

On the opposite platform a cluster of golfers were waiting for the up train. The tall bearded man with the knapsack gave up his ticket and passed out of the station. He stood uncertainly for a minute or two – then he saw the signpost: *Footpath to Warmsley Vale* – and directed his steps that way with brisk determination.

II

At Long Willows Rowley Cloade had just finished making himself a cup of tea when a shadow falling across the kitchen table made him look up.

If for just a moment he thought the girl standing just

inside the door was Lynn, his disappointment turned to surprise when he saw it was Rosaleen Cloade.

She was wearing a frock of some peasant material in bright broad stripes of orange and green – the artificial simplicity of which had run into more money than Rowley could ever have imagined possible.

Up to now he had always seen her dressed in expensive and somewhat towny clothes which she wore with an artificial air – much, he had thought, as a mannequin might display dresses that did not belong to her but to the firm who employed her.

This afternoon in the broad peasant stripes of gay colour, he seemed to see a new Rosaleen Cloade. Her Irish origin was more noticeable, the dark curling hair and the lovely blue eyes put in with the smutty finger. Her voice, too, had a softer Irish sound instead of the careful rather mincing tones in which she usually spoke.

'It's such a lovely afternoon,' she said. 'So I came for a walk.'

She added:

'David's gone to London.'

She said it almost guiltily, then flushed and took a cigarette case out of her bag. She offered one to Rowley, who shook his head, then looked round for a match to light Rosaleen's cigarette. But she was flicking unsuccessfully at an expensive-looking small gold lighter. Rowley took it from her and with one sharp movement it lit. As she bent her head towards him to light her cigarette he noticed how long and dark the lashes were that lay on her cheek and he thought to himself:

'Old Gordon knew what he was doing . . .'

Rosaleen stepped back a pace and said admiringly:

'That's a lovely little heifer you've got in the top field.'

Astonished by her interest, Rowley began to talk to her about the farm. Her interest surprised him, but it was obviously genuine and not put on, and to his surprise he found that she was quite knowledgeable on farm matters. Butter-making and dairy produce she spoke of with familiarity.

'Why, you might be a farmer's wife, Rosaleen,' he said smiling.

The animation went out of her face.

She said:

'We had a farm – in Ireland – before I came over here – before –'

'Before you went on the stage?'

She said wistfully and a trifle, it seemed to him, guiltily:

'It's not so very long ago . . . I remember it all very well.' She added with a flash of spirit, 'I could milk your cows for you, Rowley, now.'

Agatha Christie

This was quite a new Rosaleen. Would David Hunter have approved these casual references to a farming past? Rowley thought not. Old Irish landed gentry, that was the impression David tried to put over. Rosaleen's version, he thought, was nearer the truth. Primitive farm life, then the lure of the stage, the touring company to South Africa, marriage – isolation in Central Africa – escape – hiatus – and finally marriage to a millionaire in New York . . .

Yes, Rosaleen Hunter had travelled a long way since milking a Kerry cow. Yet looking at her, he found it hard to believe that she had ever started. Her face had that innocent, slightly half-witted expression, the face of one who has no history. And she looked so young – much younger than her twenty-six years.

There was something appealing about her, she had the same pathetic quality as the little calves he had driven to the butcher that morning. He looked at her as he had looked at them. Poor little devils, he had thought, a pity that they had to be killed . . .

A look of alarm came into Rosaleen's eyes. She asked uneasily: 'What are you thinking of, Rowley?'

'Would you like to see over the farm and the dairy?'

'Oh, indeed, I would.'

Amused by her interest he took her all over the farm. But when he finally suggested making her a cup of tea, an alarmed expression came into her eyes.

'Oh, no – thank you, Rowley – I'd best be getting home.' She looked down at her watch. 'Oh! how late it is! David will be back by the 5.20 train. He'll wonder where I am. I – I must hurry.' She added shyly: 'I *have* enjoyed myself, Rowley.'

And that, he thought, was true. She *had* enjoyed herself. She had been able to be natural – to be her own raw unsophisticated self. She was afraid of her brother David, that was clear. David was the brains of the family. Well, for once, she'd had an afternoon out – yes, that was it, an afternoon out just like a servant! The rich Mrs Gordon Cloade!

He smiled grimly as he stood by the gate watching her hurrying up the hill towards Furrowbank. Just before she reached the stile a man came over it – Rowley wondered if it was David but it was a bigger, heavier man. Rosaleen drew back to let him pass, then skipped lightly over the stile, her pace accentuating almost to a run.

Yes, she'd had an afternoon off – and he, Rowley, had wasted over an hour of valuable time! Well, perhaps it hadn't been wasted. Rosaleen, he thought, had seemed to like him. That might come in useful. A pretty thing – yes, and the calves this morning had been pretty . . . poor little devils.

Standing there, lost in thought, he was startled by a voice, and raised his head sharply.

Agatha Christie

A big man in a broad felt hat with a pack slung across his shoulders was standing on the footpath at the other side of the gate.

'Is this the way to Warmsley Vale?'

As Rowley stared he repeated his question. With an effort Rowley recalled his thoughts and answered:

'Yes, keep right along the path – across that next field. Turn to the left when you get to the road and about three minutes takes you right into the village.'

In the self-same words he had answered that particular question several hundred times. People took the footpath on leaving the station, followed it up over the hill, and lost faith in it as they came down the other side and saw no sign of their destination, for Blackwell Copse masked Warmsley Vale from sight. It was tucked away in a hollow there with only the tip of its church tower showing.

The next question was not quite so usual, but Rowley answered it without much thought.

'The Stag or the Bells and Motley. The Stag for choice. They're both equally good – or bad. I should think you'd get a room all right.'

The question made him look more attentively at his interlocutor. Nowadays people usually booked a room beforehand at any place they were going to . . .

The man was tall, with a bronzed face, a beard, and very blue eyes. He was about forty and not ill-looking in a tough and rather dare-devil style. It was not, perhaps, a wholly pleasant face.

Come from overseas somewhere, thought Rowley. Was there or was there not a faint Colonial twang in his accent? Curious, in some way, the face was not unfamiliar . . .

Where had he seen that face, or a face very like it, before?

Whilst he was puzzling unsuccessfully over that problem, the stranger startled him by asking:

'Can you tell me if there's a house called Furrowbank near here?'

Rowley answered slowly:

'Why, yes. Up there on the hill. You must have passed close by it – that is, if you've come along the footpath from the station.'

'Yes – that's what I did.' He turned, staring up the hill. 'So that was it – that big white new-looking house.'

'Yes, that's the one.'

'A big place to run,' said the man. 'Must cost a lot to keep up?'

A devil of a lot, thought Rowley. And *our* money . . . A stirring of anger made him forget for the moment where he was . . .

With a start he came back to himself to see the stranger staring up the hill with a curious speculative look in his eyes.

'Who lives there?' he said. 'Is it – a Mrs Cloade?'

'That's right,' said Rowley. 'Mrs Gordon Cloade.'

The stranger raised his eyebrows. He seemed gently amused.

'Oh,' he said, 'Mrs Gordon Cloade. Very nice for her!'

Then he gave a short nod.

'Thanks, pal,' he said, and shifting the pack he carried he strode on towards Warmsley Vale.

Rowley turned slowly back into the farmyard. His mind was still puzzling over something.

Where the devil had he seen that fellow before?

III

About nine-thirty that night, Rowley pushed aside a heap of forms that had been littering the kitchen table and got up. He looked absentmindedly at the photograph of Lynn that stood on the mantelpiece, then frowning, he went out of the house.

Ten minutes later he pushed open the door of the Stag Saloon Bar. Beatrice Lippincott, behind the bar counter, smiled welcome at him. Mr Rowley Cloade, she thought, was a fine figure of a man. Over a pint of bitter Rowley exchanged the usual observations with the company present, unfavourable comment was made upon the Government, the weather, and sundry particular crops.

Presently, moving up a little, Rowley was able to address Beatrice in a quiet voice:

'Got a stranger staying here? Big man? Slouch hat?'

'That's right, Mr Rowley. Came along about six o'clock. That the one you mean?'

Rowley nodded.

'He passed my place. Asked his way.'

'That's right. Seems a stranger.'

'I wondered,' said Rowley, 'who he was.'

He looked at Beatrice and smiled. Beatrice smiled back.

'That's easy, Mr Rowley, if you'd like to know.'

She dipped under the bar and out to return with a fat leather volume wherein were registered the arrivals.

She opened it at the page showing the most recent entries. The last of these ran as follows:

Enoch Arden. Cape Town. British.

Chapter 9

I

It was a fine morning. The birds were singing, and Rosaleen, coming down to breakfast in her expensive peasant dress, felt happy.

The doubts and fears that had lately oppressed her seemed to have faded away. David was in a good temper, laughing and teasing her. His visit to London on the previous day had been satisfactory. Breakfast was well cooked and well served. They had just finished it when the post arrived.

There were seven or eight letters for Rosaleen. Bills, charitable appeals, some local invitations – nothing of any special interest.

David laid aside a couple of small bills and opened the third envelope. The enclosure, like the outside of the envelope, was written in printed characters.

Dear Mr Hunter,

I think it is best to approach you rather than your sister, 'Mrs Cloade', in case the contents of this letter might come as somewhat of a shock to her. Briefly, I have news of Captain Robert Underhay, which she may be glad to hear. I am staying at the Stag and if you will call there this evening, I shall be pleased to go into the matter with you.

Yours faithfully,

Enoch Arden

A strangled sound came from David's throat. Rosaleen looked up smiling, then her face changed to an expression of alarm.

'David – David – what is it?'

Mutely he held out the letter to her. She took it and read it.

'But – David – I don't understand – what does it mean?'

'You can read, can't you?'

She glanced up at him timorously.

'David – does it mean – what are we going to do?'

He was frowning – planning rapidly in his quick far-seeing mind.

'It's all right, Rosaleen, no need to be worried. I'll deal with it –'

'But does it mean that –'

'Don't worry, my dear girl. Leave it to me. Listen,

this is what you've got to do. Pack a bag at once and go up to London. Go to the flat – and stay there until you hear from me? Understand?'

'Yes. Yes, of course I understand, but David –'

'Just do as I say, Rosaleen.' He smiled at her. He was kindly, reassuring. 'Go and pack. I'll drive you to the station. You can catch the 10.32. Tell the porter at the flats that you don't want to see any one. If any one calls and asks for you, he's to say you're out of town. Give him a quid. Understand? He's not to let any one up to see you except me.'

'Oh.' Her hands went up to her cheeks. She looked at him with scared lovely eyes.

'It's all right, Rosaleen – but it's tricky. You're not much hand at the tricky stuff. That's my look-out. I want you out of the way so that I've got a free hand, that's all.'

'Can't I stay here, David?'

'No, of course you can't, Rosaleen. Do have some sense. I've got to have a free hand to deal with this fellow whoever he is –'

'Do you think that it's – that it's –'

He said with emphasis:

'I don't think anything at the moment. The first thing is to get you out of the way. Then I can find out where we stand. Go on – there's a good girl, don't argue.'

She turned and went out of the room.

David frowned down at the letter in his hand.

Very non-committal – polite – well phrased – might mean anything. It might be genuine solicitude in an awkward situation. Might be a veiled threat. He conned its phrases over and over – 'I have news of Captain Robert Underhay' . . . 'Best to approach you' . . . 'I shall be pleased to go into the matter with you . . .' 'Mrs Cloade.' Damn it all, he didn't like those inverted commas – *Mrs Cloade . . .'*

He looked at the signature. Enoch Arden. Something stirred in his mind – some poetical memory . . . a line of verse.

II

When David strode into the hall of the Stag that evening, there was, as was usual, no one about. A door at the left was marked Coffee Room, a door on the right was marked Lounge. A door farther along was marked repressively 'For Resident Guests Only.' A passage on the right led along to the bar, from whence a faint hum of voices could be heard. A small glass-encased box was labelled Office and had a push-bell placed conveniently on the side of its sliding window.

Sometimes, as David knew by experience, you had to ring four or five times before any one condescended to come and attend to you. Except for the short period of meal times, the hall of the Stag was as deserted as Robinson Crusoe's island.

This time, David's third ring of the bell brought Miss Beatrice Lippincott along the passage from the bar, her hand patting her golden pompadour of hair into place. She slipped into the glass box and greeted him with a gracious smile.

'Good evening, Mr Hunter. Rather cold weather for the time of year, isn't it?'

'Yes – I suppose it is. Have you got a Mr Arden staying here?'

'Let me see now,' said Miss Lippincott, making rather a parade of not knowing exactly, a proceeding she always adopted as tending to increase the importance of the Stag. 'Oh, yes. Mr *Enoch* Arden. No. 5. On the first floor. You can't miss it, Mr Hunter. Up the stairs, and don't go along the gallery but round to the left and down three steps.'

Following these complicated directions, David tapped on the door of No. 5 and a voice said Come in.

He went in, closing the door behind him.

Agatha Christie

III

Coming out of the office, Beatrice Lippincott called, 'Lily.' An adenoidal girl with a giggle and pale boiled-gooseberry eyes responded to the summons.

'Can you manage for a bit, Lily? I've got to see about some linen.'

Lily said, 'Oh, yes, Miss Lippincott,' gave a giggle and added, sighing gustily: 'I do think Mr Hunter's *ever* so good-looking, don't you?'

'Ah, I've seen a lot of his type in the war,' said Miss Lippincott, with a world-weary air. 'Young pilots and such-like from the fighter station. Never could be sure about their cheques. Often had such a way with them that you'd cash the things against your better judgment. But, of course, I'm funny that way, Lily, what I like is *class*. Give me class every time. What I say is a gentleman's a gentleman even if he does drive a tractor.' With which enigmatic pronouncement Beatrice left Lily and went up the stairs.

IV

Inside room No. 5, David Hunter paused inside the door and looked at the man who had signed himself Enoch Arden.

Fortyish, knocked about a bit, a suggestion of having come down in the world – on the whole a difficult customer. Such was David's summing up. Apart from that, not easy to fathom. A dark horse.

Arden said;

'Hallo – you Hunter? Good. Sit down. What'll you have? Whisky?'

He'd made himself comfortable, David noted that. A modest array of bottles – a fire burning in the grate on this chilly spring evening. Clothes not English cut, but worn as an Englishman wears clothes. The man was the right age, too . . .

'Thanks,' David said, 'I'll have a spot of whisky.'

'Say When.'

'When. Not too much soda.'

They were a little like dogs, manoeuvring for position – circling round each other, backs stiff, hackles up, ready to be friendly or ready to snarl and snap.

'Cheerio,' said Arden.

'Cheerio.'

They set their glasses down, relaxed a little. Round One was over.

The man who called himself Enoch Arden said:

'You were surprised to get my letter?'

'Frankly,' said David, 'I don't understand it at all.'

'N-no – n-no – well, perhaps not.'

David said:

'I understand you knew my sister's first husband – Robert Underhay.'

'Yes, I knew Robert very well.' Arden was smiling, blowing clouds of smoke idly up in the air. 'As well, perhaps, as any one could know him. *You* never met him, did you, Hunter?'

'No.'

'Oh, perhaps that's as well.'

'What do you mean by that?' David asked sharply.

Arden said easily:

'My dear fellow, it makes everything much simpler – that's all. I apologize for asking you to come here, but I did think it was best to keep' – he paused – 'Rosaleen out of it all. No need to give her unnecessary pain.'

'Do you mind coming to the point?'

'Of course, of course. Well now, did you ever suspect – how shall we say – that there was anything – well – *fishy* – about Underhay's death?'

'What on earth do you mean?'

'Well, Underhay had rather peculiar ideas, you know. It may have been chivalry – it may just possibly have been for quite a different reason – but let's say that, at a particular moment some years ago, there were certain advantages to Underhay in being considered dead. He was good at managing natives – always had been. No trouble to him to get a probable story circulated with any amount of corroborative detail. All Underhay had to do was to turn up about a thousand miles away – with a new name.'

'It seems a most fantastic supposition to me,' said David.

'Does it? Does it really?' Arden smiled. He leaned forward, tapped David on the knee. 'Suppose it's true, Hunter? Eh? Suppose it's true?'

'I should require very definite proof of it.'

'Would you? Well, of course, there's no super-definite proof. Underhay himself could turn up here – in Warmsley Vale. How'd you like that for proof?'

'It would at least be conclusive,' said David dryly.

'Oh, yes, conclusive – but just a little embarrassing – for Mrs Gordon Cloade, I mean. Because then, of course, she wouldn't *be* Mrs Gordon Cloade. Awkward. You must admit, just a little bit awkward?'

'My sister,' said David, 'remarried in perfectly good faith.'

'Of course she did, my dear fellow. Of course she

did. I'm not disputing that for a second. Any judge would say the same. No actual blame could attach to her.'

'Judge?' said David sharply.

The other said as though apologetically:

'I was thinking of bigamy.'

'Just what are you driving at?' asked David savagely.

'Now don't get excited, old boy. We just want to put our heads together and see what's best to be done – best for your sister, that's to say. Nobody wants a lot of dirty publicity. Underhay – well, Underhay was always a chivalrous kind of chap.' Arden paused. 'He still is . . .'

'*Is?*' asked David sharply.

'That's what I said.'

'You say Robert Underhay is alive. Where is he now?'

Arden leaned forward – his voice became confidential.

'*Do you really want to know, Hunter?* Wouldn't it be better if you *didn't* know? Put it that, as far as *you* know, and as far as Rosaleen knows, Underhay died in Africa. Very good, and *if* Underhay is alive, he doesn't know his wife has married again, he hasn't the least idea of it. Because, of course, if he *did* know he would have come forward . . . Rosaleen, you see, has inherited a good deal of money from her second husband – well, then, of course she isn't entitled to any of that money . . . Underhay is a man with a very sensitive sense of honour. He wouldn't like her inheriting money under false pretences.' He paused. 'But of course it's possible that Underhay doesn't know anything about her second marriage. He's in a bad way, poor fellow – in a very bad way.'

'What do you mean by in a bad way?'

Arden shook his head solemnly.

'Broken down in health. He needs medical attention – special treatments – all unfortunately rather *expensive.*'

The last word dropped delicately as though into a category of its own. It was the word for which David Hunter had been unconsciously waiting.

He said:

'Expensive?'

'Yes – unfortunately everything costs money. Underhay, poor devil, is practically destitute.' He added: 'He's got practically nothing but what he stands up in . . .'

Just for a moment David's eyes wandered round the room. He noted the pack slung on a chair. There was no suitcase to be seen.

'I wonder,' said David, and his voice was not pleasant, 'if Robert Underhay is quite the chivalrous gentleman you make him out to be.'

'He was once,' the other assured him. 'But life,

123

you know, is inclined to make a fellow cynical.' He paused and added softly: 'Gordon Cloade was really an incredibly wealthy fellow. The spectacle of too much wealth arouses one's baser instincts.'

David Hunter got up.

'I've got an answer for you. Go to the devil.'

Unperturbed, Arden said, smiling:

'Yes, I thought you'd say that.'

'You're a damned blackmailer, neither more nor less. I've a good mind to call your bluff.'

'Publish and be damned? An admirable sentiment. But you wouldn't like it if I did "publish". Not that I shall. If you won't buy, I've another market.'

'What do you mean?'

'The Cloades. Suppose I go to them. "Excuse me, but would you be interested to learn that the late Robert Underhay is very much alive?" Why, man, they'll jump at it!'

David said scornfully:

'You won't get anything out of them. They're broke, every one of them.'

'Ah, but there's such a thing as a working arrangement. So much in cash on the day it's proved that Underhay is alive, that Mrs Gordon Cloade is still Mrs Robert Underhay and that consequently Gordon Cloade's will, made before his marriage, is good in law . . .'

For some few minutes David sat silent, then he asked bluntly:

'How much?'

The answer came as bluntly:

'Twenty thousand.'

'Out of the question! My sister can't touch the capital, she's only got a life interest.'

'Ten thousand, then. She can raise that, easily. There's jewellery, isn't there?'

David sat silent, then he said unexpectedly:

'All right.'

For a moment the other man seemed at a loss. It was as though the ease of his victory surprised him.

'No cheques,' he said. 'To be paid in notes!'

'You'll have to give us time – to get hold of the money.'

'I'll give you forty-eight hours.'

'Make it next Tuesday.'

'All right. You'll bring the money here.' He added before David could speak, 'I'm not meeting you at a lonely copse – or a deserted river bank, so don't you think so. You'll bring the money here – to the Stag – at nine o'clock next Tuesday evening.'

'Suspicious sort of chap, aren't you?'

'I know my way about. And I know your kind.'

'As you said, then.'

David went out of the room and down the stairs. His face was black with rage.

Beatrice Lippincott came out of the room marked No. 4. There was a communicating door between 4 and 5, though the fact could hardly be noted by an occupant in 5 since a wardrobe stood upright in front of it.

Miss Lippincott's cheeks were pink and her eyes bright with pleasurable excitement. She smoothed back her pompadour of hair with an agitated hand.

Chapter 10

Shepherd's Court, Mayfair, was a large block of luxury service flats. Unharmed by the ravages of enemy action, they had nevertheless been unable to keep up quite their pre-war standard of ease. There was service still, although not very good service. Where there had been two uniformed porters there was now only one. The restaurant still served meals, but except for breakfast, meals were not sent up to the apartments.

The flat rented by Mrs Gordon Cloade was on the third floor. It consisted of a sitting-room with a built-in cocktail bar, two bedrooms with built-in cupboards, and a superbly appointed bathroom, gleaming with tiles and chromium.

In the sitting-room David Hunter was striding up and down whilst Rosaleen sat on a big square-ended settee watching him. She looked pale and frightened.

Agatha Christie

'Blackmail!' he muttered. 'Blackmail! My God, am I the kind of man to let myself be blackmailed?'

She shook her head, bewildered, troubled.

'If I knew,' David was saying. 'If I only *knew*!'

From Rosaleen there came a small miserable sob.

He went on:

'It's this working in the dark – working blindfold –'

He wheeled round suddenly. 'You took those emeralds round to Bond Street to old Greatorex?'

'Yes.'

'How much?'

Rosaleen's voice was stricken as she said:

'Four thousand. Four thousand *pounds*. He said if I didn't sell them they ought to be reinsured.'

'Yes – precious stones have doubled in value. Oh well, we *can* raise the money. But if we do, it's only the beginning – it means being bled to death – bled, Rosaleen, bled white!'

She cried:

'Oh, let's leave England – let's get away – couldn't we go to Ireland – America – *somewhere*?'

He turned and looked at her.

'You're not a fighter, are you, Rosaleen? Cut and run is your motto.'

She wailed: 'We're wrong – all this has been wrong – very wicked.'

'Don't turn pious on me just now! I can't stand it.

We were sitting pretty, Rosaleen. For the first time in my life I was sitting pretty – and I'm not going to let it all go, do you hear? If only it wasn't this cursed fighting in the dark. You understand, don't you, that the whole thing may be bluff – nothing *but* bluff? Underhay's probably safely buried in Africa as we've always thought he was.'

She shivered.

'Don't, David. You make me afraid.'

He looked at her, saw the panic in her face, and at once his manner changed. He came over to her, sat down, took her cold hands in his.

'You're not to worry,' he said. 'Leave it all to me – and do as I tell you. You can manage that, can't you? Just do exactly as I tell you.'

'I always do, David.'

He laughed. 'Yes, you always do. We'll snap out of this, never you fear. I'll find a way of scotching Mr Enoch Arden.'

'Wasn't there a poem, David – something about a man coming back –'

'Yes.' He cut her short. 'That's just what worries me . . . But I'll get to the bottom of things, never you fear.'

She said:

'It's Tuesday night you – take him the money?'

He nodded.

129

Agatha Christie

'Five thousand. I'll tell him I can't raise the rest all at once. But I *must* stop him going to the Cloades. I *think* that was only a threat, but I can't be *sure*.'

He stopped, his eyes became dreamy, far away. Behind them his mind worked, considering and rejecting possibilities.

Then he laughed. It was a gay reckless laugh. There were men, now dead, who would have recognized it . . .

It was the laugh of a man going into action on a hazardous and dangerous enterprise. There was enjoyment in it and defiance.

'I can trust you, Rosaleen,' he said. 'Thank goodness I can trust you absolutely!'

'Trust me?' She raised her big inquiring eyes. 'To do what?'

He smiled again.

'To do exactly as you are told. That's the secret, Rosaleen, of a successful operation.'

He laughed:

'Operation Enoch Arden.'

Chapter 11

Rowley opened the big mauve envelope with some surprise. Who on earth, he wondered, could be writing to him, using that kind of stationery – and how did they manage to get it, anyway? These fancy lines had surely gone right out during the war.

'Dear Mr Rowley,' he read,
   'I hope you won't think I'm taking a liberty in writing to you this way, but if you'll excuse me, I do think there are things going on that you ought to know about.'

He noted the underlining with a puzzled look.

'Arising out of our conversation the other evening when you came in asking about a certain person. *If you could call in at the Stag I'd be very glad to tell you all about*

it. We've all of us felt down here what a wicked shame
it was about your Uncle dying and his money going the
way it did.

'Hoping you won't be angry with me, but I really do
think you ought to know what's going on.

'Yours ever,

'Beatrice Lippincott.'

Rowley stared down at this missive, his mind afire with
speculation. What on earth was all this about? Good old
Bee. He'd known Beatrice all his life. Bought tobacco
from her father's shop and passed the time of day with
her behind the counter. She'd been a good-looking girl.
He remembered as a child hearing rumours about her
during an absence of hers from Warmsley Vale. She'd
been away about a year and everybody said she'd
gone away to have an illegitimate baby. Perhaps she
had, perhaps she hadn't. But she was certainly highly
respectable and refined nowadays. Plenty of backchat
and giggles, but an almost painful propriety.

Rowley glanced up at the clock. He'd go along to
the Stag right away. To hell with all those forms.
He wanted to know what it was that Beatrice was so
anxious to tell him.

It was a little after eight when he pushed open the
door of the saloon bar. There were the usual greetings,
nods of the head, 'Evening, sir.' Rowley edged up to

the bar and asked for a Guinness. Beatrice beamed upon him.

'Glad to see you, Mr Rowley.'

'Evening, Beatrice. Thanks for your note.'

She gave him a quick glance.

'I'll be with you in a minute, Mr Rowley.'

He nodded – and drank his half pint meditatively whilst he watched Beatrice finish serving out. She called over her shoulder and presently the girl Lily came in to relieve her. Beatrice murmured, 'If you'll come with me, Mr Rowley?'

She led him along a passage and in through a door marked Private. Inside it was very small and overfurnished with plush arm-chairs, a blaring radio, a lot of china ornaments and a rather battered-looking pierrot doll thrown across the back of a chair.

Beatrice Lippincott turned off the radio and indicated a plush arm-chair.

'I'm ever so glad you came up, Mr Rowley, and I hope you didn't mind my writing to you – but I've been turning it over in my mind all over the weekend – and as I said I really felt you ought to know what's going on.'

She was looking happy and important, clearly pleased with herself.

Rowley asked with mild curiosity:

'What is going on?'

133

'Well, Mr Rowley, you know the gentleman who's staying here – Mr Arden, the one you came and asked about.'

'Yes?'

'It was the very next evening. Mr Hunter came along and asked for him.'

'Mr Hunter?'

Rowley sat up interestedly.

'Yes, Mr Rowley. No. 5, I said, and Mr Hunter nodded and went straight up. I was surprised I must say, for this Mr Arden hadn't said he knew any one in Warmsley Vale and I'd kind of taken it for granted he was a stranger here and didn't know any one in the place. Very out of temper Mr Hunter looked, as though something had happened to upset him but of course I didn't make anything of it *then.*'

She paused for breath. Rowley said nothing, just listened. He never hurried people. If they liked to take their time it suited him.

Beatrice continued with dignity:

'It was just a little later I had occasion to go up to No. 4 to see to the towels and the bed linen. That's next door to No. 5, and as it happens there's a communicating door – not that you'd know it from No. 5 because the big wardrobe there stands right across it, so that you wouldn't know there *was* a door. Of course it's always kept shut but as it happened this time it was

134

just a bit open – though *who* opened it I've no idea,
I'm *sure*!'

Again Rowley said nothing, but just nodded his
head.

Beatrice, he thought, had opened it. She had been
curious and had gone up deliberately to No. 4 to find
out what she could.

'And so you see, Mr Rowley, I couldn't help hearing
what was going on. Really, you could have knocked me
over with a feather –'

A pretty substantial feather, thought Rowley, would
be needed.

He listened, with an impassive, almost bovine face,
to Beatrice's succinct account of the conversation she
had overheard. When she had finished, she waited
expectantly.

It was fully a couple of minutes before Rowley came
out of his trance. Then he got up.

'Thanks, Beatrice,' he said. 'Thanks a lot.'

And with that he went straight out of the room.
Beatrice felt somewhat deflated. She really *did* think,
she said to herself, that Mr Rowley might have said
something.

Chapter 12

When Rowley left the Stag his steps turned automatically in the direction of home, but after walking a few hundred yards, he pulled up short and retraced his steps.

His mind took things in slowly and his first astonishment over Beatrice's revelations was only now beginning to give way to a true appreciation of the significance. If her version of what she had overheard was correct, and he had no doubt that in substance it was so, then a situation had arisen which concerned every member of the Cloade family closely. The person most fitted to deal with this was clearly Rowley's Uncle Jeremy. As a solicitor, Jeremy Cloade would know what use could best be made of this surprising information, and exactly what steps to take.

Though Rowley would have liked to take action himself, he realized rather grudgingly that it would be far better to lay the matter before a shrewd and experienced lawyer. The sooner Jeremy was in possession of this information the better, and accordingly Rowley bent his footsteps straight to Jeremy's house in the High Street.

The little maid who opened the door informed him that Mr and Mrs Cloade were still at the dinner table. She would have shown him in there, but Rowley negatived this and said he would wait in Jeremy's study till they had finished. He did not particularly want to include Frances in the colloquy. Indeed the fewer people who knew about it the better, until they should have determined on a definite course of action.

He wandered restlessly up and down Jeremy's study. On the flat-topped desk was a tin dispatch box labelled Sir William Jessamy Deceased. The shelves held a collection of legal tomes. There was an old photograph of Frances in evening dress and one of her father, Lord Edward Trenton, in riding kit. On the desk was the picture of a young man in uniform – Jeremy's son Antony, killed in the war.

Rowley winced and turned away. He sat down in a chair and stared at Lord Edward Trenton instead.

In the dining-room Frances said to her husband:

'I wonder what Rowley wants?'

Jeremy said wearily:

'Probably fallen foul of some Government regulation.

No farmer understands more than a quarter of these forms they have to fill up. Rowley's a conscientious fellow. He gets worried.'

'He's nice,' said Frances, 'but terribly slow. I have a feeling, you know, that things aren't going too well between him and Lynn.'

Jeremy murmured vacantly:

'Lynn – oh, yes, of course. Forgive me, I – I don't seem able to concentrate. The strain –'

Frances said swiftly:

'Don't think about it. It's going to be all right, I tell you.'

'You frighten me sometimes, Frances. You're so terribly reckless. You don't realize –'

'I realize everything. I'm not afraid. Really, you know, Jeremy, I'm rather enjoying myself –'

'That, my dear,' said Jeremy, 'is just what causes me such anxiety.'

She smiled.

'Come,' she said. 'You mustn't keep that bucolic young man waiting too long. Go and help him to fill up form eleven hundred and ninety-nine, or whatever it is.'

But as they came out of the dining-room the front door banged shut. Edna came to tell them that Mr Rowley had said he wouldn't wait and that it was nothing that really mattered.

Chapter 13

On that particular Tuesday afternoon, Lynn Marchmont had gone for a long walk. Conscious of a growing restlessness and dissatisfaction with herself, she felt the need for thinking things out.

She had not seen Rowley for some days. After their somewhat stormy parting on the morning she had asked him to lend her five hundred pounds they had met as usual. Lynn realized that her demand had been unreasonable and that Rowley had been well within his rights in turning it down. Nevertheless reasonableness has never been a quality that appeals to lovers. Outwardly things were the same between her and Rowley, inwardly she was not so sure. The last few days she had found unbearably monotonous, yet hardly liked to acknowledge to herself that David Hunter's sudden departure to London with his sister might have something to do with their monotony. David, she admitted ruefully, was an exciting person . . .

As for her relations, at the moment she found them all unbearably trying. Her mother was in the best of spirits and had annoyed Lynn at lunch that day by announcing that she was going to try and find a second gardener. 'Old Tom really can't keep up with things here.'

'But, darling, we can't afford it,' Lynn had exclaimed.

'Nonsense, I really think, Lynn, that Gordon would be terribly upset if he could see how the garden has gone down. He was so particular always about the border, and the grass being kept mown, and the paths in good order – and just look at it now. I feel Gordon would want it put in order again.'

'Even if we have to borrow money from his widow to do it.'

'I told you, Lynn, Rosaleen couldn't have been nicer about it. I really think she quite saw my point of view. I have a nice balance at the bank after paying all the bills. And I really think a second gardener would be an *economy*. Think of the extra vegetables we could grow.'

'We could buy a lot of extra vegetables for a good deal less than another three pounds a week.'

'I think we could get someone for less than that, dear. There are men coming out of the Services now who *want* jobs. The paper says so.'

Lynn said dryly: 'I doubt if you'll find them in Warmsley Vale – or in Warmsley Heath.'

But although the matter was left like that, the tendency of her mother to count on Rosaleen as a regular source of support haunted Lynn. It revived the memory of David's sneering words.

So, feeling disgruntled and out of temper, she set out to walk her black mood off.

Her temper was not improved by a meeting with Aunt Kathie outside the post office. Aunt Kathie was in good spirits.

'I think, Lynn dear, that we shall soon have good news.'

'What on earth do you mean, Aunt Kathie?'

Mrs Cloade nodded and smiled and looked wise.

'I've had the most astonishing communications – really astonishing. A simple happy end to all our troubles. I had one setback, but since then I've got the message to Try try try again. If at first you don't succeed, etc . . . I'm not going to betray any secrets, Lynn dear, and the last thing I should want to do would be to raise false hopes prematurely, but I have the strongest belief that things will very soon *be quite all right*. And quite time, too. I am really very worried about your uncle. He worked far too hard during the war. He really needs to retire and devote himself to his specialized studies – but of course he can't do that

Agatha Christie

without an adequate income. And sometimes he has such queer nervous fits, I am really very worried about him. He is really quite odd.'

Lynn nodded thoughtfully. The change in Lionel Cloade had not escaped her notice, nor his curious alternation of moods. She suspected that he occasionally had recourse to drugs to stimulate himself, and she wondered whether he were not to a certain extent an addict. It would account for his extreme nervous irritability. She wondered how much Aunt Kathie knew or guessed. Aunt Kathie, thought Lynn, was not such a fool as she looked.

Going down the High Street, she caught a glimpse of her Uncle Jeremy letting himself into his front door. He looked, Lynn thought, very much older just in these last three weeks.

She quickened her pace. She wanted to get out of Warmsley Vale, up on to the hills and open spaces. Setting out at a brisk pace she soon felt better. She would go for a good tramp of six or seven miles – and really think things out. Always, all her life, she had been a resolute clear-headed person. She had known what she wanted and what she didn't want. Never, until now, had she been content just to drift along . . .

Yes, that was just what it was! Drifting along! An aimless, formless method of living. Ever since she had come out of the Service. A wave of nostalgia swept over her for those war days. Days when duties were clearly defined, when life was planned and orderly – when the weight of individual decisions had been lifted from her. But even as she formulated the idea, she was horrified at herself. Was that really and truly what people were secretly feeling everywhere? Was that what, ultimately, war did to you? It was not the physical dangers – the mines at sea, the bombs from the air, the crisp *ping* of a rifle bullet as you drove over a desert track. No, it was the spiritual danger of learning how much easier life was if you ceased to *think* . . . She, Lynn Marchmont, was no longer the clear-headed resolute intelligent girl who had joined up. Her intelligence had been specialized, directed in well-defined channels. Now mistress of herself and her life once more, she was appalled at the disinclination of her mind to seize and grapple with her own personal problems.

With a sudden wry smile, Lynn thought to herself: Odd if it's really that newspaper character 'the housewife' who has come into her own through war conditions. The women who, hindered by innumerable 'shall nots', were not helped by any definite 'shalls'. Women who had to plan and think and improvise, who had to use every inch of the ingenuity they had been given, and to develop an ingenuity that they didn't know they had got! They alone, thought

Lynn now, could stand upright without a crutch, responsible for themselves and others. And she, Lynn Marchmont, well educated, clever, having done a job that needed brains and close application, was now rudderless, devoid of resolution – yes, hateful word: *drifting* . . .

The people who had stayed at home; Rowley, for instance.

But at once Lynn's mind dropped from vague generalities to the immediate personal. *Herself and Rowley.* That was the problem, the real problem – the only problem. *Did she really want to marry Rowley?*

Slowly the shadows lengthened to twilight and dusk. Lynn sat motionless, her chin cupped in her hands on the outskirts of a small copse on the hillside, looking down over the valley. She had lost count of time, but she knew that she was strangely reluctant to go home to the White House. Below her, away to the left, was Long Willows. Long Willows, her home if she married Rowley.

If! It came back to that – if – if – if!

A bird flew out of the wood with a startled cry like the cry of an angry child. A billow of smoke from a train went eddying up in the sky forming as it did so a giant question mark:

? ? ?

Shall I marry Rowley? Do I *want* to marry Rowley? Did I ever want to marry Rowley? Could I bear *not* to marry Rowley?

The train puffed away up the valley, the smoke quivered and dispersed. But the question mark did not fade from Lynn's mind.

She had loved Rowley before she went away. 'But I've come home changed,' she thought. 'I'm not the same Lynn.'

A line of poetry floated into her mind.

'Life and the world and *mine own self* are changed . . .'

And Rowley? Rowley *hadn't* changed.

Yes, that was it. Rowley hadn't changed. Rowley was where she had left him four years ago.

Did she want to marry Rowley? If not, what did she want?

Twigs cracked in the copse behind her and a man's voice cursed as he pushed his way through.

She cried out, 'David!'

'Lynn!' He looked amazed as he came crashing through the undergrowth. 'What in the name of fortune are you doing here?'

He had been running and was slightly out of breath.

'I don't know. Just thinking – sitting and thinking.' She laughed uncertainly. 'I suppose – it's getting very late.'

'Haven't you any idea of the time?'

She looked down vaguely at her wrist-watch.

'It's stopped again. I disorganize watches.'

'More than watches!' David said. 'It's the electricity in you. The vitality. The *life*.'

He came up to her, and vaguely disturbed, she rose quickly to her feet.

'It's getting quite dark. I must hurry home. What time *is* it, David?'

'Quarter past nine. I must run like a hare. I simply must catch the 9.20 train to London.'

'I didn't know you had come back here!'

'I had to get some things from Furrowbank. But I must catch this train. Rosaleen's alone in the flat – and she gets the jitters if she's alone at night in London.'

'In a service flat?' Lynn's voice was scornful.

David said sharply:

'Fear isn't logical. When you've suffered from blast –'

Lynn was suddenly ashamed – contrite. She said:

'I'm sorry. I'd forgotten.'

With sudden bitterness David cried out:

'Yes, it's soon forgotten – all of it. Back to safety! Back to tameness! Back to where we were when the whole bloody show started! Creep into our rotten little holes and play safe again. You, too, Lynn – you're just the same as the rest of them!'

She cried, 'I'm not. I'm *not*, David. I was just thinking – now –'

'Of me?'

His quickness startled her. His arm was round her, holding him to her. He kissed her with hot angry lips.

'Rowley Cloade?' he said, 'that oaf? By God, Lynn, you belong to me.'

Then as suddenly as he had taken her, he released her, almost thrusting her away from him.

'I'll miss the train.'

He ran headlong down the hillside.

'David . . .'

He turned his head, calling back:

'I'll ring you when I get to London . . .'

She watched him running through the gathering gloom, light and athletic and full of natural grace.

Then, shaken, her heart strangely stirred, her mind chaotic, she walked slowly homeward.

She hesitated a little before going in. She shrank from her mother's affectionate welcome, her questions . . .

Her mother who had borrowed five hundred pounds from people whom she despised.

'We've no right to despise Rosaleen and David,' thought Lynn as she went very softly upstairs. 'We're just the same. We'd do anything – *anything* for money.'

She stood in her bedroom, looking curiously at her face in the mirror. It was, she thought, the face of a stranger . . .

And then, sharply, anger shook her.

'If Rowley really loved me,' she thought, 'he'd have got that five hundred pounds for me somehow. He would – he *would*. He wouldn't let me be humiliated by having to take it from David – David . . .'

David had said he would ring her when he got to London.

She went downstairs, walking in a dream.

Dreams, she thought, could be very dangerous things . . .

Chapter 14

'Oh, there you are, Lynn.' Adela's voice was brisk and relieved. 'I didn't hear you come in, darling. Have you been in long?'

'Oh, yes, ages. I was upstairs.'

'I wish you'd tell me when you come in, Lynn. I'm always nervous when you're out alone after dark.'

'Really, Mums, don't you think I can look after myself?'

'Well, there have been dreadful things in the papers lately. All these discharged soldiers – they attack girls.'

'I expect the girls ask for it.'

She smiled – rather a twisted smile.

Yes, girls did ask for danger . . . Who, after all, really wanted to be safe . . . ?

'Lynn, darling, are you listening?'

Lynn brought her mind back with a jerk.

Her mother had been talking.

'What did you say, Mums?'

'I was talking about your bridesmaids, dear. I suppose they'll be able to produce the coupons all right. It's very lucky for you having all your demob ones. I'm really terribly sorry for girls who get married nowadays on just their ordinary coupons. I mean they just can't have anything new at all. Not outside, I mean. What with the state all one's undies are in nowadays one just has to go for *them*. Yes, Lynn, you really are lucky.'

'Oh, very lucky.'

She was walking round the room – prowling, picking up things, putting them down.

'Must you be so terribly restless, dear? You make me feel quite jumpy!'

'Sorry, Mums.'

'There's nothing the matter, is there?'

'What should be the matter?' asked Lynn sharply.

'Well, don't jump down my throat, darling. Now about bridesmaids. I really think you ought to ask the Macrae girl. Her mother was my closest friend, remember, and I do think she'll be hurt if –'

'I loathe Joan Macrae and always have.'

'I know, darling, but does that really matter? Marjorie will, I'm sure, feel hurt –'

'Really, Mums, it's *my* wedding, isn't it?'

'Yes, I know, Lynn, but –'

'If there is a wedding at all!'

She hadn't meant to say that. The words slipped out without her having planned them. She would have caught them back, but it was too late. Mrs Marchmont was staring at her daughter in alarm.

'Lynn, darling, what do you mean?'

'Oh, nothing, Mums.'

'You and Rowley haven't quarrelled?'

'No, of course not. Don't fuss, Mums, everything's all right.'

But Adela was looking at her daughter in real alarm, sensitive to the turmoil behind Lynn's frowning exterior.

'I've always felt you'd be so *safe* married to Rowley,' she said piteously.

'Who wants to be safe?' Lynn asked scornfully. She turned sharply. 'Was that the telephone?'

'No. Why? Are you expecting a call?'

Lynn shook her head. Humiliating to be waiting for the telephone to ring. He had said he would ring her tonight. He must. 'You're mad,' she told herself. 'Mad.'

Why did this man attract her so? The memory of his dark unhappy face rose up before her eyes. She tried to banish it, tried to replace it by Rowley's broad good-looking countenance. His slow smile, his affectionate glance. But did Rowley, she thought, *really* care about her? Surely if he'd really cared, he'd have understood that day when she came to him and begged for five hundred pounds. He'd have understood instead of being so maddeningly reasonable and matter-of-fact. Marry Rowley, live on the farm, never go away again, never see foreign skies, smell exotic smells – never again be free . . .

Sharply the telephone rang. Lynn took a deep breath, walked across the hall and picked up the receiver.

With the shock of a blow, Aunt Kathie's voice came thinly through the wire.

'Lynn? Is that you? Oh, I'm so glad. I'm afraid, you know, I've made rather a muddle – about the meeting at the Institute –'

The thin fluttering voice went on. Lynn listened, interpolated comments, uttered reassurances, received thanks.

'Such a comfort, dear Lynn, you are always so kind and so practical. I really can't imagine how I get things so muddled up.'

Lynn couldn't imagine either. Aunt Kathie's capacity for muddling the simplest issues amounted practically to genius.

'But I always do say,' finished Aunt Kathie, 'that everything goes wrong at once. Our telephone is out of order and I've had to go out to a call-box, and now

I'm here I hadn't got twopence, only halfpennies – and I had to go and ask –'

It petered out at last. Lynn hung up and went back to the drawing-room. Adela Marchmont, alert, asked: 'Was that –' and paused.

Lynn said quickly: 'Aunt Kathie.'

'What did she want?'

'Oh, just one of her usual muddles.'

Lynn sat down again with a book, glancing up at the clock. Yes – it had been too early. She couldn't expect her call yet. At five minutes past eleven the telephone rang again. She went slowly out to it. This time she wouldn't expect – it was probably Aunt Kathie again . . .

But no. 'Warmsley Vale 34? Can Miss Lynn Marchmont take a personal call from London?'

Her heart missed a beat.

'This is Miss Lynn Marchmont speaking.'

'Hold on, please.'

She waited – confused noises – then silence. The telephone service was getting worse and worse. She waited. Finally she depressed the receiver angrily. Another woman's voice, indifferent, cold, spoke, was uninterested. 'Hang up, please. You'll be called later.'

She hung up, went back towards the drawing-room, the bell rang again as she had her hand on the door. She hurried back to the telephone.

'Hallo?'

A man's voice said: 'Warmsley Vale 34? Personal call from London for Miss Lynn Marchmont.'

'Speaking.'

'Just a minute please.' Then, faintly, 'Speak up, London, you're through . . .'

And then, suddenly, David's voice:

'Lynn, is that you?'

'David!'

'I had to speak to you.'

'Yes . . .'

'Look here, Lynn, I think I'd better clear out –'

'What do you mean?'

'Clear out of England altogether. Oh, it's easy enough. I've pretended it wasn't to Rosaleen – simply because I didn't want to leave Warmsley Vale. But what's the good of it all? You and I – it wouldn't work. You're a fine girl, Lynn – and as for me, I'm a bit of a crook, always have been. And don't flatter yourself that I'd go straight for your sake. I might mean to – but it wouldn't work. No, you'd better marry the plodding Rowley. He'll never give you a day's anxiety as long as you live. I should give you hell.'

She stood there, holding the receiver, saying nothing.

'Lynn, are you still there?'

'Yes, I'm here.'

'You didn't say anything.'

'What is there to say?'

'Lynn?'

'Well . . . ?'

Strange how clearly she could feel over all that distance, his excitement, the urgency of his mood . . .

He cursed softly, said explosively, 'Oh, to hell with everything!' and rang off.

Mrs Marchmont, coming out of the drawing-room, said, 'Was that –?'

'A wrong number,' said Lynn and went quickly up the stairs.

Chapter 15

It was the custom at the Stag for guests to be called at whatever hour they named by the simple process of a loud bang on the door and the shouted information that it was 'Eight-thirty, sir,' or 'Eight o' clock' whatever the case might be. Early tea was produced if expressly stipulated for, and was deposited with a rattle of crockery on the mat outside the door.

On this particular Wednesday morning, young Gladys went through the usual formula outside No. 5, yelling out, 'Eight-fifteen, sir,' and crashing down the tray with a bang that slopped the milk out of the jug. She then went on her way, calling more people and proceeding to her other duties.

It was ten o'clock before she took in the fact that No. 5's tea was still on the mat.

She beat a few heavy raps on the door, got no reply and therupon walked in.

No. 5 was not the kind of gentleman who overslept himself, and she had just remembered that there was a convenient flat roof outside the window. It was just possible, thought Gladys, that No. 5 had done a bunk without paying his bill.

But the man registered as Enoch Arden had not done a bunk. He was lying on his face in the middle of the room and without any knowledge of medicine, Gladys had no doubt whatever that he was dead.

Gladys threw back her head and screamed, then rushed out of the room and down the stairs, still screaming.

'Ow, Miss Lippincott – Miss Lippincott – ow –'

Beatrice Lippincott was in her private room having a cut hand bandaged by Dr Lionel Cloade – the latter dropped the bandage and turned irritably as the girl burst in.

'Ow, *Miss!*'

The doctor snapped:

'What is it? What is it?'

'What's the matter, Gladys?' asked Beatrice.

'It's the gentleman in No. 5, Miss. He's lying there on the floor, dead.'

The doctor stared at the girl and then at Miss Lippincott: the latter stared at Gladys and then at the doctor.

Finally, Dr Cloade said uncertainly:

'Nonsense.'

'Dead as a doornail,' said Gladys, and added with a certain relish: ''Is 'ead's bashed in!'

The doctor looked towards Miss Lippincott.

'Perhaps I'd better –'

'Yes, please, Dr Cloade. But really – I hardly think – it seems so impossible.'

They trooped upstairs, Gladys leading the way. Dr Cloade took one look, knelt down and bent over the recumbent figure.

He looked up at Beatrice. His manner had changed. It was abrupt, authoritative.

'You'd better telephone through to the police station,' he said.

Beatrice Lippincott went out, Gladys followed her.

Gladys said in an awed whisper:

'Ow, Miss, do you think it's *murder*?'

Beatrice smoothed back her golden pompadour with an agitated hand.

'You hold your tongue, Gladys,' she said sharply. 'Saying a thing's murder before you *know* it's murder is libel and you might be had up in court for it. It'll do the Stag no good to have a lot of gossip going about.' She added, as a gracious concession: 'You can go and make yourself a nice cup of tea. I dare say you need it.'

'Yes, indeed, Miss, I do. My inside's fair turning

Agatha Christie

over! I'll bring you along a cup, too!'
    To which Beatrice did not say No.

Chapter 16

Superintendent Spence looked thoughtfully across his table at Beatrice Lippincott, who was sitting with her lips compressed tightly together.

'Thank you, Miss Lippincott,' he said. 'That's all you can remember? I'll have it typed out for you to read and then if you wouldn't mind signing it –'

'Oh, dear – I shan't have to give evidence in a police court, I do hope.'

Superintendent Spence smiled appeasingly.

'Oh, we hope it mayn't come to that,' he said mendaciously.

'It may be suicide,' Beatrice suggested hopefully.

Superintendent Spence forbore to say that a suicide does not usually cave in the back of his skull with a pair of steel fire-tongs. Instead, he replied in the same easy manner:

'Never any good jumping to conclusions. Thank

you, Miss Lippincott. Very good of you to come forward with this statement so promptly.'

When she had been ushered out, he ran over her statement in his mind. He knew all about Beatrice Lippincott, had a very good idea of how far her accuracy was to be depended upon. So much for a conversation genuinely overhead and remembered. A little extra embroidery for excitement's sake. A little extra still because murder had been done in bedroom No. 5. But take extras away and what remained was ugly and suggestive.

Superintendent Spence looked at the table in front of him. There was a wrist-watch with a smashed glass, a small gold lighter with initials on it, a lipstick in a gilt holder, and a pair of heavy steel fire-tongs, the heavy head of which was stained a rusty brown.

Sergeant Graves looked in and said that Mr Rowley Cloade was waiting. Spence nodded and the Sergeant showed Rowley in.

Just as he knew all about Beatrice Lippincott, so the Superintendent knew all about Rowley Cloade. If Rowley had come to the police station, it was because Rowley had got something to say and that something would be solid, reliable and unimaginative. It would, in fact, be worth hearing. At the same time, Rowley being a deliberate type of person, it would take some time to say. And you couldn't hurry the Rowley Cloade type.

If you did, they became rattled, repeated themselves, and generally took twice as long . . .

'Good morning, Mr Cloade. Pleased to see you. Can you throw any light on this problem of ours? The man who was killed at the Stag.'

Rather to Spence's surprise, Rowley began with a question. He asked abruptly:

'Have you identified the fellow?'

'No,' said Spence slowly. 'I wouldn't say we had. He signed the register Enoch Arden. There's nothing in his possession to show he *was* Enoch Arden.'

Rowley frowned.

'Isn't that – rather odd?'

It was exceedingly odd, but Superintendent Spence did not propose to discuss with Rowley Cloade just how odd he thought it was. Instead he said pleasantly: 'Come now, Mr Cloade, I'm the one who asks the questions. You went to see the dead man last night. Why?'

'You know Beatrice Lippincott, Superintendent? At the Stag.'

'Yes, of course. And,' said the Superintendent, taking what he hoped would be a short cut, 'I've heard her story. She came to me with it.'

Rowley looked relieved.

'Good. I was afraid she mightn't want to be mixed up with a police matter. These people are funny that way sometimes.' The Superintendent nodded. 'Well, then, Beatrice told me what she'd overheard and it seemed to me – I don't know if it does to you – decidedly fishy. What I mean is – we're, well, we're interested parties.'

Again the Superintendent nodded. He had taken a keen local interest in Gordon Cloade's death and in common with general local opinion he considered that Gordon's family had been badly treated. He endorsed the common opinion that Mrs Gordon Cloade 'wasn't a lady,' and that Mrs Gordon Cloade's brother was one of those young firebrand Commandos who, though they had had their uses in time of war, were to be looked at askance in peace-time.

'I don't suppose I need explain to you, Superintendent, that if Mrs Gordon's first husband is still alive, it will make a big difference to us as a family. This story of Beatrice's was the first intimation I had that such a state of affairs might exist. I'd never dreamed of such a thing. Thought she was definitely a widow. And I may say it shook me up a lot. Took me a bit of time to realize it, as you might say. You know, I had to let it soak in.'

Spence nodded again. He could see Rowley slowly ruminating the matter, turning it over and over in his mind.

'First of all I thought I'd better get my uncle on to it – the lawyer one.'

'Mr Jeremy Cloade?'

'Yes, so I went along there. Must have been some time after eight. They were still at dinner and I sat down in old Jeremy's study to wait for him, and I went on turning things over in my mind.'

'Yes?'

'And finally I came to the conclusion that I'd do a bit more myself before getting my uncle on to it. Lawyers, Superintendent, are all the same, I've found. Very slow, very cautious, and have to be absolutely sure of their facts before they'll move in a matter. The information I'd got had come to me in a rather hole-and-corner manner – and I wondered if old Jeremy might hem and haw a bit about acting on it. I decided I'd go along to the Stag and see this Johnnie for myself.'

'And you did so?'

'Yes. I went right back to the Stag –'

'At what time was this?'

Rowley pondered.

'Lemme see, I must have got to Jeremy's about twenty past eight or thereabouts – five minutes – well, I wouldn't like to say exactly, Spence – after half-past eight – perhaps about twenty to nine?'

'Yes, Mr Cloade?'

'I knew where the bloke was – Bee had mentioned the number of his room – so I went right up and knocked at the door and he said, "Come in," and I went in.'

Rowley paused.

'Somehow I don't think I handled the business very well. I thought when I went in that *I* was the one who was on top. But the fellow must have been rather a clever fellow. I couldn't pin him down to anything definite. I thought he'd be frightened when I hinted he'd been doing a spot of blackmail, but it just seemed to amuse him. He asked me – damned cheek – if *I* was in the market too? "You can't play your dirty game with me," I said. "*I*'ve nothing to hide." And he said rather nastily that that wasn't his meaning. The point was, he said, that *he'd* got something to sell and was I a buyer? "What do you mean?" I said. He said: "How much will you – or the family generally – pay me for the definite proof that Robert Underhay, reported dead in Africa, is really alive and kicking?" I asked him why the devil we should pay anything at all? And he laughed and said, "Because I've got a client coming this evening who certainly will pay a very substantial sum for proof positive that Robert Underhay is dead." Then – well, then, I'm afraid I rather lost my temper and told him that my family weren't used to doing that kind of dirty business. If Underhay was really alive, I said, the fact ought to be quite easy to establish. Upon that I was just stalking out when he laughed and said in what was really rather a queer tone, "I don't think you'll prove it without *my* co-operation." Funny sort of way he said that.'

'And then?'

'Well, frankly, I went home rather disturbed. Felt, you know, that I'd messed things up. Rather wished I'd left it to old Jeremy to tackle after all. I mean, dash it all, a lawyer's used to dealing with slippery customers.'

'What time did you leave the Stag?'

'I've no idea. Wait a sec. Must have been just before nine because I heard the pips for the news as I was going along the village – through one of the windows.'

'Did Arden say who it was he was expecting? The "client"?'

'No. I took it for granted it was David Hunter. Who else could it be?'

'He didn't seem in any way alarmed by the prospect?'

'I tell you the fellow was thoroughly pleased with himself and on top of the world!'

Spence indicated with a slight gesture the heavy steel tongs.

'Did you notice these in the grate, Mr Cloade?'

'Those? No – I don't think so. The fire wasn't lit.' He frowned, trying to visualize the scene. 'There were fire-irons in the grate, I'm sure, but I can't say I noticed what they were.' He added, 'Was that what –'

Agatha Christie

Spence nodded.

'Smashed his skull in.'

Rowley frowned.

'Funny. Hunter's a lightly built chap – Arden was a big man – powerful.'

The Superintendent said in a colourless voice:

'The medical evidence is that he was struck down from behind and that the blows delivered with the head of the tongs were struck from above.'

Rowley said thoughtfully:

'Of course he was a cocksure sort of a bloke – but all the same I wouldn't have turned my back with a fellow in the room whom I was trying to bleed white and who'd done some pretty tough fighting in the war. Arden can't have been a very cautious sort of chap.'

'If he *had* been cautious very likely he'd be alive now,' said the Superintendent dryly.

'I wish to God he was,' said Rowley fervently. 'As it is I feel I've mucked things up thoroughly. If only I hadn't got on my high horse and stalked off, I might have got something useful out of him. I ought to have pretended that we *were* in the market, but the thing's so damned silly. I mean, who are we to bid against Rosaleen and David? They've got the cash. None of us could raise five hundred pounds between us.'

The Superintendent picked up the gold lighter.

'Seen this before?'

A crease appeared between Rowley's brows. He said slowly:

'I've seen it somewhere, yes, but I can't remember where. Not very long ago. No – I can't remember.'

Spence did not give the lighter into Rowley's out-stretched hand. He put it down and picked up the lipstick, unsheathing it from its case.

'And this?'

Rowley grinned.

'Really, that's not in my line, Superintendent.'

Thoughtfully, Spence smeared a little on the back of his hand. He put his head on one side, studying it appreciatively.

'Brunette colouring, I should say,' he remarked.

'Funny things you policemen know,' said Rowley. He got up. 'And you don't – definitely do not – know *who* the dead man was?'

'Have you any idea yourself, Mr Cloade?'

'I only wondered,' said Rowley slowly. 'I mean – this fellow was our only clue to Underhay. Now that he's dead – well, looking for Underhay is going to be like looking for a needle in a haystack.'

'There'll be publicity, Mr Cloade,' said Spence. 'Remember that in due course a lot of this will appear in the press. If Underhay is alive and comes to read about it – well, he may come forward.'

'Yes,' said Rowley doubtfully. 'He may.'

Agatha Christie

'But you don't think so?'

'I think,' said Rowley Cloade, 'that Round One has gone to David Hunter.'

'I wonder,' said Spence. As Rowley went out, Spence picked up the gold lighter and looked at the initials D.H. on it. 'Expensive bit of work,' he said to Sergeant Graves. 'Not mass produced. Quite easily identified. Greatorex or one of those Bond Street places. Have it seen to!'

'Yes, sir.'

Then the Superintendent looked at the wrist-watch – the glass was smashed and the hands pointed to ten minutes past nine.

He looked at the Sergeant.

'Got the report on this, Graves?'

'Yes, sir. Mainspring's broken.'

'And the mechanism of the hands?'

'Quite all right, sir.'

'What, in your opinion, Graves, does the watch tell us?'

Graves murmured warily, 'Seems as though it might give us the time the crime was committed.'

'Ah,' said Spence, 'when you've been as long in the Force as I have, you'll be a leetle suspicious of anything so convenient as a smashed watch. It can be genuine – but it's a well-known hoary old trick. Turn the hands of a watch to a time that suits you – smash it – and out

172

with some virtuous alibi. But you don't catch an old bird that way. I'm keeping a very open mind on the subject of the time this crime was committed. Medical evidence is: between 8 p.m. and 11 p.m.'

Sergeant Graves cleared his throat.

'Edwards, second gardener at Furrowbank, says he saw David Hunter coming out of a side door there about 7.30. The maids didn't know he was down here. They thought he was up in London with Mrs Gordon. Shows he was in the neighbourhood all right.'

'Yes,' said Spence. 'I'll be interested to hear Hunter's own account of his doings.'

'Seems like a clear case, sir,' said Graves, looking at the initials on the lighter.

'H'm,' said the Superintendent. 'There's still this to account for.'

He indicated the lipstick.

'It had rolled under the chest of drawers, sir. Might have been there some time.'

'I've checked up,' said Spence. 'The last time a woman occupied that room was three weeks ago. I know service isn't up to much nowadays – but I still think they run a mop under the furniture once in three weeks. The Stag is kept pretty clean and tidy on the whole.'

'There's been no suggestion of a woman being mixed up with Arden.'

Agatha Christie

'I know,' said the Superintendent. 'That's why that lipstick is what I call the unknown quantity.'

Sergeant Graves refrained from saying 'Cherchez la femme.' He had a very good French accent and he knew better than to irritate Superintendent Spence by drawing attention to it. Sergeant Graves was a tactful young man.

Chapter 17

Superintendent Spence looked up at Shepherd's Court, Mayfair, before stepping inside its agreeable portal. Situated modestly in the vicinity of Shepherd Market, it was discreet, expensive and inconspicuous.

Inside, Spence's feet sunk into soft pile carpet, there was a velvet-covered settee and a jardinière full of flowering plants. A small automatic lift faced him, with a flight of stairs at one side of it. On the right of the hall was a door marked Office. Spence pushed it open and went through. He found himself in a small room with a counter, behind which was a table and a typewriter, and two chairs. One was drawn up to the table, the other, a more decorative one, was set at an angle to the window. There was no one visible.

Spying a bell inset on the mahogany counter, Spence pressed it. When nothing happened, he pressed it again. A minute or so later a door in the far wall was

opened and a resplendent person in uniform appeared.
His appearance was that of a foreign General or possibly Field Marshal, but his speech was of London and
uneducated London at that.

'Yes, sir?'

'Mrs Gordon Cloade.'

'Third floor, sir. Shall I ring through first?'

'She's here, is she?' said Spence. 'I had an idea she
might be in the country.'

'No, sir, she's been here since Saturday last.'

'And Mr David Hunter?'

'Mr Hunter's been here, too.'

'He's not been away?'

'No, sir.'

'Was he here last night?'

'Now then,' said the Field Marshal, suddenly becoming aggressive. 'What's all this about? Want to know
every one's life history?'

Silently Spence displayed his warrant card. The
Field Marshal was immediately deflated and became
co-operative.

'Sorry, I'm sure,' he said. 'Couldn't tell, could I?'

'Now then, was Mr Hunter here last night?'

'Yes, sir, he was. At least to the best of my belief he
was. That is, he didn't say he was going away.'

'Would you know if he was away?'

'Well, generally speaking, no. I don't suppose I

should. Gentlemen and ladies usually say if they're not going to be here. Leave word about letters or what they want said if any one rings up.'

'Do telephone calls go through this office?'

'No, most of the flats have their own lines. One or two prefer not to have a telephone and then we send up word on the house phone and the people come down and speak from the box in the hall.'

'But Mrs Cloade's flat has its own phone?'

'Yes, sir.'

'And as far as you know they were both here last night?'

'That's right.'

'What about meals?'

'There's a restaurant, but Mrs Cloade and Mr Hunter don't very often use it. They usually go out to dinner.'

'Breakfast?'

'That's served in the flats.'

'Can you find out if breakfast was served this morning to them?'

'Yes, sir. I can find out from room service.'

Spence nodded. 'I'm going up now. Let me know about that when I come down.'

'Very good, sir.'

Spence entered the lift and pressed the button for the third floor. There were only two flats on each landing. Spence pushed the bell of No. 9.

David Hunter opened it. He did not know the Super-intendent by sight and he spoke brusquely.

'Well, what is it?'

'Mr Hunter?'

'Yes.'

'Superintendent Spence of the Oastshire County Police. Can I have a word with you?'

'I apologize, Superintendent.' He grinned. 'I thought you were a tout. Come in.'

He led the way into a modern and charming room. Rosaleen Cloade was standing by the window and turned at their entrance.

'Superintendent Spence, Rosaleen,' said Hunter. 'Sit down, Superintendent. Have a drink?'

'No, thank you, Mr Hunter.'

Rosaleen had inclined her head slightly. She sat now, her back to the window, her hands clasped tightly on her lap.

'Smoke?' David proferred cigarettes.

'Thanks.' Spence took a cigarette, waited . . . watched David slide a hand into a pocket, slide it out, frown, look round and pick up a box of matches. He struck one and lit the Superintendent's cigarette.

'Thank you, sir.'

'Well,' said David, easily, as he lit his own cigarette. 'What's wrong at Warmsley Vale? Has our cook been dealing in the black market? She provides us with wonderful food, and I've always wondered if there was some sinister story behind it.'

'It's rather more serious than that,' said the Superintendent. 'A man died at the Stag Inn last night. Perhaps you saw it in the papers?'

David shook his head.

'No, I didn't notice it. What about him?'

'He didn't only die. He was killed. His head was stove in as a matter of fact.'

A half-choked exclamation came from Rosaleen. David said quickly:

'Please, Superintendent, don't enlarge on any details. My sister is delicate. She can't help it, but if you mention blood and horrors she'll probably faint.'

'Oh, I'm sorry,' said the Superintendent. 'But there wasn't any blood to speak of. It was murder right enough, though.'

He paused. David's eyebrows went up. He said gently:

'You interest me. Where do we come in?'

'We hoped you might be able to tell us something about this man, Mr Hunter.'

'I?'

'You called to see him on Saturday evening last. His name – or the name he was registered under – was Enoch Arden.'

'Yes, of course. I remember now.'

David spoke quietly, without embarrassment.

'Well, Mr Hunter?'

'Well, Superintendent, I'm afraid I can't help you. I know next to nothing about the man.'

'Was his name really Enoch Arden?'

'I should very much doubt it.'

'Why did you go to see him?'

'Just one of the usual hard luck stories. He mentioned certain places, war experiences, people –' David shrugged his shoulders. 'Just a touch, I'm afraid. The whole thing rather bogus.'

'Did you give him any money, sir?'

There was a fractional pause and then David said:

'Just a fiver – for luck. He'd been in the war all right.'

'He mentioned certain names that you – knew?'

'Yes.'

'Was one of those names Captain Robert Underhay?'

Now at last he got his effect. David stiffened. Behind him, Rosaleen gave a little frightened gasp.

'What makes you think that, Superintendent?' David asked at last. His eyes were cautious, probing.

'Information received,' said the Superintendent stolidly.

There was a short silence. The Superintendent was aware of David's eyes, studying him, sizing him up, striving to *know* . . . He himself waited quietly.

'Any idea who Robert Underhay was, Superintendent?' David asked.

'Suppose *you* tell me, sir.'

'Robert Underhay was my sister's first husband. He died in Africa some years ago.'

'Quite sure of that, Mr Hunter?' Spence asked quickly.

'Quite sure. That's so, isn't it, Rosaleen?' He turned to her.

'Oh, yes.' She spoke quickly and breathlessly. 'Robert died of fever – blackwater fever. It was very sad.'

'Sometimes stories get about that aren't quite true, Mrs Cloade.'

She said nothing. She was looking not at him, but at her brother. Then, after a moment, she said:

'Robert's dead.'

'From information in my possession,' said the Superintendent, 'I understand that this man, Enoch Arden, claimed to be a friend of the late Robert Underhay and at the same time informed you, Mr Hunter, that Robert Underhay was alive.'

David shook his head.

'Nonsense,' he said. 'Absolute nonsense.'

'You state definitely that the name of Robert Underhay was not mentioned?'

'Oh,' David smiled charmingly, 'it was *mentioned*. This poor fellow had known Underhay.'

'There was no question of – blackmail, Mr Hunter?'

'Blackmail? I don't understand you, Superinten-dent.'

'Don't you really, Mr Hunter? By the way, just as a matter of form, where were you last night – between, shall we say, seven and eleven?'

'Just as a matter of form, Superintendent, suppose I refuse to answer?'

'Aren't you behaving rather childishly, Mr Hunter?'

'I don't think so. I dislike – I always have disliked, being bullied.'

The Superintendent thought that was probably true.

He'd known witnesses of the David Hunter type before. Witnesses who were obstructive for the sake of being obstructive, and not in the least because they had anything to hide. The mere fact of being asked to account for their comings and goings seemed to raise a black pride and sullenness in them. They would make it a point to give the law all the trouble they could.

Superintendent Spence, though he prided himself on being a fair-minded man, had nevertheless come to Shepherd's Court with a very strong conviction that David Hunter was a murderer.

Now, for the first time, he was not so sure. The very puerility of David's defiance awoke doubts in him.

Spence looked at Rosaleen Cloade. She responded at once.

'David, why don't you tell him?'

'That's right, Mrs Cloade. We only want to clear things up –'

David broke in savagely:

'You'll stop bullying my sister, do you hear? What is it to you where I may have been, here, or at Warmsley Vale or in Timbuctoo?'

Spence said warningly:

'You'll be subpoena'd for the inquest, Mr Hunter, and there you'll have to answer questions.'

'I'll wait for the inquest, then! And now, Superintendent, will you get to hell out of here?'

'Very good, sir.' The Superintendent rose, imperturbable. 'But I've something to ask Mrs Cloade first.'

'I don't want my sister worried.'

'Quite so. But I want her to look at the body and tell me if she can identify it. I'm within my rights there. It'll have to be done sooner or later. Why not let her come down with me now and get it over? The late Mr Arden was heard by a witness to say that he knew Robert Underhay – *ergo* he may have known Mrs Underhay – and therefore Mrs Underhay may know him. If his name isn't Enoch Arden, we could do with knowing what it really is.'

Rather unexpectedly Rosaleen Cloade got up.

'I'll come, of course,' she said.

Spence expected a fresh outburst from David, but to his surprise the other grinned.

'Good for you, Rosaleen,' he said. 'I'll confess, I'm curious myself. After all, you may be able to put a name to the fellow.'

Spence said to her:

'You didn't see him yourself in Warmsley Vale?'

She shook her head.

'I've been in London since Saturday last.'

'And Arden arrived on Friday night – yes.'

Rosaleen asked: 'Do you want me to come *now*?'

She asked the question with something of the submissiveness of a little girl. In spite of himself the Superintendent was favourably impressed. There was a docility, a willingness about her which he had not expected.

'That would be very nice of you, Mrs Cloade,' he said. 'The sooner we can get certain facts definitely established the better. I haven't got a police car here, I'm afraid.'

David crossed to the telephone.

'I'll ring up the Daimler Hire. It's beyond the legal limit – but I expect you can square that, Superintendent.'

'I think that can be arranged, Mr Hunter.'

He got up. 'I'll be waiting for you downstairs.'

He went down in the lift and pushed open the office door once more.

The Field Marshal was awaiting him.

'Well?'

'Both beds slept in last night, sir. Baths and towels used. Breakfast was served to them in the flat at nine-thirty.'

'And you don't know what time Mr Hunter came in yesterday evening?'

'I can't tell you anything further, I'm afraid, sir!'

Well, that was that, Spence thought. He wondered if there was anything behind David's refusal to speak except pure childlike defiance. He must realize that a charge of murder was hovering over him. Surely he must see that the sooner he told his story the better. Never a good thing to antagonize the police. But antagonizing the police, he thought ruefully, was just what David Hunter would enjoy doing.

They talked very little on the way down. When they arrived at the mortuary Rosaleen Cloade was very pale. Her hands were shaking. David looked concerned for her. He spoke to her as though she was a small child.

'It'll be only a minute or two, mavourneen. It's nothing at all, nothing at all now. Don't get worked up. You go in with the Superintendent and I'll wait for you. And there's nothing at all to mind about. Peaceful he'll look and just as though he were asleep.'

Agatha Christie

She gave him a little nod of the head and stretched out her hand. He gave it a little squeeze.

'Be a brave girl now, alanna.'

As she followed the Superintendent she said in her soft voice: 'You must think I'm a terrible coward, Superintendent. But when they've been all dead in the house – all dead but you – that awful night in London –'

He said gently: 'I understand, Mrs Cloade. I know you went through a bad experience in the Blitz when your husband was killed. Really, it will be only a minute or two.'

At a sign from Spence the sheet was turned back. Rosaleen Cloade stood looking down at the man who had called himself Enoch Arden. Spence, unobtrusively standing to one side, was actually watching her closely.

She looked at the dead man curiously and as though wondering – she gave no start, no sign of emotion or recognition, just looked long and wonderingly at him. Then, very quietly, in an almost matter-of-fact way, she made the sign of the cross.

'God rest his soul,' she said. 'I've never seen that man in my life. I don't know who he is.'

Spence thought to himself:

'Either you're one of the finest actresses I've ever known or else you're speaking the truth.'

Later, Spence rang up Rowley Cloade.

'I've had the widow down,' he said. 'She says definitely that he's not Robert Underlay and that she's never seen him before. So that settles *that*!'

There was a pause. Then Rowley said slowly:

'*Does* it settle it?'

'I think a jury would believe her – in the absence of evidence to the contrary, of course.'

'Ye-es,' said Rowley and rang off.

Then, frowning, he picked up not the local telephone directory, but the London one. His forefingers ran methodically down the letter P. Presently he found what he wanted.

Book II

Chapter 1

I

Hercule Poirot carefully folded the last of the newspapers he had sent George out to purchase. The information they gave was somewhat meagre. Medical evidence was given that the man's skull was fractured by a series of heavy blows. The inquest had been adjourned for a fortnight. Anybody who could give information about a man named Enoch Arden believed to have lately arrived from Cape Town was asked to communicate with the Chief Constable of Oastshire.

Poirot laid the papers in a neat pile and gave himself up to meditation. He was interested. He might, perhaps, have passed the first small paragraph by without interest if it had not been for the recent visit of Mrs Lionel Cloade. But that visit had recalled to him very clearly the incidents of that day at the club during that air raid. He remembered, very distinctly, Major Porter's voice saying, 'Maybe a Mr Enoch Arden will

Agatha Christie

turn up somewhere a thousand miles away and start life anew.' He wanted now, rather badly, to know more about this man called Enoch Arden who had died by violence at Warmsley Vale.

He remembered that he was slightly acquainted with Superintendent Spence of the Oastshire police and he also remembered that young Mellon lived not very far from Warmsley Heath, and that young Mellon knew Jeremy Cloade.

It was while he was meditating a telephone call to young Mellon that George came in and announced that a Mr Rowland Cloade would like to see him.

'Aha,' said Hercule Poirot with satisfaction. 'Show him in.'

A good-looking worried young man was shown in, and seemed rather at a loss how to begin.

'Well, Mr Cloade,' said Poirot helpfully, 'and what can I do for you?'

Rowley Cloade was eyeing Poirot rather doubtfully. The flamboyant moustaches, the sartorial elegance, the white spats and the pointed-patent leather shoes all filled this insular young man with distinct misgivings.

Poirot realized this perfectly well, and was somewhat amused.

Rowley Cloade began rather heavily:

'I'm afraid I'll have to explain who I am and all that. You won't know my name –'

Poirot interrupted him:

'But yes, I know your name perfectly. Your aunt, you see, came to see me last week.'

'My aunt?' Rowley's jaw dropped. He stared at Poirot with the utmost astonishment. This so clearly was news to him, that Poirot put aside his first surmise which was that the two visits were connected. For a moment it seemed to him a remarkable coincidence that two members of the Cloade family should choose to consult him within such a short period of time, but a second later he realized that there was no coincidence – merely a natural sequence proceeding from one initial cause.

Aloud he said:

'I assume that Mrs Lionel Cloade *is* your aunt.'

If anything Rowley looked rather more astonished than before.

He said with the utmost incredulity:

'Aunt Kathie? Surely – don't you mean – Mrs *Jeremy* Cloade?'

Poirot shook his head.

'But what on earth could Aunt Kathie –'

Poirot murmured discreetly:

'She was directed to me, I understand, by spirit guidance.'

'Oh Lord!' said Rowley. He looked relieved and amused. He said, as though reassuring Poirot, 'She's quite harmless, you know.'

Agatha Christie

'I wonder,' said Poirot.

'What do you mean?'

'Is anybody – ever – quite harmless?'

Rowley stared. Poirot sighed.

'You have come to me to ask me something? – Yes?' he prompted gently.

The worried look came back to Rowley's face.

'It's rather a long story, I'm afraid –'

Poirot was afraid of it, too. He had a very shrewd idea that Rowley Cloade was not the sort of person to come to the point quickly. He leaned back and half-closed his eyes as Rowley began:

'My uncle, you see, was Gordon Cloade –'

'I know all about Gordon Cloade,' said Poirot, helpfully.

'Good. Then I needn't explain. He married a few weeks before his death – a young widow called Underhay. Since his death she has been living at Warmsley Vale – she and a brother of hers. We all understood that her first husband had died of fever in Africa. But now it seems as though that mightn't be so.'

'Ah,' Poirot sat up. 'And what has led you to that surmise?'

Rowley described the advent of Mr Enoch Arden in Warmsley Vale. 'Perhaps you have seen in the papers –'

'Yes, I have seen.' Poirot was again helpful.

Rowley went on. He described his first impression of the man Arden, his visit to the Stag, the letter he had received from Beatrice Lippincott and finally the conversation that Beatrice had overheard.

'Of course,' Rowley said, 'one can't be sure just what she *did* hear. She may have exaggerated it all a bit – or even got it wrong.'

'Has she told her story to the police?'

Rowley nodded. 'I told her she'd better.'

'I don't quite see – pardon me – why you come to *me*, Mr Cloade? Do you want me to investigate this – murder? For it is murder, I assume.'

'Lord, no,' said Rowley. 'I don't want anything of that kind. That's a police job. He was bumped off all right. No, what I'm after is this. I want you to find out who the fellow *was*.'

Poirot's eyes narrowed.

'Who do you think he was, Mr Cloade?'

'Well, I mean – Enoch Arden isn't a name. Dash it all, it's a quotation. Tennyson. I went and mugged it up. Fellow who comes back and finds out his wife has married another fellow.'

'So you think,' said Poirot quietly, 'that Enoch Arden was Robert Underhay himself?'

Rowley said slowly:

'Well, he might have been – I mean, about the right age and appearance and all that. Of course I've gone over it all with Beatrice again and again. She can't naturally remember *exactly* what they both said. The chap said Robert Underhay had come down in the world and was in bad health and needed money. Well, he might have been talking about himself, mightn't he? He seems to have said something about it wouldn't suit David Hunter's book if Underhay turned up in Warmsley Vale – sounding a bit as though he *was* there under an assumed name.'

'What evidence of identification was there at the inquest?'

Rowley shook his head.

'Nothing definite. Only the Stag people saying he was the man who'd come there and registered as Enoch Arden.'

'What about his papers?'

'He hadn't any.'

'What?' Poirot sat up in surprise. 'No papers of any kind?'

'Nothing at all. Some spare socks and a shirt and a toothbrush, etc. – but no papers.'

'No passport? No letters? Not even a ration card?'

'Nothing at all.'

'That,' said Poirot, 'is very interesting. Yes, very interesting.'

Rowley went on: 'David Hunter, that's Rosaleen Cloade's brother, had called to see him the evening after he arrived. His story to the police is that he'd had a letter from the chap saying he had been a friend of Robert Underhay's and was down and out. At his sister's request he went to the Stag and saw the fellow and gave him a fiver. That's *his* story and you bet he means to stick to it! Of course the police are keeping dark about what Beatrice heard.'

'David Hunter says he had no previous acquaintance with the man?'

'That's what he says. Anyway, I gather Hunter never met Underhay.'

'And what about Rosaleen Cloade?'

'The police asked her to look at the body in case she knew the man. She told them that he was a complete stranger to her.'

'*Eh bien*,' said Poirot. 'Then that answers your question!'

'Does it?' said Rowley bluntly. 'I think not. If the dead man *is* Underhay then Rosaleen was never my uncle's wife and she's not entitled to a penny of his money. Do you think she *would* recognize him under those circumstances?'

'You don't trust her?'

'I don't trust either of them.

'Surely there are plenty of people who could say for certain that the dead man is or is not Underhay?'

'It doesn't seem to be so easy. That's what I want you

to do. Find someone who knows Underhay. Apparently he has no living relations in this country – and he was always an unsociable lonely sort of chap. I suppose there must be old servants – friends – *someone* – but the war's broken up everything and shifted people round. *I* wouldn't know how to begin to tackle the job – anyway I haven't the time. I'm a farmer – and I'm short-handed.'

'Why me?' said Hercule Poirot.

Rowley looked embarrassed.

A faint twinkle came into Poirot's eye.

'Spirit guidance?' he murmured.

'Good Lord, no,' said Rowley horrified. 'Matter of fact,' he hesitated, 'I heard a fellow I know talk about you – said you were a wizard at these sort of things. I don't know about your fees – expensive, I expect – we're rather a stony-broke lot, but I dare say we could cough it up amongst the lot of us. That is, if you'll take it on.'

Hercule Poirot said slowly:

'Yes, I think perhaps I can help you.'

His memory, a very precise and definite memory, went back. The club bore, the rustling newspapers, the monotonous voice.

The name – he had heard the name – it would come back to him presently. If not, he could always ask Mellon . . . No, he had got it. Porter. Major Porter.

Hercule Poirot rose to his feet.

'Will you come back here this afternoon, Mr Cloade?'

'Well – I don't know. Yes, I suppose I could. But surely you can't do anything in that short time?'

He looked at Poirot with awe and incredulity. Poirot would have been less than human if he could have resisted the temptation to show off. With memories of a brilliant predecessor in his mind, he said solemnly:

'I have my methods, Mr Cloade.'

It was clearly the right thing to say. Rowley's expression became respectful in the extreme.

'Yes – of course – really – I don't know how you people do these things.'

Poirot did not enlighten him. When Rowley had gone, he sat down and wrote a short note. Giving it to George he instructed him to take it to the Coronation Club and wait for an answer.

The answer was highly satisfactory. Major Porter presented his compliments to M. Hercule Poirot and would be happy to see him and his friend at 79 Edgeway Street, Campden Hill, that afternoon at five o'clock.

Agatha Christie

At four-thirty Rowley Cloade reappeared.

'Any luck, M. Poirot?'

'But yes, Mr Cloade, we go now to see an old friend of Captain Robert Underhay's.'

'*What?*' Rowley's mouth fell open. He stared at Poirot with the amazement a small boy shows when a conjurer produces rabbits out of a hat. 'But it's *incredible*! I don't understand how you can do these things – why, it's only a few hours.'

Poirot waved a deprecating hand and tried to look modest. He had no intention of revealing the simplicity with which his conjuring trick had been done. His vanity was pleased to impress this simple Rowley.

The two men went out together, and hailing a taxi they drove to Campden Hill.

Major Porter had the first floor of a small shabby house. They were admitted by a cheerful blowsy-looking woman who took them up. It was a square room with bookshelves round it and some rather bad sporting prints. There were two rugs on the floor –

good rugs with lovely dim colour but very worn. Poirot noticed that the centre of the floor was covered with a new heavy varnish whereas the varnish round the edge was old and rubbed. He realized then that there had been other better rugs until recently – rugs that were worth good money in these days. He looked up at the man standing erect by the fireplace in his well-cut shabby suit. Poirot guessed that for Major Porter, retired Army officer, life was lived very near the bone. Taxation and increased cost of living struck hardest at the old war-horses. Some things, he guessed, Major Porter would cling to until the end. His club subscription, for instance.

Major Porter was speaking jerkily.

''Fraid I don't remember meeting you, M. Poirot. At the club, you say? Couple of years ago? Know your *name* of course.'

'This,' said Poirot, 'is Mr Rowland Cloade.'

Major Porter jerked his head in honour of the introduction.

'How d'ye do?' he said. ''Fraid I can't ask you to have a glass of sherry. Matter of fact my wine merchant has lost his stock in the Blitz. Got some gin. Filthy stuff, *I* always think. Or what about some beer?'

They accepted beer. Major Porter produced a cigarette case. 'Smoke?' Poirot accepted a cigarette. The Major struck a match and lighted Poirot's cigarette.

Agatha Christie

'*You* don't, I know,' said the Major to Rowley: 'Mind if I light my pipe?' He did so with a good deal of sucking and blowing.

'Now then,' he said when all these preliminaries had been accomplished. 'What's all this about?'

He looked from one to the other of them.

Poirot said: 'You may have read in the paper of the death of a man at Warmsley Vale?'

Porter shook his head.

'May have. Don't think so.'

'His name was Arden. Enoch Arden?'

Porter still shook his head.

'He was found at the Stag Inn with the back of his head smashed in.'

Porter frowned.

'Let me see – yes, did see something about it, I believe – some days ago.'

'Yes. I have here a photograph – it is a press photograph and not very clear, I'm afraid! What we should like to know, Major Porter, is whether you have ever seen this man before?'

He handed over the best reproduction of the dead man's face he had been able to find.

Major Porter took it and frowned at it.

'Wait a sec.' The Major took out his spectacles, adjusted them on his nose and studied the photograph more closely – then he gave a sudden start.

'God bless my soul!' he said. 'Well, I'm damned!'

'You know the man, Major?'

'Of course I know him. It's Underhay – Robert Underhay.'

'You're sure of that?' There was triumph in Rowley's voice.

'Of course I'm sure. Robert Underhay! I'd swear to it anywhere.'

Chapter 2

The telephone rang and Lynn went to answer it.

Rowley's voice spoke.

'Lynn?'

'Rowley?'

Her voice sounded depressed. He said:

'What are you up to? I never see you these days.'

'Oh, well – it's all chores – you know. Running round with a basket, waiting for fish and queueing up for a bit of quite disgusting cake. All that sort of thing. Home life.'

'I want to see you. I've got something to tell you.'

'What sort of thing?'

He gave a chuckle.

'Good news. Meet me by Rolland Copse. We're ploughing up there.'

Good news? Lynn put the receiver down. What to Rowley Cloade would be good news? Finance? Had he sold that young bull at a better price than he had hoped to get?

No, she thought, it must be more than that. As she walked up the field to Rolland Copse, Rowley left the tractor and came to meet her.

'Hallo, Lynn.'

'Why, Rowley – you look – *different*, somehow?'

He laughed.

'I should think I do. *Our luck's turned*, Lynn!'

'What *do* you mean?'

'Do you remember old Jeremy mentioning a chap called Hercule Poirot?'

'Hercule Poirot?' Lynn frowned. 'Yes, I do remember *something* –'

'Quite a long time ago. When the war was on. They were in that mausoleum of a club of his and there was an air raid.'

'Well?' Lynn demanded impatiently.

'Fellow has the wrong clothes and all that. French chap – or Belgian. Queer fellow but he's the goods all right.'

Lynn knit her brows.

'Wasn't he – a *detective*?'

'That's right. Well, you know, this fellow who was done in at the Stag. I didn't tell you but an idea was getting around that he might just possibly be Rosaleen Cloade's first husband.'

Lynn laughed.

'Simply because he called himself Enoch Arden? What an absurd idea!'

'Not so absurd, my girl. Old Spence got Rosaleen down to have a look at him. And she swore quite firmly that he *wasn't* her husband.'

'So that finished it?'

'It might have,' said Rowley. 'But for *me*!'

'For you? What did *you* do?'

'I went to this fellow Hercule Poirot. I told him we wanted another opinion. Could he rustle up someone who had actually known Robert Underhay? My word, but he's absolutely wizard that chap! Just like rabbits out of a hat. He produced a fellow who was Underhay's best friend in a few hours. Old boy called Porter.' Rowley stopped. Then he chuckled again with that note of excitement that had surprised and startled Lynn. 'Now *keep this under your hat*, Lynn. The Super swore me to secrecy – but I'd like *you* to know. The dead man is Robert Underhay.'

'What?' Lynn took a step back. She stared at Rowley blankly.

'Robert Underhay himself. Porter hadn't the least doubt. So you see, Lynn' – Rowley's voice rose excitedly – '*we've won*! After all, we've *won*! We've beaten those damned crooks!'

'What damned crooks?'

'Hunter and his sister. They're licked – out of it. Rosaleen doesn't get Gordon's money. *We* get it. It's *ours*! Gordon's will that he made before he married Rosaleen holds good and that divides it amongst us. I get a fourth share. See? *If* her first husband was alive when she married Gordon, *she was never married to Gordon at all*!'

'Are you – are you *sure* of what you're saying?'

He stared at her, for the first time he looked faintly puzzled.

'Of course I'm sure! It's elementary. Everything's all right now. It's the same as Gordon meant it to be. Everything's the same as if that precious pair had never butted in.'

Everything's the same . . . But you couldn't, Lynn thought, wash out like that something that had happened. You couldn't pretend that it had never been. She said slowly:

'What will they do?'

'Eh?' She saw that until that moment Rowley had hardly considered that question. 'I don't know. Go back where they came from, I suppose. I think, you know –' She could see him slowly following it out. 'Yes, I think we ought to do something for *her*. I mean, she married Gordon in all good faith. I gather she really believed her first husband was dead. It's not *her* fault. Yes, we must do something about her

– give her a decent allowance. Make it up between us all.'

'You like her, don't you?' said Lynn.

'Well, yes.' He considered. 'I do in a way. She's a nice kid. She knows a cow when she sees it.'

'I don't,' said Lynn.

'Oh, you'll learn,' said Rowley kindly.

'And what about – David?' asked Lynn.

Rowley scowled.

'To hell with David! It was never *his* money anyway. He just came along and sponged on his sister.'

'No, Rowley, it wasn't like that – it wasn't. He's *not* a sponger. He's – an adventurer, perhaps –'

'*And* a ruddy murderer!'

She said breathlessly:

'What do you mean?'

'Well, who do you think killed Underhay?'

She cried:

'I don't believe it! I don't believe it!'

'Of course he killed Underhay! Who else could have done it? He was down here that day. Came down by the five-thirty. I was meeting some stuff at the station and caught sight of him in the distance.'

Lynn said sharply:

'He went back to London that evening.'

'After having killed Underhay,' said Rowley triumphantly.

'You oughtn't to say things like that, Rowley. What time was Underhay killed?'

'Well – I don't know *exactly*.' Rowley slowed up – considered. 'Don't suppose we shall know until the inquest tomorrow. Some time between nine and ten, I imagine.'

'David caught the nine-twenty train back to London.'

'Look here, Lynn, how do *you* know?'

'I – I met him – he was running for it.'

'How do you know he ever caught it?'

'Because he telephoned me from London later.'

Rowley scowled angrily.

'What the hell should he telephone *you* for? Look here, Lynn, I'm damned if I –'

'Oh, what does it *matter*, Rowley? Anyway, it shows he caught that train.'

'Plenty of time to have killed Underhay and then run for the train.'

'Not if he was killed after nine o'clock.'

'Well, he may have been killed just before nine.'

But his voice was a little doubtful.

Lynn half-closed her eyes. *Was* that the truth of it? When, breathless, swearing, David had emerged from the copse, had it been a murderer fresh from his crime who had taken her in his arms? She remembered his curious excitement – the recklessness of his mood. Was that the way that murder would affect him? It might.

She had to admit it. Were David and murder so far removed from each other? *Would* he kill a man who had never done him any harm – a ghost from the past? A man whose only crime was to stand between Rosaleen and a big inheritance – between David and the enjoyment of Rosaleen's money.

She murmured:

'*Why* should he kill Underhay?'

'My God, Lynn, can you *ask*? I've just *told* you! Underhay's being alive means that *we* get Gordon's money! Anyway, Underhay was blackmailing him.'

Ah, that fell more into the pattern. David might kill a blackmailer – in fact, wasn't it just the way he *would* deal with a blackmailer? Yes, it all fell into pattern. David's haste, his excitement – his fierce, almost angry, lovemaking. And, later, his renouncement of her. 'I'd better clear out . . .' Yes, it fitted.

From a long way away, she heard Rowley's voice asking:

'What's the matter, Lynn? Are you feeling all right?'

'Yes, of course.'

'Well, for heaven's sake, don't look so glum.' He turned, looking down the hillside to Long Willows. 'Thank goodness, we can have the place smartened up a bit now – get some labour-saving gadgets put in – make it right for you. I don't want you to pig it, Lynn.'

That was to be her home – that house. Her home with Rowley . . .

And one morning at eight o'clock, David would swing by the neck until he was dead . . .

Chapter 3

With a pale determined face and watchful eyes, David had his hands on Rosaleen's shoulders.

'It will be all right, I'm telling you, it will be all right. But you must keep your head and do exactly as I tell you.'

'And if they take you away? You said that! You did say that they might take you away.'

'It's a possibility, yes. But it won't be for long. Not if you keep your head.'

'I'll do what you tell me, David.'

'There's the girl! All you have to do, Rosaleen, is to stick to your story. Hold to it that the dead man is *not* your husband, Robert Underhay.'

'They'll trap me into saying things I don't mean.'

'No – they won't. It's all right, I tell you.'

'No, it's wrong – it's been wrong all along. Taking money that doesn't belong to us. I lie awake nights thinking of it, David. Taking what doesn't belong to us. God is punishing us for our wickedness.'

He looked at her, frowning. She was cracking – yes, definitely she was cracking. There had always been that religious streak. Her conscience had never been quite stilled. Now, unless he was extremely lucky, she'd break down completely. Well, there was only one thing to be done.

'Listen, Rosaleen,' he said gently. 'Do you want me to be hanged?'

Her eyes widened in horror.

'Oh, David, you wouldn't – they couldn't –'

'There's only one person who can hang me – that's you. If you once admit, by look or sign or word, that the dead man might be Underhay, you put the rope round my neck! Do you understand that?'

Yes, that had got home. She gazed at him with wide, horrified eyes.

'I'm so stupid, David.'

'No, you're not. In any case you haven't got to be clever. You'll have to swear solemnly that the dead man is not your husband. You can do that?'

She nodded.

'Look stupid if you like. Look as if you don't understand quite what they're asking you. That will do no harm. But stand firm on the points I've gone over with you. Gaythorne will look after you. He's a very able criminal lawyer – that's why I've got him. He'll be at the inquest and he'll protect you from any heckling. But even to him *stick to your story*. For God's sake don't try to be clever or think you can help me by some line of your own.'

'I'll do it, David. I'll do exactly what you tell me.'

'Good girl. When it's all over we'll go away – to the South of France – to America. In the meantime, take care of your health. Don't lie awake at nights fretting and working yourself up. Take those sleepings things Dr Cloade prescribed for you – bromide or something. Take one every night, cheer up, and remember *there's a good time coming*!

'Now –' he looked at his watch. 'It's time to go to the inquest. It's called for eleven.'

He looked round the long beautiful drawing-room. Beauty, comfort, wealth . . . He'd enjoyed it all. A fine house, Furrowbank. Perhaps this was Goodbye . . .

He'd got himself into a jam – that was certain. But even now he didn't regret. And for the future – well, he'd go on taking chances. '*And we must take the current when it serves or lose our ventures.*'

He looked at Rosaleen. She was watching him with large appealing eyes and intuitively he knew what she wanted.

'I didn't kill him, Rosaleen,' he said gently. 'I swear it to you by every saint in your calendar!'

Chapter 4

The Inquest was held in the Cornmarket.

The coroner, Mr Pebmarsh, was a small fussy man with glasses and a considerable sense of his own importance.

Beside him sat the large bulk of Superintendent Spence. In an unobtrusive seat was a small foreign-looking man with a large black moustache. The Cloade family: the Jeremy Cloades, the Lionel Cloades, Rowley Cloade, Mrs Marchmont and Lynn – they were all there. Major Porter sat by himself, fidgeting and ill at ease. David and Rosaleen arrived last. They sat by themselves.

The coroner cleared his throat and glancing round the jury of nine local worthies, started proceedings.

Constable Peacock –

Sergeant Vane . . .

Dr Lionel Cloade . . .

'You were attending a patient professionally at the Stag, when Gladys Aitkin came to you. What did she say?'

'She informed me that the occupant of No. 5 was lying on the floor dead.'

'In consequence you went up to No. 5?'

'I did.'

'Will you describe what you found there?'

Dr Cloade described. Body of a man ... face downwards ... head injuries ... back of skull ... fire-tongs.

'You were of opinion, that the injuries were inflicted with the tongs in question?'

'Some of them unquestionably were.'

'And that several blows had been struck?'

'Yes. I did not make a detailed examination as I considered that the police should be called before the body was touched or its position altered.'

'Very proper. The man was dead?'

'Yes. He had been dead for some hours.'

'How long in your opinion had he been dead?'

'I should hesitate to be very definite about that. At least eleven hours – quite possibly thirteen or fourteen – let us say between 7.30 and 10.30 p.m. the preceding evening.'

'Thank you, Dr Cloade.'

Then came the police surgeon – giving a full and

technical description of the wounds. There was an abrasion and swelling on the lower jaw and five or six blows had been struck on the base of the skull, some of which had been delivered after death.

'It was an assault of great savagery?'

'Exactly.'

'Would great strength have been needed to inflict these blows?'

'N-no, not exactly strength. The tongs, grasped by the pincers end, could be easily swung without much exertion. The heavy steel ball which forms the head of the tongs makes them a formidable weapon. Quite a delicate person could have inflicted the injuries if, that is to say, they were struck in a frenzy of excitement.'

'Thank you, Doctor.'

Details as to the condition of the body followed – well nourished, healthy, age about forty-five. No signs of illness or disease – heart, lungs, etc., all good.

Beatrice Lippincott gave evidence of the arrival of the deceased. He had registered as Enoch Arden, Cape Town.

'Did deceased produce a ration book?'

'No, sir.'

'Did you ask him for one?'

'Not at first. I did not know how long he was staying.'

'But you did eventually ask him?'

'Yes, sir. He arrived on the Friday and on Saturday I said if he was staying more than five days would he please let me have his ration book.'

'What did he say to that?'

'He said he would give it to me.'

'But he did not actually do so?'

'No.'

'He did not say that he had lost it? Or had not got one?'

'Oh, no. He just said, "I'll look it out and bring it along."'

'Miss Lippincott, did you, on the night of Saturday, overhear a certain conversation?'

With a good deal of elaborate explanation as to the necessity she was under of visiting No. 4, Beatrice Lippincott told her tale. The coroner guided her astutely.

'Thank you. Did you mention this conversation you had overheard to anybody?'

'Yes, I told Mr Rowley Cloade.'

'Why did you tell Mr Cloade?'

'I thought he ought to know.' Beatrice flushed.

A tall thin man (Mr Gaythorne) rose and asked permission to put a question.

'In the course of the conversation between the deceased and Mr David Hunter did the deceased at any time mention definitely that he himself was Robert Underhay?'

'No – no – he didn't.'

'In fact he spoke of "Robert Underhay" as though Robert Underhay was quite another person?'

'Yes – yes, he did.'

'Thank you, Mr Coroner, that was all I wanted to get clear.'

Beatrice Lippincott stood down and Rowley Cloade was called.

He confirmed that Beatrice had repeated the story to him and then gave his account of his interview with the deceased.

'His last words to you were, "I don't think you'll prove that without *my* co-operation?" "*That*" – being the fact that Robert Underhay was still alive.'

'That's what he said, yes. And he laughed.'

'He laughed, did he? What did you take those words to mean?'

'Well – I just thought he was trying to get me to make him an offer, but afterwards I got thinking –'

'Yes, Mr Cloade – but what you thought afterwards is hardly relevant. Shall we put it that that as a result of that interview you set about trying to find some person who was acquainted with the late Robert Underhay? And that, with certain help, you were successful.'

Rowley nodded.

'That's right.'

'What time was it when you left the deceased?'

'As nearly as I can tell it was five minutes to nine.'

'What made you fix on that time?'

'As I went along the street I heard the nine o'clock chimes through an open window.'

'Did the deceased mention at what time he was expecting this client?'

'He said "At any minute."'

'He did not mention any name?'

'No.'

'David Hunter!'

There was just a faint soft buzz as the inhabitants of Warmsley Vale craned their necks to look at the tall thin bitter-looking young man who stood defiantly facing the coroner.

The preliminaries went rapidly. The coroner continued:

'You went to see the deceased on Saturday evening?'

'Yes. I received a letter from him asking for assistance and stating he had known my sister's first husband in Africa.'

'You have got that letter?'

'No, I don't keep letters.'

'You have heard the account given by Beatrice Lippincott of your conversation with the deceased. Is that a true account?'

'Quite untrue. The deceased spoke of knowing my late brother-in-law, complained of his own bad luck and of having come down in the world, and begged for some financial assistance which, as is usual, he was quite confident of being able to repay.'

'Did he tell you that Robert Underhay was still alive?'

David smiled:

'Certainly not. He said, "*If* Robert were still alive I know he would help me."'

'That is quite different from what Beatrice Lippincott tells us.'

'Eavesdroppers,' said David, 'usually hear only a portion of what goes on and frequently get the whole thing wrong owing to supplying the missing details from their own fertile imaginations.'

Beatrice flounced angrily and exclaimed, 'Well, I never –' The coroner said repressively, 'Silence, please.'

'Now, Mr Hunter, did you visit the deceased again on the night of Tuesday –'

'No, I did not.'

'You have heard Mr Rowley Cloade say that the deceased expected a visitor?'

'He may have expected a visitor. If so, I was not that visitor. I'd given him a fiver before. I thought that was quite enough for him. There was no proof that he'd ever known Robert Underhay. My sister, since she inherited a large income from her husband, has been the target of every begging letter-writer and every sponger in the neighbourhood.'

223

Quietly he let his eyes pass over the assembled Cloades.

'Mr Hunter, will you tell us where you were on the evening of Tuesday?'

'Find out!' said David.

'Mr Hunter!' The coroner rapped the table. 'That is a most foolish and ill-advised thing to say.'

'Why should I tell you where I was, and what I was doing? Time enough for that when you accuse me of murdering the man.'

'If you persist in that attitude it may come to that sooner than you think. Do you recognize *this*, Mr Hunter?'

Leaning forward, David took the gold cigarette lighter into his hand. His face was puzzled. Handing it back, he said slowly: 'Yes, it's mine.'

'When did you have it last?'

'I missed it –' He paused.

'Yes, Mr Hunter?' The coroner's voice was suave.

Gaythorne fidgeted, seemed about to speak. But David was too quick for him.

'I had it last Friday – Friday morning. I don't remember seeing it since.'

Mr Gaythorne rose.

'With your permission, Mr Coroner. You visited the deceased Saturday evening. Might you not have left the lighter there then?'

'I might have, I suppose,' David said slowly. 'I certainly don't remember seeing it after Friday –' He added: 'Where was it found?'

The coroner said:

'We shall go into that later. You can stand down now, Mr Hunter.'

David moved slowly back to his seat. He bent his head and whispered to Rosaleen Cloade.

'Major Porter.'

Hemming and hawing a little, Major Porter took the stand. He stood there, an erect soldierly figure, as though on parade. Only the way he moistened his lips showed the intense nervousness from which he was suffering.

'You are George Douglas Porter, late Major of the Royal African Rifles?'

'Yes.'

'How well did you know Robert Underhay?'

In a parade-ground voice Major Porter barked out places and dates.

'You have viewed the body of the deceased?'

'Yes.'

'Can you identify that body?'

'Yes. It is the body of Robert Underhay.'

A buzz of excitement went round the court.

'You state that positively and without the least doubt?'

Agatha Christie

'I do.'

'There is no possibility of your being mistaken?'

'None.'

'Thank you, Major Porter. Mrs Gordon Cloade.'

Rosaleen rose. She passed Major Porter. He looked at her with some curiosity. She did not even glance at him.

'Mrs Cloade, you were taken by the police to see the body of the deceased?'

She shivered.

'Yes.'

'You stated definitely that it was the body of a man completely unknown to you?'

'Yes.'

'In view of the statement just made by Major Porter would you like to withdraw or amend your own statement?'

'No.'

'You still assert definitely that the body was not that of your husband, Robert Underhay?'

'It was not my husband's body. It was a man I had never seen in my life.'

'Come now, Mrs Cloade, Major Porter has definitely recognized it as the body of his friend Robert Underhay.'

Rosaleen said expressionlessly:

'Major Porter is mistaken.'

'You are not under oath in this court, Mrs Cloade. But it is likely that you will be under oath in another court shortly. Are you prepared then to swear that the body is not that of Robert Underhay but of an unknown stranger?'

'I am prepared to swear that it is not the body of my husband but of a man quite unknown to me.'

Her voice was clear and unfaltering. Her eyes met the coroner unshrinkingly.

He murmured: 'You can stand down.'

Then, removing his pince-nez, he addressed the jury.

They were there to discover how this man came to his death. As to that, there could be little question. There could be no idea of accident or suicide. Nor could there be any suggestion of manslaughter. There remained only one verdict – wilful murder. As to the identity of the dead man, that was not clearly established.

They had heard one witness, a man of upright character and probity whose word could be relied upon, say that the body was that of a former friend of his, Robert Underhay. On the other hand Robert Underhay's death from fever in Africa had been established apparently to the satisfaction of the local authorities and no question had then been raised. In contradiction of Major Porter's statement, Robert Underhay's widow, now

Agatha Christie

Mrs Gordon Cloade, stated positively that the body was *not* that of Robert Underhay. These were diametrically opposite statements. Passing from the question of identity they would have to decide if there was any evidence to show whose hand had murdered the deceased. They might think that the evidence pointed to a certain person, but a good deal of evidence was needed before a case could be made out – evidence and motive and opportunity. The person must have been seen by someone in the vicinity of the crime at the appropriate time. If there was not such evidence the best verdict was that of Wilful Murder without sufficient evidence to show by whose hand. Such a verdict would leave the police free to pursue the necessary inquiries.

He then dismissed them to consider their verdict.

They took three quarters of an hour.

They returned a verdict of Wilful Murder against David Hunter.

Chapter 5

'I was afraid they'd do it,' said the coroner apologetically. 'Local prejudice! Feeling rather than logic.'

The coroner, the Chief Constable, Superintendent Spence and Hercule Poirot were all in consultation together after the inquest.

'You did your best,' said the Chief Constable.

'It's premature, to say the least of it,' said Spence frowning. 'And it hampers us. Do you know M. Hercule Poirot? He was instrumental in bringing Porter forward.'

The coroner said graciously:

'I have heard of you, M. Poirot,' and Poirot made an unsuccessful attempt to look modest.

'M. Poirot's interested in the case,' said Spence with a grin.

'Truly, that is so,' said Poirot. 'I was in it, as you might say, before there *was* a case.'

Agatha Christie

And in answer to their interested glances he told of the queer little scene in the club when he had first heard a mention of Robert Underhay's name.

'That's an additional point in Porter's evidence when the case comes to trial,' said the Chief Constable thoughtfully. 'Underhay actually *planned* a pretended death – and spoke of using the name of Enoch Arden.'

The Chief Constable murmured: 'Ah, but will that be admissible as evidence? Words spoken by a man who is now dead?'

'It may not be admissible as evidence,' said Poirot thoughtfully. 'But it raises a very interesting and suggestive line of thought.'

'What *we* want,' said Spence, 'is not suggestion, but a few concrete facts. Someone who actually saw David Hunter at the Stag or near it on Tuesday evening.'

'It ought to be easy,' said the Chief Constable, frowning.

'If it was abroad in my country it would be easy enough,' said Poirot. 'There would be a little café where someone takes the evening coffee – but in provincial England!' He threw up his hands.

The Superintendent nodded.

'Some of the folks are in the pubs, and will stay in the pubs till closing time, and the rest of the population are inside their houses listening to the nine o'clock news. If you ever go along the main street here

230

between eight-thirty and ten it's completely deserted. Not a soul.'

'He counted on that?' suggested the Chief Constable.

'Maybe,' said Spence. His expression was not a happy one.

Presently the Chief Constable and the coroner departed. Spence and Poirot were left together.

'You do not like the case, no?' asked Poirot sympathetically.

'That young man worries me,' said Spence. 'He's the kind that you never know where you are with them. When they're most innocent of a business, they act as though they were guilty. And when they're guilty – why, you'd take your oath they were angels of light!'

'*You* think he *is* guilty?' asked Poirot.

'Don't you?' Spence countered.

Poirot spread out his hands.

'I should be interested to know,' he said, 'just exactly how much you have against him?'

'You don't mean legally? You mean in the way of probability?'

Poirot nodded.

'There's the lighter,' said Spence.

'Where did you find it?'

'Under the body.'

'Fingerprints on it?'

'None.'

'Ah,' said Poirot.

'Yes,' said Spence. 'I don't like that too much myself. Then the dead man's watch has stopped at 9.10. That fits in with the medical evidence quite nicely – and with Rowley Cloade's evidence that Underhay was expecting his client at any minute – presumably that client was almost due.'

Poirot nodded.

'Yes – it is all very neat.'

'And the thing you can't get away from, to my mind, M. Poirot, is that he's the only person (he and his sister, that is to say) who has the ghost or shadow of a motive. Either David Hunter killed Underhay – or else Underhay was killed by some outsider who followed him here for some reason that we know nothing about – and that seems wildly improbable.'

'Oh, I agree, I agree.'

'You see, there's no one in Warmsley Vale who could possibly have a motive – unless by a coincidence someone is living here (other than the Hunters) who had a connection with Underhay in the past. I never rule out coincidence, but there hasn't been a hint or suggestion of anything of the kind. The man was a stranger to every one but that brother and sister.'

Poirot nodded.

'To the Cloade family Robert Underhay would be

the apple of their eye to be kept alive by every possible precaution. Robert Underhay, alive and kicking, means the certainty of a large fortune divided amongst them.'

'Again, *mon ami*, I agree with you enthusiastically. Robert Underhay, alive and kicking, is what the Cloade family needs.'

'So back we come – Rosaleen and David Hunter are the only two people who have a motive. Rosaleen Cloade was in London. But David, we know, was in Warmsley Vale that day. He arrived at 5.30 at Warmsley Heath station.'

'So now we have Motive, written very big and the fact that at 5.30 and onward to some unspecified time, he was on the spot.'

'Exactly. Now take Beatrice Lippincott's story. I believe that story. She overheard what she says she overheard, though she may have gingered it up a little, as is only human.'

'Only human as you say.'

'Apart from knowing the girl, I believe her because she couldn't have invented some of the things. She'd never heard of Robert Underhay before, for instance. So I believe her story of what passed between the two men and not David Hunter's.'

'I, too,' said Poirot. 'She strikes me as a singularly truthful witness.'

'We've confirmation that her story is true. What do you suppose the brother and sister went off to London for?'

'That is one of the things that has interested me most.'

'Well, the money position's like this. Rosaleen Cloade has only a life interest in Gordon Cloade's estate. She can't touch the capital – except, I believe, for about a thousand pounds. But jewellery, etc., is hers. The first thing she did on going to town was to take some of the most valuable pieces round to Bond Street and sell them. She wanted a large sum of cash quickly – in other words she had to pay a blackmailer.'

'You call that evidence against David Hunter?'

'Don't you?'

Poirot shook his head.

'Evidence that there was blackmail, yes. Evidence of intent to commit murder, no. You cannot have it both ways, *mon cher*. Either that young man was going to pay up, or else he was planning to kill. You have produced evidence that he was planning to *pay*.'

'Yes – yes, perhaps that is so. But he may have changed his mind.'

Poirot shrugged his shoulders.

'I know his type,' said the Superintendent thoughtfully. 'It's a type that's done well during the war. Any amount of physical courage. Audacity and a reckless disregard of personal safety. The sort that will face any odds. It's the kind that is likely to win the V.C. – though, mind you, it's often a posthumous one. Yes, in wartime, a man like that is a hero. But in peace – well, in peace such men usually end up in prison. They like excitement and they can't run straight, and they don't give a damn for society – and finally they've no regard for human life.'

Poirot nodded.

'I tell you,' the Superintendent repeated, 'I *know* the type.'

There was some few minutes of silence.

'*Eh bien*,' said Poirot at last. 'We agree that we have here the *type* of a killer. But that is all. It takes us no further.'

Spence looked at him with curiosity.

'You're taking a great interest in this business, M. Poirot?'

'Yes.'

'Why, if I may ask?'

'Frankly,' Poirot spread out his hands, 'I do not quite know. Perhaps it is because when two years ago, I am sitting very sick in my stomach (for I did not like air raids, and I am not very brave though I endeavour to put up the good appearance) when, as I say, I am sitting with a sick feeling here,' Poirot clasped his stomach expressively, 'in the smoking-room of my friend's club, there, droning away, is the club bore, the good Major Porter, recounting a long history to which nobody listens; but me, I listen, because I am wishful to distract myself from the bombs, and because the facts he is relating seem to me interesting and suggestive. And I think to myself that it is possible that some day something may come of the situation he recounts. And now something *has* come of it.'

'The unexpected has happened, eh?'

'On the contrary,' Poirot corrected him. 'It is the *expected* that has happened – which in itself is sufficiently remarkable.'

'You expected murder?' Spence asked sceptically.

'No, no, no! But a wife remarries. Possibility that first husband is still alive? He *is* alive. He may turn up? He *does* turn up! There may be blackmail. There *is* blackmail! Possibility, therefore, that blackmailer may be silenced? *Ma foi*, he is silenced!'

'Well,' said Spence, eyeing Poirot rather doubtfully. 'I suppose these things run pretty close to type. It's a common sort of crime – blackmail resulting in murder.'

'Not interesting, you would say? Usually, no. But this case is interesting, because, you see,' said Poirot placidly, '*it is all wrong*.'

'All wrong? What do you mean by all wrong?'

'None of it is, how shall I put it, *the right shape*?'

Spence stared. 'Chief Inspector Japp,' he remarked, 'always said you have a tortuous mind. Give me an instance of what you call wrong?'

'Well, the dead man, for instance, *he* is all wrong.'

Spence shook his head.

'You do not feel that?' Poirot asked. 'Oh, well, perhaps I am fanciful. Then take this point. Underhay arrives at the Stag. He writes to David Hunter. Hunter receives that letter the next morning – at breakfast time?'

'Yes, that's so. He admits receiving a letter from Arden then.'

'That was the first intimation, was it not, of the arrival of Underhay in Warmsley Vale? What is the first thing he does – *bundles his sister off to London!*'

'That's quite understandable,' said Spence. 'He wants a clear hand to deal with things his own way. He may have been afraid the woman would have been weak. He's the leading spirit, remember. Mrs Cloade is entirely under his thumb.'

'Oh, yes, that shows itself plainly. So he sends her to London and calls on this Enoch Arden. We have a pretty clear account of their conversation from Beatrice Lippincott, and the thing that sticks out, a mile, as you say, is that David Hunter *was not sure whether the man he was talking to was Robert Underhay or not. He suspected* it, but he didn't *know.*'

'But there's nothing odd about that, M. Poirot. Rosaleen Hunter married Underhay in Cape Town and went with him straight to Nigeria. Hunter and Underhay never met. Therefore though, as you say, Hunter *suspected* that Arden was Underhay, he couldn't *know* it for a fact – because he had never met the man.'

Poirot looked at Superintendent Spence thoughtfully.

'So there is nothing there that strikes you as – peculiar?' he asked.

'I know what you're driving at. Why didn't Underhay say straight out that he *was* Underhay? Well, I think that's understandable, too. Respectable people who are doing something crooked like to preserve appearances. They like to put things in such a way that it keeps them in the clear – if you know what I mean. No – I don't think that that is so very remarkable. You've got to allow for human nature.'

'Yes,' said Poirot. 'Human nature. That, I think, is perhaps the real answer as to why I am interested in this case. I was looking round the Coroner's Court, looking at all the people, looking particularly at the Cloades – so many of them, all bound by a common interest, all so different in their characters, in their thoughts and feelings. All of them dependent for many years on the strong man, the power in the family, on Gordon Cloade! I do not mean, perhaps, directly dependent.

They had all their independent means of existence. But they had come, they must have come, consciously or unconsciously, to lean on him. And what happens – I will ask you this, Superintendent – *What happens to the ivy when the oak round which it clings is struck down?*'

'That's hardly a question in my line,' said Spence.

'You think not? I think it is. Character, *mon cher*, does not stand still. It can gather strength. It can also deteriorate. What a person really *is*, is only apparent when the test comes – that is, the moment when you stand or fall on your own feet.'

'I don't really know what you are getting at, M. Poirot.' Spence looked bewildered. 'Anyway, the Cloades are all right now. Or will be, once the legal formalities are through.'

That, Poirot reminded him, might take some time. 'There is still Mrs Gordon Cloade's evidence to shake. After all, a woman should know her own husband when she sees him?'

He put his head a little on one side and gazed inquiringly at the big Superintendent.

'Isn't it worth while to a woman *not* to recognize her husband if the income of a couple of million pounds depends on it?' asked the Superintendent cynically. 'Besides, if he wasn't Robert Underhay, why was he killed?'

'That,' murmured Poirot, 'is indeed the question.'

Chapter 6

Poirot left the police station frowning to himself. His steps grew slower as he walked. In the market square he paused, looking about him. There was Dr Cloade's house with its worn brass plate, and a little way along was the post office. On the other side was Jeremy Cloade's house. In front of Poirot, set back a little, was the Roman Catholic Church of the Assumption, a small modest affair, a shrinking violet compared to the aggressiveness of St Mary's which stood arrogantly in the middle of the square facing the Cornmarket, and proclaiming the dominance of the Protestant religion.

Moved by an impulse Poirot went through the gate and along the path to the door of the Roman Catholic building. He removed his hat, genuflected in front of the altar and knelt down behind one of the chairs. His prayers were interrupted by the sound of stifled heartbroken sobs.

He turned his head. Across the aisle a woman in a dark dress was kneeling, her head buried in her hands. Presently she got up and, still sobbing under her breath, went towards the door. Poirot, his eyes wide with interest, got up and followed her. He had recognized Rosaleen Cloade.

She stood in the porch, fighting for control, and there Poirot spoke to her, very gently:

'Madame, can I help you?'

She showed no signs of surprise, but answered with the simplicity of an unhappy child.

'No,' she said. 'No one can help me.'

'You are in very bad trouble. That is it, is it not?'

She said: 'They've taken David away . . . I'm all alone. They say he killed – But he didn't! He didn't!'

She looked at Poirot and said: 'You were there today? At the inquest. I saw you!'

'Yes. If I can help you, Madame, I shall be very glad to do so.'

'I'm frightened. David said I'd be safe as long as he was there to look after me. But now they've taken him away – I'm afraid. He said – they all wanted me dead. That's a dreadful thing to say. But perhaps it's true.'

'Let me help you, Madame.'

She shook her head.

'No,' she said. 'No one can help me. I can't go

to confession, even. I've got to bear the weight of my wickedness all alone. I'm cut off from the mercy of God.'

'Nobody,' said Hercule Poirot, 'is cut off from the mercy of God. You know that well, my child.'

Again she looked at him – a wild unhappy look.

'I'd have to confess my sins – to confess. If I could confess –'

'Can't you confess? You came to the church for that, did you not?'

'I came to get comfort – comfort. But what comfort is there for me? I'm a sinner.'

'We are all sinners.'

'But you'd have to repent – I'd have to say – to tell –' Her hands went up to her face. 'Oh, the lies I've told – the lies I've told.'

'You told a lie about your husband? About Robert Underhay? It *was* Robert Underhay who was killed here, wasn't it?'

She turned sharply on him. Her eyes were suspicious, wary. She cried out sharply:

'I tell you it was *not* my husband. It wasn't the least like him!'

'The dead man was not in the least like your husband?'

'No,' she said defiantly.

'Tell me,' said Poirot, 'what *was* your husband like?'

Her eyes stared at him. Then her face hardened into alarm. Her eyes grew dark with fear.

She cried out:

'I'll not talk to you any more!'

Going swiftly past him, she ran down the path and passed through the gate out into the market square.

Poirot did not try and follow her. Instead he nodded his head with a good deal of satisfaction.

'Ah,' he said. 'So that is *that*!'

He walked slowly out into the square.

After a momentary hesitation he followed the High Street until he came to the Stag, which was the last building before the open country.

In the doorway of the Stag he met Rowley Cloade and Lynn Marchmont.

Poirot looked at the girl with interest. A handsome girl, he thought, and intelligent also. Not the type he himself admired. He preferred something softer, more feminine. Lynn Marchmont, he thought, was essentially a modern type – though one might, with equal accuracy, call it an Elizabethan type. Women who thought for themselves, who were free in language, and who admired enterprise and audacity in men.

'We're very grateful to you, M. Poirot,' said Rowley. 'By Jove, it really was quite like a conjuring trick.'

Which was exactly what it had been, Poirot reflected! Asked a question to which you knew the answer, there was no difficulty whatsoever in performing a trick with the requisite frills. He quite appreciated that to the simple Rowley, the production of Major Porter out of the blue, so to speak, had been as breathtaking as any number of rabbits produced from the conjurer's hat.

'How you go about these things beats me,' said Rowley.

Poirot did not enlighten him. He was, after all, only human. The conjurer does not tell his audience how the trick was done.

'Anyway, Lynn and I are no end grateful,' Rowley went on.

Lynn Marchmont, Poirot thought, was not looking particularly grateful. There were lines of strain round her eyes, her fingers had a nervous trick of twining and intertwining themselves.

'It's going to make a lot of difference to our future married life,' said Rowley.

Lynn said sharply:

'How do you know? There are all sorts of formalities and things, I'm sure.'

'You are getting married, when?' asked Poirot politely.

'June.'

'And you have been engaged since when?'

'Nearly six years,' said Rowley. 'Lynn's just come out of the Wrens.'

'And is it forbidden to marry in the Wrens, yes?'

Lynn said briefly:

'I've been overseas.'

Poirot noticed Rowley's swift frown. He said shortly:

'Come on, Lynn. We must get going. I expect M. Poirot wants to get back to town.'

Poirot said smilingly:

'But I'm not going back to town.'

'What?'

Rowley stopped dead, giving a queer wooden effect.

'I am staying here, at the Stag, for a short while.'

'But – but why?'

'*C'est un beau paysage,*' Poirot said placidly.

Rowley said uncertainly:

'Yes, of course . . . But aren't you – well, I mean, busy?'

'I have made my economies,' said Poirot, smiling. 'I do not need to occupy myself unduly. No, I can enjoy my leisure and spend my time where the fancy takes me. And my fancy inclines to Warmsley Vale.'

He saw Lynn Marchmont raise her head and gaze at him intently. Rowley, he thought, was slightly annoyed.

'I suppose you play golf?' he said. 'There's a much better hotel at Warmsley Heath. This is a very one-horse sort of place.'

'My interests,' said Poirot, 'lie entirely in Warmsley Vale.'

Lynn said:

'Come along, Rowley.'

Half reluctantly, Rowley followed her. At the door, Lynn paused and then came swiftly back. She spoke to Poirot in a quiet low voice.

'They arrested David Hunter after the inquest. Do you – do you think they were right?'

'They had no alternative, Mademoiselle, after the verdict.'

'I mean – do you think he did it?'

'Do *you*?' said Poirot.

But Rowley was back at her side. Her face hardened to a poker smoothness. She said:

'Goodbye, M. Poirot. I – I hope we meet again.'

'Now, I wonder,' said Poirot to himself.

Presently, after arranging with Beatrice Lippincott about a room, he went out again. His steps led him to Dr Lionel Cloade's house.

'Oh!' said Aunt Kathie, who opened the door, taking a step or two backwards. 'M. Poirot!'

'At your service, Madame.' Poirot bowed. 'I came to pay my respects.'

'Well, that's very nice of you, I'm sure. Yes – well – I suppose you'd better come in. Sit down – I'll move Madame Blavatsky – and perhaps a cup of tea – only the cake is terribly stale. I meant to go to Peacocks for some, they do have Swiss roll sometimes on a

Wednesday – but an inquest puts one's household routine out, don't you think so?'

Poirot said that he thought that was entirely understandable.

He had fancied that Rowley Cloade was annoyed by the announcement of his stay in Warmsley Vale. Aunt Kathie's manner, without any doubt, was far from welcoming. She was looking at him with something not far from dismay. She said, leaning forward and speaking in a hoarse conspiratorial whisper:

'You won't tell my husband, will you, that I came and consulted you about – well, about we know what?'

'My lips are sealed.'

'I mean – of course I'd no idea at the time – that Robert Underhay, poor man, so *tragic* – was actually *in* Warmsley Vale. That seems to me still a most *extraordinary* coincidence!'

'It would have been simpler,' agreed Poirot, 'if the Ouija board had directed you straight to the Stag.'

Aunt Kathie cheered up a little at the mention of the Ouija board.

'The way things come about in the spirit world seem quite incalculable,' she said. 'But I do feel, M. Poirot, that there is a *purpose* in it all. Don't you feel that in life? That there is always a *purpose*?'

'Yes, indeed, Madame. Even that I should sit here, now, in your drawing-room, there is a purpose in that.'

'Oh, is there?' Mrs Cloade looked rather taken aback. 'Is there, really? Yes, I suppose so . . . You're on your way back to London, *of course*?'

'Not at present. I stay for a few days at the Stag.'

'At the *Stag*? Oh – at the Stag! But that's where – oh, M. Poirot, do you think you are *wise*?'

'I have been guided to the Stag,' said Poirot solemnly.

'*Guided?* What do you mean?'

'Guided by *you*.'

'Oh, but I never meant – I mean, I had no *idea*. It's all so dreadful, don't you think so?'

Poirot shook his head sadly, and said:

'I have been talking to Mr Rowley Cloade and Miss Marchmont. They are getting married, I hear, quite soon?'

Aunt Kathie was immediately diverted.

'Dear Lynn, she is such a sweet girl – and so very good at figures. Now, I have no head for figures – no head at all. Having Lynn home is an absolute blessing. If I get in a terrible muddle she always straightens things out for me. Dear girl, I do hope she will be happy. Rowley, of course, is a splendid person, but possibly – well, a little *dull*. I mean dull to a girl who has seen as much of the world as Lynn has. Rowley, you see, has been here on his farm all through the war – oh, quite rightly, of course – I mean the Government wanted him to – that side of it is *quite* all right – not white feathers or things like that as they did in the Boer War – but what I mean is, it's made him rather limited in his ideas.'

'Six years' engagement is a good test of affection.'

'Oh, it *is*! But I think these girls, when they come home, they get rather restless – and if there is someone else about – someone, perhaps, who has led an adventurous life –'

'Such as David Hunter?'

'There isn't anything between them,' Aunt Kathie said anxiously. 'Nothing *at all.* I'm *quite* sure of that! It would have been dreadful if there had been, wouldn't there, with his turning out a *murderer*? His own brother-in-law, too! Oh, no, M. Poirot, please don't run away with the idea that there's any kind of an understanding between Lynn and David. Really, they seemed to quarrel more than anything else every time they met. What I felt is that – oh, dear, I think that's my husband coming. You will remember, won't you, M. Poirot, *not* a word about our first meeting? My poor dear husband gets so annoyed if he thinks that – oh, Lionel dear, here is M. Poirot who so cleverly brought that Major Porter down to see the body.'

Dr Cloade looked tired and haggard. His eyes, pale blue, with pin-point pupils, wandered vaguely round the room.

'How do you do, M. Poirot; on your way back to town?'

'*Mon Dieu*, another who packs me back to London!' thought Poirot.

Aloud he said patiently:

'No, I remain at the Stag for a day or so.'

'The Stag?' Lionel Cloade frowned. 'Oh? Police want to keep you here for a bit?'

'No. It is my own choice.'

'Indeed?' The doctor suddenly flashed a quick intelligent look. 'So you're not satisfied?'

'Why should you think that, Dr Cloade?'

'Come, man, it's true, isn't it?' Twittering about tea, Mrs Cloade left the room. The doctor went on: 'You've a feeling, haven't you, that something's wrong?'

Poirot was startled.

'It is odd that you should say that. Do you, then, feel that yourself?'

Cloade hesitated.

'N-n-o. Hardly that . . . perhaps it's just a feeling of *unreality*. In books the blackmailer gets slugged. Does he in real life? Apparently the answer is Yes. But it seems unnatural.'

'Was there anything unsatisfactory about the medical aspect of the case? I ask unofficially, of course.'

Dr Cloade said thoughtfully:

'No, I don't think so.'

'Yes – there is something. I can see there is something.'

When he wished, Poirot's voice could assume an almost hypnotic quality. Dr Cloade frowned a little, then he said hesitatingly:

'I've no experience, of course, of police cases. And anyway medical evidence isn't the hard-and-fast, cast-iron business that laymen or novelists seem to think. We're fallible – medical science is fallible. What's diagnosis? A guess, based on a very little knowledge, and some indefinite clues which point in more than one direction. I'm pretty sound, perhaps, at diagnosing measles because, at my time of life, I've seen hundreds of cases of measles and I know an extraordinary wide variation of signs and symptoms. You hardly ever get what a text book tells you is a "typical case" of measles. But I've known some queer things in my time – I've seen a woman practically on the operating table ready for her appendix to be whipped out – and paratyphoid diagnosed just in time! I've seen a child with skin trouble pronounced as a case of serious vitamin deficiency by an earnest and conscientious young doctor – and the local vet, comes along and mentions to the mother that the cat the child is hugging has got ringworm and that the child has caught it!

'Doctors, like every one else, are victims of the preconceived idea. Here's a man, obviously murdered, lying with a bloodstained pair of fire-tongs beside him. It would be nonsense to say he was hit with anything else, and yet, speaking out of complete inexperience of people with their heads smashed in, I'd have suspected something rather different – something not so smooth and round – something – oh, I don't know, something with a more cutting edge – a brick, something like that.'

'You did not say so at the inquest?'

'No – because I don't really know. Jenkins, the police surgeon, was satisfied, and he's the fellow who counts. But there's the preconceived idea – weapon lying beside the body. *Could* the wound have been inflicted with that? Yes, it *could*. But if you were shown the wound and asked what made it – well, I don't know whether you'd say it, because it really doesn't make sense – I mean if you had two fellows, one hitting him with a brick and one with the tongs –' The doctor stopped, shook his head in a dissatisfied way. 'Doesn't make sense, does it?' he said to Poirot.

'Could he have fallen on some sharp object?'

Dr Cloade shook his head.

'He was lying face down in the middle of the floor – on a good thick old-fashioned Axminster carpet.'

He broke off as his wife entered the room.

'Here's Kathie with the cat-lap,' he remarked.

Aunt Kathie was balancing a tray covered with

crockery, half a loaf of bread and some depressing-looking jam in the bottom of a 2-lb. pot.

'I *think* the kettle was boiling,' she remarked doubtfully as she raised the lid of the teapot and peered inside.

Dr Cloade snorted again and muttered: 'Cat-lap,' with which explosive word he left the room.

'Poor Lionel, his nerves are in a terrible state since the war. He worked much too hard. So many doctors away. He gave himself no rest. Out morning, noon, and night. I wonder he didn't break down completely. Of course he looked forward to retiring as soon as peace came. That was all fixed up with Gordon. His hobby, you know, is botany with special reference to medicinal herbs in the Middle Ages. He's writing a book on it. He was looking forward to a quiet life and doing the necessary research. But then, when Gordon died like that – well, you know what things are, M. Poirot, nowadays. Taxation and everything. He can't afford to retire and it's made him very bitter. And really it *does* seem unfair. Gordon's dying like that, without a will – well, it really quite shook my faith. I mean, I really couldn't see the *purpose* in that. It seemed, I couldn't help feeling, a *mistake*.'

She sighed, then cheered up a little.

'But I get some lovely reassurances from the other side. "Courage and patience and a way will be found."

And really, when that nice Major Porter stood up today and said in such a firm manly way that the poor murdered man was Robert Underhay – well, I saw that a way *had* been found! It's wonderful, isn't it, M. Poirot, how things do turn out for the best?'

'Even murder,' said Hercule Poirot.

Chapter 7

Poirot entered the Stag in a thoughtful mood, and shivering slightly for there was a sharp east wind. The hall was deserted. He pushed open the door of the lounge on the right. It smelt of stale smoke and the fire was nearly out. Poirot tiptoed along to the door at the end of the hall labelled 'Residents Only'. Here there was a good fire, but in a large arm-chair, comfortably toasting her toes, was a monumental old lady who glared at Poirot with such ferocity that he beat an apologetic retreat.

He stood for a moment in the hall looking from the glass-enclosed empty office to the door labelled in firm old-fashioned style COFFEE-ROOM. By experience of country hotels Poirot knew well that the only time coffee was served there was somewhat grudgingly for breakfast and that even then a good deal of watery hot milk was its principal component. Small cups of a treacly and muddy liquid called Black Coffee were served not in the COFFEE-ROOM but in the Lounge. The Windsor Soup, Vienna Steak and Potatoes, and Steamed Pudding which comprised Dinner would be obtainable in the COFFEE-ROOM at seven sharp. Until then a deep peace brooded over the residential area of the Stag.

Poirot went thoughtfully up the staircase. Instead of turning to the left where his own room, No. 11, was situated, he turned to the right and stopped before the door of No. 5. He looked round him. Silence and emptiness. He opened the door and went in.

The police had done with the room. It had clearly been freshly cleaned and scrubbed. There was no carpet on the floor. Presumably the 'old-fashioned Axminster' had gone to the cleaners. The blankets were folded on the bed in a neat pile.

Closing the door behind him, Poirot wandered round the room. It was clean and strangely barren of human interest. Poirot took in its furnishings – a writing-table, a chest of drawers of good old-fashioned mahogany, an upright wardrobe of the same (the one presumably that masked the door into No. 4), a large brass double bed, a basin with hot and cold water – tribute to modernity and the servant shortage – a large but rather uncomfortable arm-chair, two small chairs, an old-fashioned Victorian grate with a poker and a pierced shovel belonging to the same set as the fire-tongs; a heavy marble mantelpiece and a solid marble fire-curb with squared corners.

It was at these last that Poirot bent and looked. Moistening his finger he rubbed it along the right-hand corner and then inspected the result. His finger was slightly black. He repeated the performance with another finger on the left-hand corner of the curb. This time his finger was quite clean.

'Yes,' said Poirot thoughtfully to himself. 'Yes.'

He looked at the fitted washbasin. Then he strolled to the window. It looked out over some leads – the roof of a garage, he fancied, and then to a small back alley. An easy way to come and go unseen from room No. 5. But then it was equally easy to walk upstairs to No. 5 unseen. He had just done it himself.

Quietly, Poirot withdrew, shutting the door noiselessly behind him. He went along to his own room. It was decidedly chilly. He went downstairs again, hesitated, and then, driven by the chill of the evening, boldly entered the Residents Only, drew up a second arm-chair to the fire and sat down.

The monumental old lady was even more formidable seen close at hand. She had iron-grey hair, a flourishing moustache and, when presently she spoke, a deep and awe-inspiring voice.

'This Lounge,' she said, 'is Reserved for Persons staying in the hotel.'

'I am staying in the hotel,' replied Hercule Poirot.

The old lady meditated for a moment or two before returning to the attack. Then she said accusingly:

'You're a foreigner.'

'Yes,' replied Hercule Poirot.

'In my opinion,' said the old lady, 'you should all Go Back.'

'Go back where?' inquired Poirot.

'To where you came from,' said the old lady firmly. She added as a kind of rider, *sotto voce:* 'Foreigners!' and snorted.

'That,' said Poirot mildly, 'would be difficult.'

'Nonsense,' said the old lady. 'That's what we fought the war for, isn't it? So that people could go back to their proper places and stay there.'

Poirot did not enter into a controversy. He had already learnt that every single individual had a different version of the theme, 'What did we fight the war for?'

A somewhat hostile silence reigned.

'I don't know what things are coming to,' said the old lady. 'I really don't. Every year I come and stay in this place. My husband died here sixteen years ago. He's buried here. I come every year for a month.'

'A pious pilgrimage,' said Poirot politely.

'And every year things get worse and worse. No service! Food uneatable! Vienna steaks indeed! A steak's either rump or fillet steak – not chopped-up horse!'

Poirot shook his head sadly.

'One good thing – they've shut down the aerodrome,' said the old lady. 'Disgraceful it was, all those young airmen coming in here with those dreadful girls. Girls, indeed! I don't know what their mothers are thinking of nowadays. Letting them gad about as they do. I blame the Government. Sending the mothers to work in factories. Only let 'em off if they've got young children. Young children, stuff and nonsense! Any one can look after a baby! A baby doesn't go running round after soldiers. Girls from fourteen to eighteen, they're the ones that need looking after! Need their mothers. It takes a mother to know just what a girl is up to. Soldiers! Airmen! That's all they think about. Americans! Niggers! Polish riff-raff!'

Indignation at this point made the old lady cough. When she had recovered, she went on, working herself into a pleasurable frenzy and using Poirot as a target for her spleen.

'Why do they have barbed wire round their camps? To keep the soldiers from getting at the girls? No, to keep the girls from getting at the soldiers! Man-mad, that's what they are! Look at the way they dress.

Agatha Christie

Trousers! Some poor fools wear shorts – they wouldn't if they knew what they looked like from behind!'

'I agree with you, Madame, indeed I agree with you.'

'What do they wear on their heads? Proper hats? No, a twisted-up bit of stuff, and faces covered with paint and powder. Filthy stuff, all over their mouths. Not only red nails – but red *toe*-nails!'

The old lady paused explosively and looked at Poirot expectantly. He sighed and shook his head.

'Even in church,' said the old lady. 'No hats. Sometimes not even those silly scarves. Just that ugly crimped, permanently waved hair. Hair? Nobody knows what hair is nowadays. *I* could *sit* on my hair when I was young.'

Poirot stole a glance at the iron-grey bands. It seemed impossible that this fierce old woman could ever have been young!

'Put her head in here the other night, one of them did,' the old lady went on. 'Tied up in an orange scarf and painted and powdered. I looked at her. I just LOOKED at her! She soon went away!

'*She* wasn't a Resident,' went on the old lady. 'No one of *her* type staying here, I'm glad to say! So what was she doing coming out of a man's bedroom? Disgusting, I call it. I spoke about it to that Lippincott girl – but she's just as bad as any of them – go a mile for anything that wears trousers.'

Some faint interest stirred in Poirot's mind.

'Coming out of a man's bedroom?' he queried.

The old lady fell upon the topic with zest.

'That's what I said. Saw her with my own eyes. No. 5.'

'What day was that, Madame?'

'The day before there was all that fuss about a man being murdered. Disgraceful that such a thing could happen *here*! This used to be a very decent old-fashioned type of place. But *now* –'

'And what hour of the day was this?'

'Day? It wasn't day at all. Evening. Late evening, too. Perfectly disgraceful. Past ten o'clock. I go up to bed at a quarter-past ten. Out she comes from No. 5 as bold as brass, stares at me, then dodges back inside again, laughing and talking with the man there.'

'You heard *him* speak?'

'Aren't I telling you so? She dodges back inside and he calls out, "Oh, go on, get out of here. I'm fed up." That's nice way for a man to talk to a girl. But they ask for it! Hussies!'

Poirot said, 'You did not report this to the police?'

She fixed him with a basilisk stare and totteringly rose out of her chair. Standing over him and glaring down on him, she said:

'I have never had *anything* to do with the police. The police indeed! *I*, in a *police* court?'

Quiverering with rage and with one last malevolent glance at Poirot she left the room.

Poirot sat for a few minutes thoughtfully caressing his moustache, then he went in search of Beatrice Lippincott.

'Oh, yes, M. Poirot, you mean old Mrs Leadbetter? Canon Leadbetter's widow. She comes here every year, but of course between ourselves she is rather a trial. She's really frightfully rude to people sometimes, and she doesn't seem to understand that things are different nowadays. She's nearly eighty, of course.'

'But she is clear in her mind? She knows what she is saying?'

'Oh, yes. She's quite a sharp old lady – rather too much so sometimes.'

'Do you know who a young woman was who visited the murdered man on Tuesday night?'

Beatrice looked astonished.

'I don't remember a young woman coming to visit him at any time. What was she like?'

'She was wearing an orange scarf round her head and I should fancy a good deal of make-up. She was in No. 5 talking to Arden at a quarter past ten on Tuesday night.'

'Really, M. Poirot, I've no idea whatsoever.'

Thoughtfully Poirot went along in search of Superintendent Spence.

Spence listened to Poirot's story in silence. Then he leaned back in his chair and nodded his head slowly.

'Funny, isn't it?' he said. 'How often you come back to the same old formula. *Cherchez la femme.*'

The Superintendent's French accent was not as good as Sergeant Graves', but he was proud of it. He got up and went across the room. He came back holding something in his hand. It was a lipstick in a gilt cardboard case.

'We had this indication all along that there *might* be a woman mixed up in it,' he said.

Poirot took the lipstick and smeared a little delicately on the back of his hand. 'Good quality,' he said. 'A dark cherry red – worn by a brunette probably.'

'Yes. It was found on the floor of No. 5. It had rolled under the chest of drawers and of course just possibly it might have been there some time. No fingerprints on it. Nowadays, of course, there isn't the range of lipsticks there used to be – just a few standard makes.'

'And you have no doubt made your inquiries?'

Spence smiled.

'Yes,' he said; 'as you put it, we have made our inquiries. Rosaleen Cloade uses this type of lipstick. So does Lynn Marchmont. Frances Cloade uses a more subdued colour. Mrs Lionel Cloade doesn't use lipstick at all. Mrs Marchmont uses a pale mauve shade. Beatrice Lippincott doesn't appear to use anything as expensive as this – nor does the chambermaid, Gladys.'

He paused.

'You have been thorough,' said Poirot.

'Not thorough enough. It looks now as though an outsider is mixed up in it – some woman, perhaps, that Underhay knew in Warmsley Vale.'

'And who was with him at a quarter past ten on Tuesday evening?'

'Yes,' said Spence. He added with a sigh, 'This lets David Hunter out.'

'It *does?*'

'Yes. His lordship has consented to make a statement at last. After his solicitor had been along to make him see reason. Here's his account of his own movements.'

Poirot read a neat typed memorandum.

Left London 4.16 train for Warmsley Heath. Arrived there 5.30. Walked to Furrowbank by footpath.

'His reason for coming down,' the Superintendent broke in, 'was, according to him, to get certain things he'd left behind, letters and papers, a cheque-book, and to see if some shirts had come back from the laundry – which, of course, they hadn't! My word, laundry's a problem nowadays. Four ruddy weeks since they've been to our place – not a clean towel left in our house, and the wife washes all my things herself now.'

After this very human interpolation the Superintendent returned to the itinerary of David's movements.

'Left Furrowbank at 7.25 and states he went for a walk as he had missed the 7.20 train and there would be no train until the 9.20.'

'In what direction did he go for a walk?' asked Poirot.

The Superintendent consulted his notes.

'Says by Downe Copse, Bats Hill and Long Ridge.'

'In fact, a complete circular tour round the White House!'

'My word, you pick up local geography quickly, M. Poirot!'

Poirot smiled and shook his head.

'No, I did not know the places you named. I was making a guess.'

'Oh, you were, were you?' The Superintendent cocked his head on one side.

'Then, according to him, when he was up on Long Ridge, he realized he was cutting it rather fine and fairly hared it for Warmsley Heath station, going across country. He caught the train by the skin of his teeth, arrived at Victoria 10.45, walked to Shepherd's Court, arriving there at eleven o'clock, which latter statement is confirmed by Mrs Gordon Cloade.'

'And what confirmation have you of the rest of it?'

'Remarkably little – but there is some. Rowley Cloade and others saw him arrive at Warmsley Heath. The maids at Furrowbank were out (he had his own key of course) so they didn't see him, but they found a cigarette stump in the library which I gather intrigued them and also found a good deal of confusion in the linen cupboard. Then one of the gardeners was there working late – shutting up greenhouses or something and he caught sight of him. Miss Marchmont met him up by Mardon Wood – when he was running for the train.'

'Did any one see him catch the train?'

'No – but he telephoned from London to Miss Marchmont as soon as he got back – at 11.05.'

'That is checked?'

'Yes, we'd already put through an inquiry about calls from that number. There was a Toll call out at 11.04 to Warmsley Vale 34. That's the Marchmonts' number.'

'Very, very interesting,' murmured Poirot.

But Spence was going on painstakingly and methodically.

'Rowley Cloade left Arden at five minutes to nine. He's quite definite it wasn't earlier. About 9.10 Lynn Marchmont sees Hunter up at Mardon Wood. Granted he's run all the way from the Stag, would he have had time to meet Arden, quarrel with him, kill him and get to Mardon Wood? We're going into it and I don't think it can be done. However, now we're starting again. Far from Arden being killed at nine o'clock, he was alive at *ten minutes past ten* – that is unless your old lady is dreaming. He was either killed by the woman who dropped the lipstick, the woman in the orange scarf – or by somebody who came in *after* that woman left. And whoever did it, deliberately put the hands of the watch back to nine-ten.'

'Which if David Hunter had not happened to meet Lynn Marchmont in a very unlikely place would have been remarkably awkward for him?' said Poirot.

'Yes, it would. The 9.20 is the last train up from Warmsley Heath. It was growing dark. There are always golfers going back by it. Nobody would have noticed Hunter – indeed the station people don't know him by sight. And he didn't take a taxi at the other end. So we'd only have his sister's word for it that he arrived back at Shepherd's Court when he said he did.'

Poirot was silent and Spence asked:

'What are you thinking about, M. Poirot?'

Poirot said, 'A long walk round the White House. A meeting in Mardon Woods. A telephone call later . . . And Lynn Marchmont is engaged to Rowley

Agatha Christie

Cloade . . . I should like very much to know what was said over that telephone call.'

'It's the human interest that's getting you?'

'Yes,' said Poirot. 'It is always the human interest.'

Chapter 8

It was getting late, but there was still one more call that Poirot wanted to make. He went along to Jeremy Cloade's house.

There he was shown into Jeremy Cloade's study by a small, intelligent-looking maid.

Left alone, Poirot gazed interestedly round him. All very legal and dry as dust, he thought, even in his home. There was a large portrait of Gordon Cloade on the desk. Another faded one of Lord Edward Trenton on a horse, and Poirot was examining the latter when Jeremy Cloade came in.

'Ah, pardon.' Poirot put the photo-frame down in some confusion.

'My wife's father,' said Jeremy, a faint self-congratulatory note in his voice. 'And one of his best horses, Chestnut Trenton. Ran second in the Derby in 1924. Are you interested in racing?'

'Alas, no.'

'Runs away with a lot of money,' said Jeremy dryly. 'Lord Edward came a crash over it – had to go and live abroad. Yes, an expensive sport.'

But there was still the note of pride in his voice.

He himself, Poirot judged, would as soon throw his money in the street as invest it in horseflesh, but he had a secret admiration and respect for those who did.

Cloade went on:

'What can I do for you, M. Poirot? As a family, I feel we owe you a debt of gratitude – for finding Major Porter to give evidence of identification.'

'The family seems very jubilant about it,' said Poirot.

'Ah,' said Jeremy dryly. 'Rather premature to rejoice. Lot of water's got to pass under the bridge yet. After all, Underhay's death was accepted in Africa. Takes years to upset a thing of this kind – and Rosaleen's evidence was very positive – very positive indeed. She made a good impression you know.'

It seemed almost as though Jeremy Cloade was unwilling to bank upon any improvement in his prospects.

'I wouldn't like to give a ruling one way or the other,' he said. 'Couldn't say how a case would go.'

Then, pushing aside some papers with a fretful, almost weary gesture, he said:

'But you wanted to see me?'

'I was going to ask you, Mr Cloade, if you are really quite certain your brother did not leave a will? A will made subsequent to his marriage, I mean?'

Jeremy looked surprised.

'I don't think there's ever been any idea of such a thing. He certainly didn't make one before leaving New York.'

'He might have made one during the two days he was in London.'

'Gone to a lawyer there?'

'Or written one out himself.'

'And got it witnessed? Witnessed by whom?'

'There were three servants in the house,' Poirot reminded him. 'Three servants who died the same night he did.'

'H'm – yes – but if by any chance he *did* do what you suggest, well, the will was destroyed too.'

'That is just the point. Lately a great many documents believed to have perished completely have actually been deciphered by a new process. Incinerated inside home safes, for instance, but not so destroyed that they cannot be read.'

'Well, really, M. Poirot, that is a most remarkable idea of yours . . . Most remarkable. But I don't think – no, I really don't believe there is anything in it . . . So far as I know there was no safe in the house in Sheffield Terrace. Gordon kept all valuable papers, etc., at his

273

office – and there was certainly no will there.'

'But one might make inquiries?' Poirot was persistent. 'From the A.R.P. officials, for instance? You would authorize me to do that?'

'Oh, certainly – certainly. Very kind of you to offer to undertake such a thing. But I haven't any belief whatever, I'm afraid, in your success. Still – well, it is an offchance, I suppose. You – you'll be going back to London at once, then?'

Poirot's eyes narrowed. Jeremy's tone had been unmistakably eager. Going back to London . . . Did they *all* want him out of the way?

Before he could answer, the door opened and Frances Cloade came in.

Poirot was struck by two things. First, by the fact that she looked shockingly ill. Secondly, by her very strong resemblance to the photograph of her father.

'M. Hercule Poirot has come to see us, my dear,' said Jeremy rather unnecessarily.

She shook hands with him and Jeremy Cloade immediately outlined to her Poirot's suggestion about a will.

Frances looked doubtful.

'It seems a very outside chance.'

'M. Poirot is going up to London and will very kindly make inquiries.'

'Major Porter, I understand, was an Air Raid Warden in that district,' said Poirot.

A curious expression passed over Mrs Cloade's face. She said:

'Who is Major Porter?'

Poirot shrugged his shoulders.

'A retired Army officer, living on his pension.'

'He really *was* in Africa?'

Poirot looked at her curiously.

'Certainly, Madame. Why not?'

She said almost absently, 'I don't know. He puzzled me.'

'Yes, Mrs Cloade,' said Poirot. 'I can understand that.'

She looked sharply at him. An expression almost of fear came into her eyes.

Turning to her husband she said:

'Jeremy, I feel very much distressed about Rosaleen. She is all alone at Furrowbank and she must be frightfully upset over David's arrest. Would you object if I asked her to come here and stay?'

'Do you really think that is advisable, my dear?' Jeremy sounded doubtful.

'Oh – advisable? I don't know! But one is human. She is such a helpless creature.'

'I rather doubt if she will accept.'

'I can at any rate make the offer.'

The lawyer said quietly: 'Do so if it will make you feel happier.'

'Happier!'

The word came out with a strange bitterness. Then she gave a quick doubtful glance at Poirot.

Poirot murmured formally:

'I will take my leave now.'

She followed him out into the hall.

'You are going up to London?'

'I shall go up tomorrow, but for twenty-four hours at most. And then I return to the Stag – where you will find me, Madame, if you want me.'

She demanded sharply:

'Why should I want you?'

Poirot did not reply to the question, merely said:

'I shall be at the Stag.'

Later that night out of the darkness Frances Cloade spoke to her husband.

'I don't believe that man is going to London for the reason he said. I don't believe all that about Gordon's having made a will. Do you believe it, Jeremy?'

A hopeless, rather tired voice answered her:

'No, Frances. No – he's going for some other reason.'

'What reason?'

'I've no idea.'

Frances said, 'What are we going to do, Jeremy? What are we going to *do*?'

Presently he answered:

'I think, Frances, there's only one thing to be done –'

Chapter 9

Armed with the necessary credentials from Jeremy Cloade, Poirot had got the answers to his questions. They were very definite. The house was a total wreck. The site had been cleared only quite recently in preparation for rebuilding. There had been no survivors except for David Hunter and Mrs Cloade. There had been three servants in the house: Frederick Game, Elizabeth Game and Eileen Corrigan. All three had been killed instantly. Gordon Cloade had been brought out alive, but had died on the way to hospital without recovering consciousness. Poirot took the names and addresses of the three servants' next-of-kin. 'It is possible,' he said, 'that they may have spoken to their friends something in the way of gossip or comment that might give me a pointer to some information I badly need.'

The official to whom he was speaking looked sceptical.

Agatha Christie

The Games had come from Dorset, Eileen Corrigan from County Cork.

Poirot next bent his steps towards Major Porter's rooms. He remembered Porter's statement that he himself was a Warden and he wondered whether he had happened to be on duty on that particular night and whether he had seen anything of the incident in Sheffield Terrace.

He had, besides, other reasons for wanting a word with Major Porter.

As he turned the corner of Edgeway Street he was startled to see a policeman in uniform standing outside the particular house for which he was making. There was a ring of small boys and other people standing staring at the house. Poirot's heart sank as he interpreted the signs.

The constable intercepted Poirot's advance.

'Can't go in here, sir,' he said.

'What has happened?'

'You don't live in the house, do you, sir?' Poirot shook his head. 'Who was it you were wishing to see?'

'I wished to see a Major Porter.'

'You a friend of his, sir?'

'No, I should not describe myself as a friend. What has happened?'

'Gentleman has shot himself, I understand. Ah, here's the Inspector.'

The door had opened and two figures came out. One was the local Inspector, the other Poirot recognized as Sergeant Graves from Warmsley Vale. The latter recognized him and promptly made himself known to the Inspector.

'Better come inside,' said the latter.

The three men re-entered the house.

'They telephoned through to Warmsley Vale,' Graves explained. 'And Superintendent Spence sent me up.'

'Suicide?'

The Inspector answered:

'Yes. Seems a clear case. Don't know whether having to give evidence at the inquest preyed upon his mind. People are funny that way sometimes, but I gather he's been depressed lately. Financial difficulties and one thing and another. Shot himself with his own revolver.'

Poirot asked: 'Is it permitted that I go up?'

'If you like, M. Poirot. Take M. Poirot up, Sergeant.'

'Yes, sir.'

Graves led the way up to the first-floor room. It was much as Poirot remembered it: the dim colours of the old rugs, the books. Major Porter was in the big arm-chair. His attitude was almost natural, just the head slumped forward. His right arm hung down at his side – below it, on the rug, lay the revolver.

Agatha Christie

There was still a very faint smell of acrid gunpowder in the air.

'About a couple of hours ago, they think,' said Graves. 'Nobody heard the shot. The woman of the house was out shopping.'

Poirot was frowning, looking down on the quiet figure with the small scorched wound in the right temple.

'Any idea why he should do it, M. Poirot?' asked Graves.

He was respectful to Poirot because he had seen the Superintendent being respectful – though his private opinion was that Poirot was one of these frightful old dug-outs.

Poirot replied absently:

'Yes – yes, there was a very good reason. That is not the difficulty.'

His glance shifted to a small table at Major Porter's left hand. There was a big solid glass ashtray on it, with a pipe and a box of matches. Nothing there. His eye roamed round the room. Then he crossed to an open roll-top desk.

It was very tidy. Papers neatly pigeon-holed. A small leather blotter in the centre, a pen-tray with a pen and two pencils, a box of paper-clips and a book of stamps. All very neat and orderly. An ordinary life and an orderly death – of course – that was it – that was what was missing!

He said to Graves:

'Didn't he leave any note – any letter for the coroner?'

Graves shook his head.

'No, he didn't – sort of thing one would have expected an ex-Army man to do.'

'Yes, that is very curious.'

Punctilious in life, Major Porter had not been punctilious in death. It was all wrong, Poirot thought, that Porter had left no note.

'Bit of a blow for the Cloades this,' said Graves. 'It will set them back. They'll have to hunt about for someone else who knew Underhay intimately.'

He fidgeted slightly. 'Anything more you want to see, M. Poirot?'

Poirot shook his head and followed Graves from the room.

On the stairs they met the landlady. She was clearly enjoying her own state of agitation and started a voluble discourse at once. Graves adroitly detached himself and left Poirot to receive the full spate.

'Can't seem to catch my breath properly. 'Eart, that's what it is. Angina Pectoria, my mother died of – fell down dead as she was crossing the Caledonian Market. Nearly dropped down myself when I found him – oh, it did give me a turn! Never suspected anything of the kind, though 'e 'ad been low in 'is spirits for a long time. Worried over money, I think, and didn't eat enough to keep himself alive. Not that he'd ever accept a bite from us. And then yesterday he 'ad to go down to a place in Oastshire – Warmsley Vale – to give evidence in an inquest. Preyed on his mind, that did. He come back looking *awful*. Tramped about all last night. Up and down – up and down. A murdered gentleman it was and a friend of his, by all accounts. Poor dear, it did upset him. Up and down – up and down. And when I was out doing my bit of shopping – and 'aving to queue ever so long for the fish, I went up to see if he'd like a nice cuppa tea – and there he was, poor gentleman, the revolver dropped out of his hand, leaning back in his chair. Gave me an awful turn it did. 'Ad to 'ave the police in and everything. What's the world coming to, that's what I say?'

Poirot said slowly:

'The world is becoming a difficult place to live in – except for the strong.'

Chapter 10

It was past eight o'clock when Poirot got back to the Stag. He found a note from Frances Cloade asking him to come and see her. He went out at once.

She was waiting for him in the drawing-room. He had not seen that room before. The open windows gave on a walled garden with pear trees in bloom. There were bowls of tulips on the tables. The old furniture shone with beeswax and elbow-grease and the brass of the fender and coal-scuttle were brightly gleaming.

It was, Poirot thought, a very beautiful room.

'You said I should want you, M. Poirot. You were quite right. There is something that must be told – and I think you are the best person to tell it to.'

'It is always easier, Madame, to tell a thing to someone who already has a very good idea of what it is.'

'You think you know what I am going to say?'

Poirot nodded.

'Since when –'

She left the question unfinished, but he replied promptly:

'Since the moment when I saw the photograph of your father. The features of your family are very strongly marked. One could not doubt that you and he were of the same family. The resemblance was equally strong in the man who came here calling himself Enoch Arden.'

She sighed – a deep unhappy sigh.

'Yes – yes, you're right – although poor Charles had a beard. He was my second cousin, M. Poirot, somewhat the black sheep of the family. I never knew him very well but we played together as children – and now I've brought him to his death – an ugly sordid death –'

She was silent for a moment or two. Poirot said gently:

'You will tell me –'

She roused herself.

'Yes, the story has got to be told. We were desperate for money – that's where it begins. My husband – my husband was in serious trouble – the worst kind of trouble. Disgrace, perhaps imprisonment lay ahead of him – still lies ahead of him for that matter. Now understand this, M. Poirot, the plan I made and carried out was *my* plan; my husband had nothing to do with it. It wasn't his sort of plan in any case – it would have been far too risky. But I've never minded taking risks. And I've always been, I suppose, rather unscrupulous. First of all, let me say, I applied to Rosaleen Cloade for a loan. I don't know whether, left to herself, she would have given it to me or not. But her brother stepped in. He was in an ugly mood and he was, or so I thought, unnecessarily insulting. When I thought of this scheme I had no scruples at all about putting it into operation.

'To explain matters, I must tell you that my husband had repeated to me last year a rather interesting piece of information which he had heard at his club. You were there, I believe, so I needn't repeat it in detail. But it opened up the possibility that Rosaleen's first husband might not be dead – and of course in that case she would have no right at all to any of Gordon's money. It was, of course, only a vague possibility, but it was there at the back of our minds, a sort of outside chance that might possibly come true. And it flashed into my mind that something could be done by *using* that possibility. Charles, my cousin, was in this country, down on his luck. He's been in prison, I'm afraid, and he wasn't a scrupulous person, but he did well in the war. I put the proposition before him. It was, of course, blackmail, neither more nor less. But we thought that we had a good chance of getting away with it. At worst,

I thought, David Hunter would refuse to play. I didn't think that he would go to the police about it – people like him aren't fond of the police.'

Her voice hardened.

'Our scheme went well. David fell for it better than we hoped. Charles, of course, could not definitely pose as "Robert Underhay". Rosaleen could give that away in a moment. But fortunately she went up to London and that left Charles a chance of at least suggesting that he might be Robert Underhay. Well, as I say, David appeared to be falling for the scheme. He was to bring the money on Tuesday evening at nine o'clock. Instead –'

Her voice faltered.

'We should have known that David was – a dangerous person. Charles is dead – murdered – and but for me he would be alive. I sent him to his death.'

After a little she went on in a dry voice:

'You can imagine what I have felt like ever since.'

'Nevertheless,' said Poirot, 'you were quick enough to see a further development of the scheme? It was you who induced Major Porter to identify your cousin as "Robert Underhay"?'

But at once she broke out vehemently:

'No, I swear to you, no. Not that! No one was more astonished . . . Astonished? We were dumbfounded! when this Major Porter came down and gave evidence that Charles – *Charles!* – was Robert Underhay. I couldn't understand it – I *still* can't understand it!'

'But *someone* went to Major Porter. Someone persuaded him or bribed him – to identify the dead man as Underhay?'

Frances said decisively:

'It was not I. And it was not Jeremy. Neither of us would do such a thing. Oh, I dare say that sounds absurd to you! You think that because I was ready to blackmail, that I would stoop just as easily to fraud. But in my mind the two things are worlds apart. You must understand that I felt – indeed I still feel – that we have a *right* to a portion of Gordon's money. What I had failed to get by fair means I was prepared to get by foul. But deliberately to swindle Rosaleen out of everything, by manufacturing evidence that she was not Gordon's wife at all – oh, no, indeed, M. Poirot, I would not do a thing like that. Please, *please*, believe me.'

'I will at least admit,' said Poirot slowly, 'that every one has their own particular sins. Yes, I will believe that.'

Then he looked at her sharply.

'Do you know, Mrs Cloade, that Major Porter shot himself this afternoon?'

She shrank back, her eyes wide and horrified.

'Oh, no, M. Poirot – *no!*'

'Yes, Madame. Major Porter, you see, was *au fond*

287

an honest man. Financially he was in very low water, and when temptation came he, like many other men, failed to resist it. It may have seemed to him, he can have made himself feel, that his lie was almost morally justified. He was already deeply prejudiced in his mind against the woman his friend Underhay had married. He considered that she had treated his friend disgracefully. And now this heartless little gold-digger had married a millionaire and had got away with her second husband's fortune to the detriment of his own flesh and blood. It must have seemed tempting to him to put a spoke in her wheel – no more than she deserved. And merely by identifying a dead man he himself would be made secure for the future. When the Cloades got their rights, he would get his cut . . . Yes – I can see the temptation . . . But like many men of his type he lacked imagination. He was unhappy, very unhappy, at the inquest. One could see that. In the near future he would have to repeat his lie upon oath. Not only that; a man was now arrested, charged with murder – and the identity of the dead man supplied a very potent motive for that charge.

'He went back home and faced things squarely. He took the way out that seemed best to him.'

'He shot himself?'

'Yes.'

Frances murmured: 'He didn't say who – who –'

Slowly Poirot shook his head.

'He had his code. There was no reference whatever as to who had instigated him to commit perjury.'

He watched her closely. Was there an instant flash of relief, of relaxed tension? Yes, but that might be natural enough in any case . . .

She got up and walked to the window. She said:

'So we are back where we were.'

Poirot wondered what was passing in her mind.

Chapter 11

Superintendent Spence, the following morning, used almost Frances' words:

'So we're back where we started,' he said with a sigh. 'We've got to find who this fellow Enoch Arden really was.'

'I can tell you that, Superintendent,' said Poirot. 'His name was Charles Trenton.'

'Charles Trenton!' The Superintendent whistled. 'H'm! One of the Trentons – I suppose *she* put him up to it – Mrs Jeremy, I mean . . . However, we shan't be able to prove her connection with it. *Charles* Trenton? I seem to remember –'

Poirot nodded.

'Yes. He has a record.'

'Thought so. Swindling hotels if I remember rightly. Used to arrive at the Ritz, go out and buy a Rolls, subject to a morning's trial, go round in the Rolls to all the most expensive shops and buy stuff – and I can tell you a man who's got his Rolls outside waiting to take his purchases back to the Ritz doesn't get his cheques queried! Besides, he had the manner and the breeding. He'd stay a week or so and then, just when suspicions began to arise, he'd quietly disappear, selling the various items cheap to the pals he'd picked up. Charles Trenton. H'm –' He looked at Poirot. 'You find out things, don't you?'

'How does your case progress against David Hunter?'

'We shall have to let him go. There *was* a woman there that night with Arden. It doesn't only depend on that old tartar's word. Jimmy Pierce was going home, got pushed out of the Load of Hay – he gets quarrelsome after a glass or two. He saw a woman come out of the Stag and go into the telephone box outside the post office – that was just after ten. Said it wasn't any one he knew, thought it was someone staying at the Stag. "A tart from London," is what *he* called her.'

'He was not very near her?'

'No, right across the street. Who the devil *was* she, M. Poirot?'

'Did he say how she was dressed?'

'Tweed coat, he said, orange scarf round her head. Trousers and a lot of make-up. Fits with the old lady's description.'

'Yes, it fits.' Poirot was frowning.

Spence asked:

'Well, who was she, where did she come from, where did she go? You know our train service. The 9.20's the last train up to London – and the 10.03 the other way. Did that woman hang about all night and go up on the 6.18 in the morning? Had she got a car? Did she hitch-hike? We've sent out all over the place – but no results.'

'What about the 6.18?'

'It's always crowded – mostly men, though. I think they'd have noticed a woman – that type of woman, that's to say. I suppose she might have come and left by car, but a car's noticed in Warmsley Vale nowadays. We're off the main road, you see.'

'No cars noticed out that night?'

'Only Dr Cloade's. He was out on a case – over Middlingham way. You'd think someone would have noticed a strange woman in a car.'

'It need not have been a stranger,' Poirot said slowly. 'A man slightly drunk and a hundred yards away might not recognize a local person whom he did not know very well. Someone, perhaps, dressed in a different way from their usual way.'

Spence looked at him questioningly.

'Would this young Pierce recognize, for instance, Lynn Marchmont? She has been away for some years.'

'Lynn Marchmont was at the White House with her mother at that time,' said Spence.

'Are you sure?'

'Mrs Lionel Cloade – that's the scatty one, the doctor's wife – says she telephoned to her there at ten minutes past ten. Rosaleen Cloade was in London. Mrs Jeremy – well, I've never seen her in slacks and she doesn't use much make-up. Anyway, she isn't young.'

'Oh, *mon cher*. Poirot leaned forward. 'On a dim night, with feeble street lights, can one tell youth or age under a mask of make-up?'

'Look here, Poirot,' said Spence, 'what are you getting at?'

Poirot leaned back and half-closed his eyes.

'Slacks, a tweed coat, an orange scarf enveloping the head, a great deal of make-up, a dropped lipstick. It is suggestive.'

'Think you're the oracle at Delphi,' growled the Superintendent. 'Not that I know what the oracle at Delphi was – sort of thing young Graves gives himself airs about knowing – doesn't help his police work any. Any more cryptic pronnouncements, M. Poirot?'

'I told you,' said Poirot, 'that this case was the wrong shape. As an instance I said to you that the dead man was all wrong. So he was, as Underhay. Underhay was clearly an eccentric, chivalrous individual, old-fashioned and reactionary. The man at the Stag was a blackmailer; he was neither chivalrous, old-fashioned, nor reactionary, nor was he particularly eccentric – therefore he was not Underhay. He could not be Underhay, for *people do not change*. The interesting thing was that Porter said he was Underhay.'

'Leading you to Mrs Jeremy?'

'The likeness led me to Mrs Jeremy. A very distinctive cast of countenance, the Trenton profile. To permit myself a little play on words, as Charles Trenton the dead man *is* the right shape. But there are still questions to which we require answers. Why did David Hunter permit himself to be blackmailed so readily? Is he the kind of man who lets himself be blackmailed? One would say very decidedly, no. So he too acts out of character. Then there is Rosaleen Cloade. Her whole behaviour is incomprehensible – but there is one thing I should like to know very much. Why is she afraid? Why does she think that something will happen to her now that her brother is no longer there to protect her? Someone – or something has given her that fear. And it is not that she fears losing her fortune – no, it is more than that. It is for her *life* that she is afraid . . .'

'Good Lord, M. Poirot, you don't think –'

'Let us remember, Spence, that as you said just now, we are back where we started. That is to say, the Cloade family are back where they started. Robert Underhay died in Africa. And Rosaleen Cloade's life stands between them and the enjoyment of Gordon Cloade's money –'

'Do you honestly think that one of them would do that?'

'I think this. Rosaleen Cloade is twenty-six, and though mentally somewhat unstable, physically she is strong and healthy. She may live to be seventy, she may live longer still. Forty-four years, let us say. Don't you think, Superintendent, that forty-four years may be too long for someone to contemplate?'

Chapter 12

When Poirot left the police station he was almost at once accosted by Aunt Kathie. She had several shopping-bags with her and came up to him with a breathless eagerness of manner.

'So terrible about poor Major Porter,' she said. 'I can't help feeling that his outlook on life must have been very materialistic. Army life, you know. Very narrowing, and though he had spent a good deal of his life in India, I'm afraid he never took advantage of the spiritual opportunities. It would be all *pukka* and *chota hazri* and *tiffin* and pig-sticking – the narrow Army round. To think that he might have sat as a *chela* at the feet of some *guru*! Ah, the missed opportunities, M. Poirot, how sad they are!'

Aunt Kathie shook her head and relaxed her grip on one of the shopping-bags. A depressed-looking bit of cod slipped out and slithered into the gutter. Poirot retrieved it and in her agitation Aunt Kathie let a second bag slip, whereupon a tin of golden syrup began a gay career rolling along the High Street.

'Thank you so much, M. Poirot.' Aunt Kathie grasped the cod. He ran after the golden syrup. 'Oh, thank you – so clumsy of me – but really I have been so upset. That unfortunate man – yes, it *is* sticky, but really I don't like to use your clean handkerchief. Well, it's very kind of you – as I was saying, in life we are in death – and in death we are in life – I should never be surprised to see the astral body of any of my dear friends who have passed over. One might, you know, just pass them in the street. Why – only the other night I –'

'You permit?' Poirot rammed the cod firmly into the depths of the bag. 'You were saying – yes?'

'Astral bodies,' said Aunt Kathie. 'I asked, you know, for twopence – because I only had halfpennies. But I thought at the time the face was familiar – only I couldn't *place* it. I still can't – but I think now it must be someone who has Passed Over – perhaps some time ago – so that my remembrance was very uncertain. It is wonderful the way people are *sent* to one in one's need – even if it's only a matter of pennies for telephones. Oh, dear, quite a queue at Peacocks – they must have got either trifle or Swiss roll! I hope I'm not too late!'

Mrs Lionel Cloade plunged across the road and

joined herself to the tail end of a queue of grim-faced women outside the confectioner's shop.

Poirot went on down the High Street. He did not turn in at the Stag. Instead he bent his steps towards the White House.

He wanted very much to have a talk with Lynn Marchmont, and he suspected that Lynn Marchmont would not be averse to having a talk with him.

It was a lovely morning – one of those summer mornings in spring that have a freshness denied to a real summer's day.

Poirot turned off from the main road. He saw the footpath leading up past Long Willows to the hillside above Furrowbank. Charles Trenton had come that way from the station on the Friday before his death. On his way down the hill, he had met Rosaleen Cloade coming up. He had not recognized her, which was not surprising since he was not Robert Underhay, and she, naturally, had not recognized him for the same reason. But she had sworn when shown the body that she had not even glanced at the face of the man she had passed on the footpath? If so, what had she been thinking about? Had she, by any chance, been thinking of Rowley Cloade?

Poirot turned along the small side road which led to the White House. The garden of the White House was looking very lovely. It held many flowering shrubs, lilacs and laburnums, and in the centre of the lawn was a big old gnarled apple tree. Under it, stretched out in a deck-chair, was Lynn Marchmont.

She jumped nervously when Poirot, in a formal voice, wished her 'Good morning!'

'You did startle me, M. Poirot. I didn't hear you coming across the grass. So you are still here – in Warmsley Vale?'

'I am still here – yes.'

'Why?'

Poirot shrugged his shoulders.

'It is a pleasant out-of-the-world spot where one can relax. I relax.'

'I'm glad you are here,' said Lynn.

'You do not say to me like the rest of your family, 'When do you go back to London, M. Poirot?' and wait anxiously for the answer.'

'Do they want you to go back to London?'

'It would seem so.'

'I don't.'

'No – I realize that. Why, Mademoiselle?'

'Because it means that you're not satisfied. Not satisfied, I mean, that David Hunter did it.'

'And you want him so much – to be innocent?'

He saw a faint flush creep up under her bronzed skin.

'Naturally, I don't want to see a man hanged for what he didn't do.'

'Naturally – oh, yes!'

'And the police are simply prejudiced against him because he's got their backs up. That's the worst of David – he likes antagonizing people.'

'The police are not so prejudiced as you think, Miss Marchmont. The prejudice against him was in the minds of the jury. They refused to follow the coroner's guidance. They gave a verdict against him and so the police had to arrest him. But I may tell you that they are very far from satisfied with the case against him.'

She said eagerly:

'Then they may let him go?'

Poirot shrugged his shoulders.

'Who do they think did do it, M. Poirot?'

Poirot said slowly: 'There was a woman at the Stag that night.'

Lynn cried:

'I don't understand *anything*. When we thought the man was Robert Underhay it all seemed so simple. Why did Major Porter say it was Underhay if it wasn't? Why did he shoot himself? We're back now where we started.'

'You are the third person to use that phrase!'

'Am I?' She looked startled. 'What are *you* doing, M. Poirot?'

'Talking to people. That is what I do. Just talk to people.'

'But you don't ask them things about the murder?'

Poirot shook his head.

'No, I just – what shall we say – pick up gossip.'

'Does that help?'

'Sometimes it does. You would be surprised how much I know of the everyday life of Warmsley Vale in the last few weeks. I know who walked where, and who they met, and sometimes what they said. For instance, I know that the man Arden took the footpath to the village passing by Furrowbank and asking the way of Mr Rowley Cloade, and that he had a pack on his back and no luggage. I know that Rosaleen Cloade had spent over an hour at the farm with Rowley Cloade and that she had been happy there, unlike her usual self.'

'Yes,' said Lynn, 'Rowley told me that. He said she was like someone having an afternoon out.'

'Aha, he said that?' Poirot paused and went on, 'Yes, I know a lot of the comings and goings. And I have heard a lot about people's difficulties – yours and your mother's, for example.'

'There's no secret about any of us,' said Lynn. 'We've all tried to cadge money off Rosaleen. That's what you mean, isn't it?'

'I did not say so.'

'Well, it's true! And I suppose you've heard things about me and Rowley and David.'

'But you are going to marry Rowley Cloade?'

'Am I? I wish I knew . . . That's what I was trying to decide that day – when David burst out of the wood. It was like a great question mark in my brain. Shall I? Shall I? Even the train in the valley seemed to be asking the same thing. The smoke made a fine question mark in the sky.'

Poirot's face took on a curious expression. Lynn misunderstood it. She cried out:

'Oh, don't you see, M. Poirot, it's all so difficult. It isn't a question of David at all. It's *me*! I've changed. I've been away for three – four years. Now I've come back I'm not the same person who went away. That's the tragedy everywhere. People coming home changed, having to readjust themselves. You can't go away and lead a different kind of life and *not* change!'

'You are wrong,' said Poirot. 'The tragedy of life is that *people do not change.*'

She stared at him, shaking her head. He insisted:

'But yes. It is so. Why did you go away in the first place?'

'Why? I went into the Wrens. I went on service.'

'Yes, yes, but why did you join the Wrens in the first place? You were engaged to be married. You were in love with Rowley Cloade. You could have worked, could you not, as a land girl, here in Warmsley Vale?'

'I could have, I suppose, but I wanted –'

'*You wanted to get away.* You wanted to go abroad, to

see life. You wanted, perhaps, *to get away from Rowley Cloade* . . . And now you are restless, you still want – to get away! Oh, no, Mademoiselle, people do not change!'

'When I was out East, I longed for home,' Lynn cried defensively.

'Yes, yes, where you are not, there you will want to be! That will always be so, perhaps, with you. You make a picture to yourself, you see, a picture of Lynn Marchmont coming home . . . But the picture does not come true, because the Lynn Marchmont whom you imagine is not the real Lynn Marchmont. She is the Lynn Marchmont you would like to be.'

Lynn asked bitterly:

'So, according to you, I shall never be satisfied anywhere?'

'I do not say that. But I do say that, when you went away, you were dissatisfied with your engagement, and that now you have come back, you are still dissatisfied with your engagement.'

Lynn broke off a leaf and chewed it meditatively.

'You're rather a devil at knowing things, aren't you, M. Poirot?'

'It is my *métier*,' said Poirot modestly. 'There is a further truth, I think, that you have not yet recognized.'

Lynn said sharply:

'You mean David, don't you? You think I am in love with David?'

'That is for you to say,' murmured Poirot discreetly.

'And I – don't know! There's something in David that I'm afraid of – but there's something that draws me, too . . .' She was silent a moment and then went on: 'I was talking yesterday to his Brigadier. He came down here when he heard David was arrested to see what he could do. He's been telling me about David, how incredibly daring he was. He said David was one of the bravest people he'd ever had under him. And yet, you know, M. Poirot, in spite of all he said and his praise, I had the feeling that he wasn't sure, not absolutely sure that David hadn't done this!'

'And are you not sure, either?'

Lynn gave a crooked, rather pathetic smile.

'No – you see, I've never trusted David. *Can* you love someone you don't trust?'

'Unfortunately, yes.'

'I've always been unfair to David – because I didn't trust him. I've believed quite a lot of the beastly local gossip – hints that David wasn't David Hunter at all – but just a boy friend of Rosaleen's. I was ashamed when I met the Brigadier and he talked to me about having known David as a boy in Ireland.'

'*C'est épatant*,' murmured Poirot, 'how people can get hold of the wrong end of a stick!'

'What do you mean?'

'Just what I say. Tell me, did Mrs Cloade – the

doctor's wife, I mean – did she ring up on the night of the murder?'

'Aunt Kathie? Yes, she did.'

'What about?'

'Some incredible muddle she had got into over some accounts.'

'Did she speak from her own house?'

'Why no, actually her telephone was out of order. She had to go out to a call-box.'

'At ten minutes past ten?'

'Thereabouts. Our clocks never keep particularly good time.'

'Thereabouts,' said Poirot thoughtfully. He went on delicately:

'That was not the only telephone call you had that evening?'

'No.' Lynn spoke shortly.

'David Hunter rang you up from London?'

'Yes.' She flared out suddenly, 'I suppose you want to know what *he* said?'

'Oh, indeed I should not presume –'

'You're welcome to know! He said he was going away – clearing out of my life. He said he was no good to me and that he never would run straight – not even for my sake.'

'And since that was probably true you did not like it,' said Poirot.

'I hope he will go away – that is, if he gets acquitted all right . . . I hope they'll both go away to America or somewhere. Then, perhaps, we shall be able to stop thinking about them – we'll learn to stand on our own feet. We'll stop feeling ill will.'

'Ill will?'

'Yes. I felt it first one night at Aunt Kathie's. She gave a sort of party. Perhaps it was because I was just back from abroad and rather on edge – but I seemed to feel it in the air eddying all round us. Ill will to her – to Rosaleen. Don't you see, *we were wishing her dead* – all of us! Wishing her dead . . . And that's awful, to wish that someone who's never done you any harm – may die –'

'Her death, of course, is the only thing that can do you any practical good.' Poirot spoke in a brisk and practical tone.

'You mean do us good financially? Her mere being here has done us harm in all the ways that matter! Envying a person, resenting them, cadging off them – it isn't *good* for one. Now, there she is, at Furrowbank, all alone. She looks like a ghost – she looks scared to death – she looks – oh! she looks as though she's going off her head. And she won't let us help! Not one of us. We've all tried. Mums asked her to come and stay with us, Aunt Frances asked her there. Even Aunt Kathie went along and offered to be with her at Furrowbank. But she won't have anything to do with us now and I don't blame her. She wouldn't even see Brigadier Conroy. I think she's ill, ill with worry and fright and misery. And we're doing nothing about it because she won't let us.'

'Have *you* tried? You, yourself?'

'Yes,' said Lynn. 'I went up there yesterday. I said, was there anything I could do? She looked at me –' Suddenly she broke off and shivered. 'I think she hates me. She said, "*You, least of all.*" David told her, I think, to stop on at Furrowbank, and she always does what David tells her. Rowley took her up eggs and butter from Long Willows. I think he's the only one of us she likes. She thanked him and said he'd always been kind. Rowley, of course, *is* kind.'

'There are people,' said Poirot, 'for whom one has great sympathy – great pity, people who have too heavy a burden to bear. For Rosaleen Cloade I have great pity. If I could, I would help her. Even now, if she would listen –'

With sudden resolution he got to his feet.

'Come, Mademoiselle,' he said, 'let us go up to Furrowbank.'

'You want me to come with you?'

'If you are prepared to be generous and understanding –'

Lynn cried:

'I am – indeed I am –'

Chapter 13

It took them only about five minutes to reach Furrow-bank. The drive wound up an incline through carefully massed banks of rhododendrons. No trouble or expense had been spared by Gordon Cloade to make Furrowbank a show-place.

The parlourmaid who answered the front door looked surprised to see them and a little doubtful as to whether they could see Mrs Cloade. Madam, she said, wasn't up yet. However, she ushered them into the drawing-room and went upstairs with Poirot's message.

Poirot looked round him. He was contrasting this room with Frances Cloade's drawing-room – the latter such an intimate room, so characteristic of its mistress. The drawing-room at Furrowbank was strictly impersonal – speaking only of wealth tempered by good taste. Gordon Cloade had seen to the latter – everything in the room was of good quality and of

Agatha Christie

artistic merit, but there was no sign of any selectiveness, no clue to the personal tastes of the room's mistress. Rosaleen, it seemed, had not stamped upon the place any individuality of her own.

She had lived in Furrowbank as a foreign visitor might live at the Ritz or at the Savoy.

'I wonder,' thought Poirot, 'if the other –'

Lynn broke the chain of his thought by asking him of what he was thinking, and why he looked so grim.

'The wages of sin, Mademoiselle, are said to be death. But sometimes the wages of sin seem to be luxury. Is that any more endurable, I wonder? To be cut off from one's own home life. To catch, perhaps, a single glimpse of it when the way back to it is barred –'

He broke off. The parlourmaid, her superior manner laid aside, a mere frightened middle-aged woman, came running into the room, stammering and choking with words she could hardly get out.

'Oh Miss Marchmont! Oh, sir, the mistress – upstairs – she's very bad – she doesn't speak and I can't rouse her and her hand's so cold.'

Sharply, Poirot turned and ran out of the room. Lynn and the maid came behind him. He raced up to the first floor. The parlourmaid indicated the open door facing the head of the stairs.

It was a large beautiful bedroom, the sun pouring

in through the open windows on to pale beautiful rugs.

In the big carved bedstead Rosaleen was lying – apparently asleep. Her long dark lashes lay on her cheeks, her head turned naturally into the pillow. There was a crumpled-up handkerchief in one hand. She looked like a sad child who had cried itself to sleep.

Poirot picked up her hand and felt for the pulse. The hand was ice-cold and told him what he already guessed.

He said quietly to Lynn:

'She has been dead some time. She died in her sleep.'

'Oh, sir – oh – what shall we do?' The parlourmaid burst out crying.

'Who was her doctor?'

'Uncle Lionel,' said Lynn.

Poirot said to the parlourmaid: 'Go and telephone to Dr Cloade.' She went out of the room, still sobbing. Poirot moved here and there about the room. A small white cardboard box beside the bed bore a label, 'One powder to be taken at bedtime.' Using his handkerchief, he pushed the box open. There were three powders left. He moved across to the mantelpiece, then to the writing-table. The chair in front of it was pushed aside, the blotter was open. A sheet of paper was there, with words scrawled in an unformed childish hand.

Agatha Christie

'I don't know what to do . . . I can't go on . . . I've been so wicked. I must tell someone and get peace . . . I didn't mean to be so wicked to begin with. I didn't know all that was going to come of it. I must write down –'

The words sprawled off in a dash. The pen lay where it had been flung down. Poirot stood looking down at those written words. Lynn still stood by the bed looking down at the dead girl.

Then the door was pushed violently open and David Hunter strode breathlessly into the room.

'David,' Lynn started forward. 'Have they released you? I'm so glad –'

He brushed her words aside, as he brushed her aside, thrusting her almost roughly out of the way as he bent over the still white figure.

'Rosa! Rosaleen . . .' He touched her hand, then he swung round on Lynn, his face blazing with anger. His words came high and deliberate!

'So you've killed her, have you? You've got rid of her at last! You got rid of me, sent me to gaol on a trumped-up charge, and then, amongst you all, you put her out of the way! All of you? Or just one of you? I don't care which it is! You killed her! You wanted the damned money – now you've got it! Her death gives it to you! You'll all be out of Queer Street now. You'll all be rich – a lot of dirty murdering thieves, that's what you are! You weren't able to touch her so long as I was by. I knew how to protect my sister – she was never one to be able to protect herself. But when she was alone here, you saw your chance and you took it.' He paused, swayed slightly, and said in a low quivering voice, '*Murderers.*'

Lynn cried out:

'No, David. No, you're wrong. None of us would kill her. We wouldn't do such a thing.'

'One of you killed her, Lynn Marchmont. And you know that as well as I do!'

'I swear we didn't, David. I swear we did nothing of the kind.'

The wildness of his gaze softened a little.

'Maybe it wasn't *you*, Lynn –'

'It wasn't, David, I swear it wasn't –'

Hercule Poirot moved forward a step and coughed. David swung round on him.

'I think,' said Poirot, 'that your assumptions are a little over-dramatic. Why jump to the conclusion that your sister was murdered?'

'You say she wasn't murdered? Do you call *this*' – he indicated the figure on the bed – 'a natural death? Rosaleen suffered from nerves, yes, but she had no organic weakness. Her heart was sound enough.'

'Last night,' said Poirot, 'before she went to bed, she sat writing here –'

David strode past him, bent over the sheet of paper.

313

'Do not touch it,' Poirot warned him.

David drew back his hand, and read the words as he stood motionless.

He turned his head sharply and looked searchingly at Poirot.

'Are you suggesting suicide? Why should Rosaleen commit suicide?'

The voice that answered the question was not Poirot's. Superintendent Spence's quiet Oastshire voice spoke from the open doorway:

'Supposing that last Tuesday night Mrs Cloade wasn't in London, but in Warmsley Vale? Suppose she went to see the man who had been blackmailing her? Suppose that in a nervous frenzy she killed him?'

David swung round on him. His eyes were hard and angry.

'My sister was in London on Tuesday night. She was there in the flat when I got in at eleven o'clock.'

'Yes,' said Spence, 'that's your story, Mr Hunter. And I dare say you'll stick to it. But I'm not obliged to believe that story. And in any case, isn't it a little late' – he gestured towards the bed – 'the case will never come to court now.'

Chapter 14

'He won't admit it,' said Spence. 'But I think he knows she did it.' Sitting in his room at the police station he looked across the table at Poirot. 'Funny how it was *his* alibi we were so careful about checking. We never gave much thought to *hers*. And yet there's no corroboration at all for her being in the flat in London that night. We've only got his word that she was there. We knew all along that only two people had a motive for doing away with Arden – David Hunter and Rosaleen Cloade. I went bald-headed for *him* and passed *her* by. Fact is, she seemed such a gentle thing – even a bit half-witted – but I dare say that partly explains it. Very likely David Hunter hustled her up to London for just that reason. He may have realized that she'd lose her head, and he may have known that she's the kind who gets dangerous when they panic. Another funny thing: I've often seen her going about in an orange linen frock – it was a favourite colour of hers. Orange scarves – a striped orange frock, an orange beret. And yet, even when old Mrs Leadbetter described a young woman with her head tied up in an orange scarf I still didn't tumble to it that it must have been Mrs Gordon herself. I still think the girl wasn't quite all there – wasn't wholly responsible. The way you describe her as haunting the R.C. church here sounds as though she was half off her head with remorse and a sense of guilt.'

'She had a sense of guilt, yes,' said Poirot.

Spence said thoughtfully, 'She must have attacked Arden in a kind of frenzy. I don't suppose he had the least idea of what was coming to him. He wouldn't be on his guard with a slip of a girl like that.' He ruminated for a moment or two in silence, then he remarked, 'There's still one thing I'm not quite clear about. *Who got at Porter?* You say it wasn't Mrs Jeremy? Bet you it was all the same!'

'No,' said Poirot. 'It was not Mrs Jeremy. She assured me of that and I believe her. I have been stupid over that. I should have known who it was. Major Porter himself told me.'

'He told you?'

'Oh, indirectly, of course. He did not know that he had done so.'

'Well, who was it?'

Poirot put his head a little on one side.

'Is it permitted, first, that I ask you two questions?'

The Superintendent looked surprised.

'Ask anything you like.'

'Those sleeping-powders in a box by Rosaleen Cloade's bed. What were they?'

The Superintendent looked more surprised.

'Those? Oh, they were quite harmless. Bromide. Soothing to the nerves. She took one every night. We analysed them, of course. They were quite all right.'

'Who prescribed them?'

'Dr Cloade.'

'When did he prescribe them?'

'Oh, some time ago.'

'What poison was it that killed her?'

'Well, we haven't actually got the report yet, but I don't think there's much doubt about it. Morphia and a pretty hefty dose of it.'

'Was any morphia found in her possession?'

Spence looked curiously at the other man.

'No. What are you getting at, M. Poirot?'

'I will pass now to my second question,' said Poirot evasively. 'David Hunter put through a call from London to Lynn Marchmont at 11.5 on that Tuesday night. You say you checked up on calls. That was the only outgoing call from the flat in Shepherd's Court. Were there any incoming calls?'

'One. At 10.15. Also from Warmsley Vale. It was put through from a public call box.'

'I see.' Poirot was silent for a moment or two.

'What's the big idea, M. Poirot?'

'That call was answered? The operator, I mean, got a response from the London number.'

'I see what you mean,' said Spence slowly. 'There must have been *someone* in the flat. It couldn't be David Hunter – he was in the train on his way back. It looks, then, as if it must have been Rosaleen Cloade. And if so, Rosaleen Cloade couldn't have been at the Stag a few minutes earlier. What you're getting at, M. Poirot, is that the woman in the orange scarf, *wasn't* Rosaleen Cloade. And if so, it wasn't Rosaleen Cloade who killed Arden. But then why did she commit suicide?'

'The answer to that,' said Poirot, 'is very simple. She did not commit suicide. Rosaleen Cloade was killed!'

'*What?*'

'She was deliberately and cold-bloodedly murdered.'

'But who killed Arden? We've eliminated David –'

'It was not David.'

'And now you eliminate Rosaleen? But dash it all, those two were the only ones with a shadow of a motive!'

'Yes,' said Poirot. '*Motive*. It was that which has led

us astray. If A has a motive for killing C and B has a motive for killing D – well, it does not seem to make sense, does it, that A should kill D and B should kill C?'

Spence groaned. 'Go easy, M. Poirot, go easy. I don't even begin to understand what you are talking about with your A's and B's and C's.'

'It is complicated,' said Poirot, 'it is very complicated. Because, you see, you have here *two different kinds of crime* – and consequently you have, you *must* have, two different murderers. Enter First Murderer, and enter Second Murderer.'

'Don't quote Shakespeare,' groaned Spence. 'This isn't Elizabethan Drama.'

'But yes, it is very Shakespearian – there are here all the emotions – the human emotions – in which Shakespeare would have revelled – the jealousies, the hates – the swift passionate actions. And here, too, is successful opportunism. "*There is a tide in the affairs of men which taken at its flood leads on to fortune . . .*" Someone acted on that, Superintendent. To seize opportunity and turn it to one's own ends – that has been triumphantly accomplished – under your nose so to speak!'

Spence rubbed his nose irritably.

'Talk sense, M. Poirot,' he pleaded. 'If it's possible, just say what you mean.'

'I will be very clear – clear as crystal. We have here, have we not, three deaths? You agree to that, do you not? Three people are dead.'

Spence looked at him curiously.

'I should certainly say so . . . You're not going to make me believe that one of the three is still alive?'

'No, no,' said Poirot. 'They are dead. But *how* did they die? How, that is to say, would you classify their deaths?'

'Well, as to that, M. Poirot, you know my views. One murder, and two suicides. But according to you the last suicide isn't a suicide. It's another murder.'

'According to me,' said Poirot, '*there has been one suicide*, one accident and one murder.'

'Accident? Do you mean Mrs Cloade poisoned herself by accident? Or do you mean Major Porter's shooting himself was an accident?'

'No,' said Poirot. 'The accident was the death of Charles Trenton – otherwise Enoch Arden.'

'Accident!' The Superintendent exploded. '*Accident?* You say that a particularly brutal murder, where a man's head is stove in by repeated blows, is an *accident!*'

Quite unmoved by the Superintendent's vigour, Poirot replied calmly:

'When I say an accident, I mean that there was no intent to kill.'

'No intent to kill – when a man's head is battered in! Do you mean that he was attacked by a lunatic?'

'I think that that is very near the truth – though not quite in the sense you mean it.'

'Mrs Gordon was the only batty woman in this case. I've seen her looking very queer sometimes. Of course, Mrs Lionel Cloade is a bit bats in the belfry – but she'd never be violent. Mrs Jeremy has got her head screwed on the right way if any one has. By the way, you say that it was *not* Mrs Jeremy who bribed Porter?'

'No. I know who it was. As I say, it was Porter himself who gave it away. One simple little remark – ah, I could kick myself, as you say, all round the town, for not noticing it at the time.'

'And then your anonymous A B C lunatic murdered Rosaleen Cloade?' Spence's voice was more and more sceptical.

Poirot shook his head vigorously.

'By no means. This is where the First Murderer exits and Second Murderer enters. Quite a different type of crime this, no heat, and no passion. Cold deliberate murder and I intend Superintendent Spence, to see that her murderer is hanged for that murder.'

He got up as he spoke and moved towards the door.

'Hi!' cried Spence. 'You've got to give me a few names. You can't leave it like this.'

'In a very little while – yes, I will tell you. But there is something for which I wait – to be exact, a letter from across the sea.'

'Don't talk like a ruddy fortune-teller! Hi – Poirot.'

But Poirot had slipped away.

He went straight across the square and rang the bell of Dr Cloade's house. Mrs Cloade came to the door and gave her usual gasp at seeing Poirot. He wasted no time.

'Madame, I must speak to you.'

'Oh, of course – do come in – I'm afraid I haven't had much time to dust, but –'

'I want to ask you something. How long has your husband been a morphia addict?'

Aunt Kathie immediately burst into tears.

'Oh dear, oh dear – I did so hope nobody would ever know – it began in the war. He was so dreadfully overtired and had such dreadful neuralgia. And since then he's been trying to lessen the dose – he has indeed. But that's what makes him so dreadfully irritable sometimes –'

'That is one of the reasons why he has needed money, is it not?'

'I suppose so. Oh, dear, M. Poirot. He has promised to go for a cure –'

'Calm yourself, Madame, and answer me one more little question. On the night when you telephoned to

Lynn Marchmont, you went out to the call-box outside the post office, did you not? Did you meet anybody in the square that night?'

'Oh, no, M. Poirot, not a *soul*.'

'But I understood you had to borrow twopence because you had only halfpennies.'

'Oh, yes. I had to ask a woman who came out of the box. She gave me two pennies for one halfpenny –'

'What did she look like, this woman?'

'Well, rather actressy, if you know what I mean. An orange scarf round her head. The funny thing was that I'm almost sure I'd met her somewhere. Her face seemed very familiar. She must, I think, have been someone who had passed over. And yet, you know, I couldn't remember where and how I had known her.'

'Thank you, Mrs Cloade,' said Hercule Poirot.

Chapter 15

Lynn came out of the house and glanced up at the sky.

The sun was getting low, there was no red in the sky but a rather unnatural glow of light. A still evening with a breathless feel about it. There would be, she thought, a storm later.

Well, the time had come now. She couldn't put things off any longer. She must go to Long Willows and tell Rowley. She owed him that at least – to tell him herself. Not to choose the easy way of the written word.

Her mind was made up – quite made up – she told herself and yet she felt a curious reluctance. She looked round her and thought: 'It's goodbye to all this – to my own world – my own way of life.'

For she had no illusions. Life with David was a gamble – an adventure that was as likely to turn out badly as to turn out well. He himself had warned her . . .

The night of the murder, over the telephone.

And now, a few hours ago, he had said:

'I meant to go out of your life. I was a fool – to think I could leave you behind me. We'll go to London and be married by special licence – oh, yes, I'm not going to give you the chance of shilly-shallying about. You've got roots here, roots that hold you down. I've got to pull you up by the roots.' He had added: 'We'll break it to Rowley when you're actually Mrs David Hunter. Poor devil, it's the best way to break it to him.'

But to that she did not agree, though she had not said so at the time. No, she must tell Rowley herself.

It was to Rowley she was going now!

The storm was just starting as Lynn tapped at the door of Long Willows. Rowley opened it and looked astonished to see her.

'Hallo, Lynn, why didn't you ring up and say you were coming? I might have been out.'

'I want to talk to you, Rowley.'

He stood aside to let her pass and followed her into the big kitchen. The remains of his supper were on the table.

'I'm planning to get an Aga or an Esse put in here,' he said. 'Easier for you. And a new sink – steel –'

She interrupted. 'Don't make plans, Rowley.'

'You mean because that poor kid isn't buried yet? I suppose it does seem rather heartless. But she never struck me as a particularly happy person. Sickly, I suppose. Never got over that damned air raid. Anyway, there it is. She's dead and in her grave and oh the difference to me – or rather to us –'

Lynn caught her breath.

'No, Rowley. There isn't any "us". That's what I came to tell you.'

He stared at her. She said quietly, hating herself, but steadfast in her purpose:

'*I'm going to marry David Hunter, Rowley.*'

She did not know quite what she expected – protests, perhaps an angry outburst – but she certainly did not expect Rowley to take it as he did.

He stared at her for a minute or two, then he went across and poked at the stove, turning at last in an almost absentminded manner.

'Well,' he said, 'let's get it clear. You're going to marry David Hunter. Why?'

'Because I love him.'

'You love me.'

'No. I did love you – when I went away. But it's been four years and I've – I've changed. We've both changed.'

'You're wrong . . .' he said quietly. 'I haven't changed.'

327

'Well, perhaps you haven't changed so much.'

'I haven't changed at all. I haven't had much chance to change. I've just gone plodding on here. *I* haven't dropped from parachutes or swarmed up cliffs by night or wound an arm round a man in the darkness and stabbed him –'

'Rowley –'

'*I* haven't been to the war. *I* haven't fought. *I* don't know what war is! I've led a nice safe life here, down on the farm. Lucky Rowley! But as a husband, you'd be ashamed of me!'

'No, Rowley – oh, no! It isn't that at all.'

'But I tell you it is!' He came nearer to her. The blood was welling up in his neck, the veins of his forehead were starting out. That look in his eyes – she had seen it once as she passed a bull in a field. Tossing its head, stamping its foot, slowly lowering its head with the great horns. Goaded to a dull fury, a blind rage . . .

'*Be quiet*, Lynn, *you*'ll listen to *me* for a change. I've missed what I ought to have had. I've missed my chance of fighting for my country. I've seen my best friend go and be killed. I've seen my girl – *my* girl – dress up in uniform and go overseas. I've been Just the Man She Left Behind Her. *My* life's *been hell* – don't you understand, Lynn? It's been hell. And then you came back – and since then it's been worse hell.

Ever since that night at Aunt Kathie's when I saw you looking at David Hunter across the table. But *he's not going to have you, do you hear?* If you're not for me, then no one shall have you. What do you think I am?'

'Rowley –'

She had risen, was retreating a step at a time. She was terrified. This man was not a man any longer, he was a brute beast.

'*I've killed two people,*' said Rowley Cloade. '*Do you think I shall stick at killing a third?*'

'Rowley –'

He was upon her now, his hands round her throat . . .

'I can't bear any more, Lynn –'

The hands tightened round her neck, the room whirled, blackness, spinning blackness, suffocation – everything going dark . . .

And then, suddenly a cough. A prim, slightly artificial cough.

Rowley paused, his hands relaxed, fell to his sides. Lynn, released, sank in a crumpled heap on the floor.

Just inside the door, Hercule Poirot stood apologetically coughing.

'I hope,' he said, 'that I do not intrude? I knocked. Yes, indeed, I knocked, but no one answered . . . I suppose you were busy?'

For a moment the air was tense, electric. Rowley

stared. It looked for a moment as though he might fling himself on Hercule Poirot, but finally he turned away. He said in a flat empty voice:

'You turned up – just in the nick of time.'

Chapter 16

Into an atmosphere quivering with danger Hercule Poirot brought his own atmosphere of deliberate anticlimax.

'The kettle, it is boiling?' he inquired.

Rowley said heavily – stupidly – 'Yes, it's boiling.'

'Then you will, perhaps, make some coffee? Or some tea if it is easier.'

Like an automaton Rowley obeyed.

Hercule Poirot took a large clean handkerchief from his pocket; he soaked it in cold water, wrung it out and came to Lynn.

'There, Mademoiselle, if you fasten that round your throat – so. Yes, I have the safety-pin. There, that will at once ease the pain.'

Croaking hoarsely, Lynn thanked him. The kitchen of Long Willows, Poirot fussing about – it all had for her the quality of a nightmare. She felt horribly ill, and her throat was paining her badly. She staggered to her feet and Poirot guided her gently to a chair and put her into it.

'There,' he said, and over his shoulder:

'The coffee?' he demanded.

'It's ready,' said Rowley.

He brought it. Poirot poured out a cup and took it to Lynn.

'Look here,' said Rowley, 'I don't think you understand. I tried to strangle Lynn.'

'Tscha, tscha,' said Poirot in a vexed voice. He seemed to be deploring a lapse of bad taste on Rowley's part.

'Two deaths I've got on my conscience,' said Rowley. 'Hers would have been the third – if you hadn't arrived.'

'Let us drink up our coffee,' said Poirot, 'and not talk of deaths. It is not agreeable for Mademoiselle Lynn.'

'My God!' said Rowley. He stared at Poirot.

Lynn sipped her coffee with difficulty. It was hot and strong. Presently she felt her throat less painful, and the stimulant began to act.

'There, that is better, yes?' said Poirot.

She nodded.

'Now we can talk,' said Poirot. 'When I say that, I mean, really, that *I* shall talk.'

'How much do you know?' said Rowley heavily. 'Do you know that I killed Charles Trenton?'

'Yes,' said Poirot. 'I have known that for some time.'

The door burst open. It was David Hunter.

'Lynn,' he cried. 'You never told me –'

He stopped, puzzled, his eyes going from one to the other.

'*What's the matter with your throat?*'

'Another cup,' said Poirot. Rowley took one from the dresser. Poirot received it, filled it with coffee and handed it to David. Once more, Poirot dominated the situation.

'Sit down,' he said to David. 'We will sit here and drink coffee, and you shall all three listen to Hercule Poirot while he gives you a lecture on crime.'

He looked round on them and nodded his head.

Lynn thought:

'This is some fantastic nightmare. It isn't *real*!'

They were all, it seemed, under the sway of this absurd little man with the big moustaches. They sat there, obediently – Rowley the killer; she, his victim; David, the man who loved her – all holding cups of coffee, listening to this little man who in some strange way dominated them all.

'What causes crime?' Hercule Poirot demanded rhetorically. 'It is a question, that. What stimulus is needed?

Agatha Christie

What inbred predisposition does there have to be? Is
every one capable of crime – of *some* crime? And what
happens – that is what I have asked myself from the
beginning, what happens when people who have been
protected from real life – from its assaults and ravages
– are suddenly deprived of that protection?'

'I am speaking, you see, of the Cloades. There is only
one Cloade here, and so I can speak very freely. From
the beginning the problem has fascinated me. Here
is a whole family who circumstances have prevented
from ever having to stand on their own feet. Though
each one of the family had a life of his or her own,
a profession, yet really they have never escaped from
the shadow of a beneficent protection. They have had,
always, freedom from fear. They have lived in security
– and a security which was unnatural and artificial.
Gordon Cloade was always there behind them.

'What I say to you is this, there is no telling what a
human character is, until the test comes. To most of us
the test comes early in life. A man is confronted quite
soon with the necessity to stand on his own feet, to
face dangers and difficulties and to take his own line of
dealing with them. It may be the straight way, it may be
the crooked way – whichever it is, a man usually learns
early just what he is made of.

'But the Cloades had no opportunity of knowing
their own weaknesses until the time when they were

suddenly shorn of protection and were forced, quite unprepared, to face difficulty. One thing, and one thing only, stood between them and the resumption of security, the life of Rosaleen Cloade. I am quite certain in my own mind that every single one of the Cloades thought at one time or another, "If Rosaleen was to die –"'

Lynn shivered. Poirot paused, letting the words sink in, then went on:

'The thought of death, *her* death, passed through every mind – of that I am certain. Did the further thought of murder pass through also? And did the thought, in one particular instance, go beyond thinking and become action.'

Without a change of voice he turned to Rowley:

'Did *you* think of killing her?'

'Yes,' said Rowley. 'It was the day she came to the farm. There was no one else there. I thought then – I could kill her quite easily. She looked pathetic – and very pretty – like the calves I'd sent to market. You can see how pathetic they are – but you send them off just the same. I wondered, really, that she wasn't afraid . . . She would have been, if she'd known what was in my mind . . . Yes, it was in my mind when I took the lighter from her to light her cigarette.'

'She left it behind, I suppose. That's how you got hold of it.'

Rowley nodded.

'I don't know why I *didn't* kill her,' he said wonderingly. 'I thought of it. One could have faked it up as an accident, or something.'

'It was not your type of crime,' said Poirot. 'That is the answer. The man you did kill, you killed in a rage – and you did not really *mean* to kill him, I fancy?'

'Good Lord, no. I hit him on the jaw. He went over backwards and hit his head on that marble fender. I couldn't believe it when I found he was dead.'

Then suddenly he shot a startled glance at Poirot: 'How did you know that?'

'I think,' said Poirot, 'that I have reconstructed your actions fairly accurately. You shall tell me if I am wrong. You went to the Stag, did you not, and Beatrice Lippincott told you about the conversation she had overheard? Thereupon you went, as you have said, to your uncle's, Jeremy Cloade, to get his opinion as a solicitor upon the position. Now something happened there, something that made you change your mind about consulting him. I think I know what that something was. *You saw a photograph –*'

Rowley nodded.

'Yes, it was on the desk. I suddenly realized the likeness. I realized too why the fellow's face had seemed so familiar. I tumbled to it that Jeremy and Frances were getting some relation of hers to put up a stunt and get money out of Rosaleen. It made me see red. I went headlong back to the Stag and up to No. 5 and accused the fellow of being a fraud. He laughed and admitted it – said David Hunter was going to come across all right with the money that very evening. I just saw red when I realized that my own family was, as I saw it, double-crossing me. I called him a swine and hit him. He went down as I said.'

There was a pause. Poirot said: 'And then?'

'It was the lighter,' said Rowley slowly. 'It fell out of my pocket. I'd been carrying it about meaning to give it back to Rosaleen when I saw her. It fell down on the body, and I saw the initials, D.H. It was David's, not hers.

'Ever since that party at Aunt Kathie's I'd realized – well, never mind all that. I've sometimes thought I'm going mad – perhaps I *am* a bit mad. First Johnnie going – and then the war – I – I can't talk about things but sometimes I'd feel blind with rage – and now Lynn – and this fellow. I dragged the dead man into the middle of the room and turned him over on his face. Then I picked up those heavy steel tongs – well, I won't go into details. I wiped off fingerprints, cleaned up the marble curb – then I deliberately put the hands of the wrist-watch at ten minutes past nine and smashed it. I took away his ration book and his papers – I thought his identity might be traced through them. Then I got out. It seemed to me that with Beatrice's story of what she'd overheard, David would be for it all right.'

'And then,' said Poirot, 'you came to *me*. It was a pretty little comedy that you played there, was it not, asking me to produce some witnesses that knew Underhay? It was already clear to me that Jeremy Cloade had repeated to his family the story that Major Porter had told. For nearly two years all the family had cherished a secret hope that Underhay might turn up. That wish influenced Mrs Lionel Cloade in her manipulation of the Ouija board – unconsciously, but it was a very revealing accident.

'*Eh bien*, I perform my "conjuring trick". I flatter myself that I impress you and really it is *I* who am the complete mug. Yes and there in Major Porter's room, he says, after he offers me a cigarette, he says to you, "You don't, do you?"

'*How did he know that you did not smoke?* He is supposed only that moment to have met you. Imbecile that I am, I should have seen the truth then – that already you and Major Porter, you had made your little arrangement together! No wonder he was nervous that morning. Yes, *I* am to be the mug, *I* am to bring Major Porter down to identify the body. But I do not go on being the mug for ever – no, I am not the mug now, am I?'

He looked round angrily and then went on:

'But then, Major Porter went back on that arrangement. He does not care to be a witness upon oath in a murder trial, and the strength of the case against David Hunter depends very largely upon the identity of the dead man. So Major Porter backs out.'

'He wrote to me he wouldn't go through with it,' said Rowley thickly. 'The damned fool. Didn't he see we'd gone too far to stop? I came up to try to drive some sense into him. I was too late. He'd said he'd rather shoot himself than perjure himself when it was a question of murder. The front door wasn't locked – I went up and found him.

'I can't tell you what I felt like. It was as though I was a murderer twice over. If only he'd waited – if he'd only let me talk to him.'

'There was a note there?' Poirot asked. 'You took it away?'

'Yes – I was in for things now. Might as well go the whole hog. The note was to the coroner. It simply said that he'd given perjured evidence at the inquest. The dead man was *not* Robert Underhay. I took the note away and destroyed it.'

Rowley struck his fist on the table. 'It was like a bad dream – a horrible nightmare! I'd begun this thing and I'd got to go on with it. I wanted the money to get Lynn – and I wanted Hunter to hang. And then – I couldn't understand it – the case against him broke down. Some story about a woman – a woman who was with Arden later. I couldn't understand, I *still* can't understand. What woman? How could a woman be in there talking to Arden after he was dead?'

'There was no woman,' said Poirot.

'But, M. Poirot,' Lynn croaked. 'That old lady. She *saw* her. She heard her.'

'Aha,' said Poirot. 'But what did she see? And what did she hear? She saw someone in trousers, with a light tweed coat. She saw a head completely enveloped in an orange scarf arranged turbanwise and a face covered with make-up and a lipsticked mouth. She saw that in a dim light. And what did she hear? She saw the "hussy" draw back into No. 5 and from within the room she heard a man's voice saying, "Get out of here, my girl." *Eh bien*, it was a *man* she saw and a *man* she heard! But it was a very ingenious idea, Mr Hunter,' Poirot added, turning placidly to David.

'What do you mean?' David asked sharply.

'It is now to *you* that I will tell a story. You come along to the Stag at nine o'clock or thereabouts. You come not to murder, but to *pay*. What do you find? You find the man who had been blackmailing you lying on the floor, murdered in a particularly brutal manner. You can think fast, Mr Hunter, and you realize at once that you are in imminent danger. You have not been seen entering the Stag by any one as far as you know and your first idea is to clear out as soon as possible, catch the 9.20 train back to London and swear hard that you have not been near Warmsley Vale. To catch the train your only chance is to run across country. In doing so you run unexpectedly into Miss Marchmont and you also realize that you cannot catch the train. You see the smoke of it in the valley. She too, although you do not know it, has seen the smoke, but she has not consciously realized that it indicates *that you cannot catch the train*, and when you tell her that the time is *nine-fifteen* she accepts your statement without any doubt.

'To impress on her mind that you do catch the train, you invent a very ingenious scheme. In fact, you now have to plan an entirely new scheme to divert suspicion from yourself.

'You go back to Furrowbank, letting yourself in quietly with your key and you help yourself to a scarf of your sister's, you take one of her lipsticks, and you also proceed to make up your face in a highly theatrical manner.

'You return to the Stag at a suitable time, impress your personality on the old lady who sits in the Residents Only room and whose peculiarities are common gossip at the Stag. Then you go up to No. 5. When you hear her coming to bed, you come out into the passage, then withdraw hurriedly inside again, and proceed to say loudly, "You'd better get out of here, my girl."'

Poirot paused.

'A very ingenious performance,' he observed.

'Is that true, David?' cried Lynn. 'Is it true?'

David was grinning broadly.

'I think a good deal of myself as a female impersonator. Lord, you should have seen that old gorgon's face!'

'But how could you be here at ten o'clock and yet telephone to me from London at eleven?' demanded Lynn perplexedly.

David Hunter bowed to Poirot.

'All explanations by Hercule Poirot,' he remarked. 'The man who knows everything. How did I do it?'

'Very simply,' said Poirot. 'You rang up your sister at the flat from the public call-box and gave her certain precise instructions. At eleven-four exactly she put through a toll call to Warmsley Vale 34. When Miss Marchmont came to the phone the operator verified the number, then saying no doubt "A call from London," or "Go ahead London," something of that kind?'

Lynn nodded.

'Rosaleen Cloade then replaced the receiver. *You*,' Poirot turned to David, 'carefully noting the time, dialled 34, got it, pressed Button A, said "London wants you" in a slightly disguised voice and then spoke.

The lapse of a minute or two would be nothing strange in a telephone call these days, and would only strike Miss Marchmont as a reconnection.'

Lynn said quietly:

'So *that's* why you rang me up, David?'

Something in her tone, quiet as it was, made David look at her sharply.

He turned to Poirot and made a gesture of surrender.

'No doubt about it. You *do* know everything! To tell the truth I was scared stiff. I had to think up something. After I'd rung Lynn, I walked five miles to Dasleby and went up to London by the early milk train. Slipped into the flat in time to rumple the bed and have breakfast with Rosaleen. It never entered my head that the police would think *she'd* done it.

'And of course *I* hadn't the remotest idea who *had* killed him! I simply couldn't imagine who could have *wanted* to kill him. Absolutely nobody had a motive as far as I could see, except for myself and Rosaleen.'

'That,' said Poirot, 'has been the great difficulty. *Motive.* You and your sister had a motive for killing Arden. Every member of the Cloade family had a motive for killing Rosaleen.'

David said sharply:

'She *was* killed, then? It wasn't suicide?'

'No. It was a carefully premeditated well-thought-out crime. Morphia was substituted for bromide in one of her sleeping-powders – one towards the bottom of the box.'

'In the *powders*.' David frowned. 'You don't mean – you *can't* mean *Lionel Cloade*?'

'Oh, no,' said Poirot. 'You see, practically *any* of the Cloades could have substituted the morphia. Aunt Kathie could have tampered with the powders before they left the surgery. Rowley here came up to Furrowbank with butter and eggs for Rosaleen. Mrs Marchmont came there. So did Mrs Jeremy Cloade. Even Lynn Marchmont came. And one and all they had a motive.'

'Lynn didn't have a motive,' cried David.

'We all had motives,' said Lynn. 'That's what you mean?'

'Yes,' said Poirot. 'That is what has made the case difficult. David Hunter and Rosaleen Cloade had a motive for killing Arden – but they did *not* kill him. All of you Cloades had a motive for killing Rosaleen Cloade and yet none of you killed her. This case is, always has been, *the wrong way round*. Rosaleen Cloade was killed by the person who had *most to lose* by her death.' He turned his head slightly. '*You* killed her, Mr Hunter . . .'

'I?' David cried. 'Why on earth should I kill my own sister?'

'You killed her because she wasn't your sister.

Rosaleen Cloade died by enemy action in London nearly two years ago. The woman you killed was a young Irish housemaid, Eileen Corrigan, whose photograph I received from Ireland today.'

He drew it from his pocket as he spoke. With lightning swiftness David snatched it from him, leapt to the door, jumped through it, and banging it behind him, was gone. With a roar of anger Rowley charged headlong after him.

Poirot and Lynn were left alone.

Lynn cried out, 'It's not true. It can't be true.'

'Oh, yes, it is true. You saw half the truth once when you fancied David Hunter was not her brother. Put it the other way and it all falls into shape. This Rosaleen was a Catholic (Underhay's wife was *not* a Catholic), troubled by conscience, wildly devoted to David. Imagine his feelings on that night of the Blitz, his sister dead, Gordon Cloade dying – all that new life of ease and money snatched away from him, and then he sees this girl, very much the same age, the only survivor except for himself, blasted and unconscious. Already no doubt he has made love to her and he has no doubt he can make her do what he wants.

'He had a way with woman,' Poirot added dryly, without looking at Lynn who flushed.

'He is an opportunist, he snatches his chance of fortune. He identifies her as his sister. She returns to consciousness to find him at her bedside. He persuades and cajoles her into accepting the role.

'But imagine their consternation when the first blackmailing letter arrives. All along I have said to myself, "Is Hunter really the type of man to let himself be blackmailed so easily?" It seemed, too, that he was actually uncertain whether the man blackmailing him was Underhay or not. But how *could* he be uncertain? Rosaleen Cloade could tell him at once if the man were her husband or not. Why hurry her up to London before she has a chance to catch a glimpse of the man? Because – there could only be one reason – because he could not risk the man getting a glimpse of *her*. If the man *was* Underhay, he must not discover that Rosaleen Cloade was not Rosaleen Cloade at all. No, there was only one thing to be done. Pay up enough to keep the blackmailer quiet, and then – do a flit – go off to America.

'And then, unexpectedly, the blackmailing stranger is murdered – and Major Porter identifies him as Underhay. Never in his life has David Hunter been in a tighter place! Worse still, the girl herself is beginning to crack. Her conscience is becoming increasingly active. She is showing signs of mental breakdown. Sooner or later she will confess, give the whole thing away, render him liable to criminal prosecution. Moreover, he finds her demands on him increasingly irksome.

He has fallen in love with you. So he decides to cut his losses. Eileen must die. He substitutes morphia for one of the powders prescribed for her by Dr Cloade, urges her on to take them every night, suggests to her fears of the Cloade family. David Hunter will not be suspected since the death of his sister means that her money passes back to the Cloades.

'That was his trump card: lack of motive. As I told you – this case was always the wrong way round.'

The door opened and Superintendent Spence came in.

Poirot said sharply, '*Eh bien?*'

Spence said, 'It's all right. We've got him.'

Lynn said in a low voice:

'Did he – say anything?'

'Said he'd had a good run for his money –'

'Funny,' added the Superintendent, 'how they always talk at the wrong moment . . . We cautioned him, of course. But he said, "Cut it out, man. I'm a gambler – but I know when I've lost the last throw."'

Poirot murmured:

'"There is a tide in the affairs of men
Which, taken at its flood, leads on to fortune . . ."

'Yes, the tide sweeps in – but it also ebbs – and may carry you out to sea.'

Chapter 17

It was a Sunday morning when Rowley Cloade, answering a knock at the farm door, found Lynn waiting outside.

He stepped back a pace.

'Lynn!'

'Can I come in, Rowley?'

He stood back a little. She passed him and went into the kitchen. She had been at church and was wearing a hat. Slowly, with an almost ritual air, she raised her hands, took off the hat and laid it down on the window-sill.

'*I've come home, Rowley.*'

'What on earth do you mean?'

'Just that. I've come home. This is home – here, with you. I've been a fool not to know it before – not to know journey's end when I saw it. Don't you understand, Rowley, I've come *home*!'

Agatha Christie

'You don't know what you're saying, Lynn. I – I tried to kill you.'

'I know.' Lynn gave a grimace and put her fingers gingerly to her throat. 'Actually, it was just when I thought you *had* killed me, that I began to realize what a really thundering fool I'd been making of myself!'

'I don't understand,' said Rowley.

'Oh, don't be stupid. I always wanted to marry you, didn't I? And then I got out of touch with you – you seemed to me so tame – so *meek* – I felt life would be so safe with you – so dull. I fell for David because he was dangerous and attractive – and, to be honest, because he knows women much too well. But none of that was *real*. When you caught hold of me by the throat and said if I wasn't for you, no one should have me – well – I knew then that I was *your* woman! Unfortunately it seemed that I was going to know it – just too late . . . Luckily Hercule Poirot walked in and saved the situation. And I *am* your woman, Rowley!'

Rowley shook his head.

'It's impossible, Lynn. I've killed two men – murdered them –'

'Rubbish,' cried Lynn. 'Don't be pigheaded and melodramatic. If you have a row with a hulking big man and hit him and he falls down and hits his head on a fender – *that* isn't murder. It's not even legally murder.'

'It's manslaughter. You go to prison for it.'

'Possibly. If so, I shall be on the step when you come out.'

'And there's Porter. I'm morally responsible for his death.'

'No, you're not. He was a fully adult responsible man – he could have turned down your proposition. One can't blame any one else for the things one decides to do with one's eyes open. You suggested dishonesty to him, he accepted it and then repented and took a quick way out. He was just a weak character.'

Rowley shook his head obstinately.

'It's no good, old girl. You can't marry a gaol-bird.'

'I don't think you're going to gaol. A policeman would have been round for you before now if so.'

Rowley stared.

'But damn it all, manslaughter – bribing Porter –'

'What makes you think the police know anything about all that or ever will?'

'That fellow Poirot knows.'

'He isn't the police. I'll tell you what the police think. They think David Hunter killed Arden as well as Rosaleen, now they know he was in Warmsley Vale that evening. They won't charge him with it because it isn't necessary – and besides, I believe you can't be arrested twice on the same charge. But as long as they *think* he did it, they won't look for any one else.'

'But that chap Poirot –'

'He told the Superintendent it was an accident, and I gather the Superintendent just laughed at him. If you ask me I think Poirot will say nothing to any one. He's rather a dear –'

'No, Lynn. I can't let you risk it. Apart from anything else I – well, I mean, can I trust myself? What I mean is, it wouldn't be *safe* for you.'

'Perhaps not . . . But you see, Rowley, I *do* love you – and you've had such a hell of a time – and I've never, really, *cared* very much for being safe –'